THE FALL OF
CRAZY
HOUSE

JIMMY PATTERSON BOOKS FOR YOUNG ADULT READERS

JAMES PATTERSON PRESENTS

Stalking Jack the Ripper by Kerri Maniscalco
Hunting Prince Dracula by Kerri Maniscalco
Escaping from Houdini by Kerri Maniscalco
Capturing the Devil by Kerri Maniscalco
Girls of Paper and Fire by Natasha Ngan
Girls of Storm and Shadow by Natasha Ngan
Gunslinger Girl by Lyndsay Ely
Twelve Steps to Normal by Farrah Penn
Campfire by Shawn Sarles
96 Words for Love by Rachel Roy and Ava Dash
Once & Future by Cori McCarthy and Amy Rose Capetta
When We Were Lost by Kevin Wignall

THE MAXIMUM RIDE SERIES BY JAMES PATTERSON

The Angel Experiment
School's Out—Forever
Saving the World and Other Extreme Sports
The Final Warning
MAX
FANG
ANGEL
Nevermore
Maximum Ride Forever

THE CONFESSIONS SERIES BY JAMES PATTERSON

Confessions of a Murder Suspect
Confessions: The Private School Murders
Confessions: The Paris Mysteries
Confessions: The Murder of an Angel

THE WITCH & WIZARD SERIES BY JAMES PATTERSON

Witch & Wizard
The Gift
The Fire
The Kiss
The Lost

NONFICTION BY JAMES PATTERSON

Med Head

STAND-ALONE NOVELS BY JAMES PATTERSON

Crazy House
The Fall of Crazy House
Expelled
Cradle and All
First Love
Homeroom Diaries

For exclusives, trailers, and other information, visit jimmypatterson.org.

THE FALL OF CRAZY HOUSE

JAMES PATTERSON
AND GABRIELLE CHARBONNET

JIMMY Patterson Books
Little, Brown and Company
New York Boston London

Copyright © 2019 by James Patterson

JIMMY Patterson Books / Little, Brown and Company
Hachette Book Group
1290 Avenue of the Americas, New York, NY 10104
JimmyPatterson.org

First Edition: April 2019

JIMMY Patterson Books is an imprint of Little, Brown and Company, a division of Hachette Book Group, Inc. The Little, Brown name and logo are trademarks of Hachette Book Group, Inc. The JIMMY Patterson Books® name and logo are trademarks of JBP Business, LLC.

Library of Congress Cataloging-in-Publication Data

Names: Patterson, James, 1947- author. | Charbonnet, Gabrielle, author.
Title: The fall of Crazy House / James Patterson and Gabrielle Charbonnet.
Description: First edition. | New York ; Boston : Little, Brown and Company, 2019. | "JIMMY Patterson Books." | Summary: Eighteen-year-old twins Becca and Cassie, now trained, fearless fighters, hold the key to defeating the despotic United regime and freeing the people of the former United States, but at what cost?
Identifiers: LCCN 2019001483 | ISBN 9780316433747 (alk. paper)
Subjects: | CYAC: Government, Resistance to—Fiction. | Sisters—Fiction. | Twins—Fiction. | Science fiction.
Classification: LCC PZ7.P27653 Fal 2019 | DDC [Fic]—dc23
LC record available at https://lccn.loc.gov/2019001483

10 9 8 7 6 5 4 3 2 1

LSC-C

Printed in the United States of America

THE FALL OF
CRAZY
HOUSE

1

CASSIE

MY HEART WAS BEATING SO hard I was sure the United soldiers could hear it. It radiated out from my sore, bruised chest, ricocheting off the unyielding trees, the ice daggers hanging from every branch. The woods vibrated with my heartbeat, echoing *life*…or death. *Life*…or death. Over and over.

My hands were numb and I clutched my rifle by instinct rather than feel. With every breath I pulled in, more lung cells froze, iced over, became hard and brittle. I would never recover. Recovering wasn't even the point anymore.

It was me against United soldiers, and my heartbeat betrayed my position every second.

For the last hour, I'd been holding steady, but in the Resistance, simply *staying alive* is the lamest possible default. As much as I wanted to sink into the snow, the ice, and into oblivion, I knew I had to act. And the *only* action that made sense, the *only* plan that could possibly work, had a price so high that my brain shied away from it like a nervous horse from a rattlesnake back on our farm.

Once more I sluggishly evaluated already-discarded options. Every one of them ended with me dead, the Uniteds winning, and the rest of the camp fatally compromised. I didn't mind dying—I'd lost that fear ages ago in the Crazy House. Death was bearable, even *preferable* at this point. Failure wasn't. The days, weeks, *months* of incessant, soul-crushing, body-breaking training had ensured that the merest *thought* of failure was enough to make every neuron in my brain implode.

As I picked up the faintest sounds of heavy military boots crunching toward me through the thin top layer of ice, my mind focused painfully on the one choice that remained. It was unbearable—the worst choice possible—and the *only* one that might not lead to failure.

Shit shit shit. I had to do it. It was the only way. Gulping convulsively, I tapped the comm on my coat collar. "Beck, come in," I breathed.

My twin sister's voice, tired and cranky, came back. "Becca here. 'Sup?"

2

SEVENTEEN YEARS IN AN AG cell hadn't prepared me for anything riskier than corn fungus or more difficult than confronting a slacker on my science-a-thon team. The last twelve months had been a one-eighty from my previous life, but the constant that remained had been Becca. Reckless, ridiculous Rebecca. My identical twin. And by identical I mean that we share virtually no similarities except our looks...and a fierce, unbreakable, unshakeable love for each other, no matter what. In everything else—taste in food, clothes, boys, music, weapons—she's totally nuts.

"I'm on the ridge," I told Becca quietly, my lips stiff and thick with cold. "I need...I need you to flank east and take out as many of the Uniteds as possible. To give me cover."

On the other end, Becca was silent. For twenty-seven heartbeats. I knew she was calculating the odds, figuring out the plan, realizing that she was going to be sacrificed for the good of the camp and *me*. Realizing that I was sending her to die.

Death was nothing, but I was *terrified* of losing my *sister*, the only family I had left. Like I said, the worst choice possible. War had put me in this position. War puts everyone in this position.

Becca's voice came back with only the slightest waver. "Roger that, Cass. Leaving now."

Becca's comm clicked off just as I opened my mouth to say, *No, don't! I changed my mind!*

My quick breaths were like punches against my breastbone. I tapped my comm again. "This is Cassie," I told the relay. "I'm heading toward the mountain. United's hot on my tail. Expect company."

"Copy that," said a voice through the crackly comm system.

Much closer now, a branch snapped, sounding like a boulder shattering in these hard, icy woods. The United soldiers were sweeping the area. They were almost on me. Becca should be in place now. Suddenly my cold-slowed reactions burst into animal-survival mode, my muscles twitching, my whole being consumed by a primitive refusal to be prey. *It was now or never.*

3

WITH EVERY COLD, CRAMPED MUSCLE screaming, I broke out of my hiding place and quickly took my bearings. I couldn't see the United soldiers yet but heard them coming up the ridge I was on.

Feeling much, much older than eighteen, I snuck toward the edge of the woods. I'd been motionless for so long that my hands and feet felt dead, making me clumsy, loosening my hold on my rifle. I stumbled against a rough-barked pine, whacking my shoulder, and bit down a grunt of pain.

Then I heard shouts. The first sound of gunfire made me stiffen, whipping my head toward the sound. Oh, God, that was Becca. That was Becca giving me cover. I crouched as I heard a spray of bullets and a choked scream.

Becca! I took an unconscious step in her direction. *No, don't turn back,* I ordered myself.

After a few more steps through snow halfway to my knees, I caved and looked back. Through the woods I saw that Becca was still standing, blooms of red like poppies spreading over her white winter gear. She was yelling and flipping the bird with one hand, because of being Becca.

Then a new volley of bullets knocked her off her feet, flung her backward to land heavily on the hard-packed snow. My mouth opened to scream but no sound came out. I clamped numb fingers against my lips as my knees gave way and I sank into the snow. The noise of firing guns bounced around inside my head, making me dizzy. The bullets kept hitting, making Becca's limp body twitch grotesquely.

My sister. The only family I had left. I had ordered her to die so that I could live.

Gulping down nausea, choking on pointless sobs, I clutched my rifle and raced away from Becca's blood-soaked body. I'd been trained for exactly this. I would deal with my emotions later. Right now our camp was depending on me. This fight wasn't over. I ran through the trees, knowing my boots left obvious footprints in the snow.

After everything we'd been through, Becca was dead and I was alone.

4

BECCA HAD BOUGHT ME TIME and a decent head start, but the Uniteds kept coming, following me easily. Every so often I ducked behind a rock, lay down some ribbons of cover fire. I heard screams and had no reaction to them. Sometimes their bullets struck trees so close to me that hot, splintery shards of bark hit my frozen cheeks, stinging like needles.

The objective should be right ahead of me, right around this— suddenly I windmilled to a stop, going up on my toes, trying to keep my weight back. This *should* be a United entrenchment, a for- tified location for their high-powered weapons. But it was a *cliff,* a sheer drop-off—all the maps I had were wrong! They'd led me to this cliff, and a long way down was a roaring, frigidly cold river. Goddamnit! How had this happened? Rifle shots shredded trees behind me. Someone had given me inaccurate maps. *Why?*

Realization seeped into the frozen paths of my brain, and a bit- ter smile crossed my face. I knew why.

Again, my only choice was the worst one possible: I had to jump. The river below might be shallow, making this jump a suicide. There might be sharp rocks on the bottom waiting to break my neck, my spine, my skull. This might be where it ends. This might be where I failed.

Had Becca died for nothing? Would I get picked off now, so easily?

No.

In war there was no place for emotion. Zero.

"One, two, three!" I hissed, and jumped before I could think myself out of it. I fell for a surprisingly long time and then I hit freezing water as hard as concrete.

5

SOMETIMES THE HOT WATER RUNS out and you're stuck taking a cold shower and it feels like a *huge hardship*. Well, I'm here to tell you that you're a pathetic, weak *loser* who should never *mention* the words *cold shower* again. Being slammed into this river—there were no words for this kind of cold. I was shocked almost to unconsciousness, stunned, instantly wracked with consuming pain from a cold so cold that it felt like fire. It knocked every coherent thought out of my head and I was dumbfounded when I bobbed up to the surface and my lungs told me to breathe.

Seconds later, bullets hissed with steam as they sliced the water around me. I looked up to see gray-garbed United soldiers at the top of the cliff, pointing their weapons at me. I was still holding my rifle, my fingers frozen around it. With my last effort, I raised my gun and fired. I hit a United soldier, who screamed and fell headfirst into the fast-moving water about twenty yards away.

Well, what was one more? I'd already killed Becca.

The harsh current swept me roughly downstream and I was barely able to keep my chin above water. Hypothermia was setting in—my brain was foggy and I couldn't feel my body, could hardly remember what I was doing or why I was here. Still, something kept me trying to head to the other side of the river. But the current was too strong. I was freezing to death. Literally.

I had nearly made peace with my slow death when my sister's face popped into my brain. *Don't you let me sacrifice myself for nothing,* she scolded. *My ass is dead and you better swim like a goddamn eel to the other side, you hear me?*

Becca mad is not a good situation. I moved one arm, then the other.

Swim, you bitch! she snapped.

So I did. Inch by painful inch, the other shore got closer.

Somehow my boots hit the bottom. I crawled upward on the icy sand, dragging myself away from the punishing river. I couldn't feel anything, except the violent shivering of my body. I was so tired. So, so tired. Tears leaked from my eyes, burning my frozen cheeks.

Dimly, a sound reached my ears. A steady rhythm. It was—a slow clap.

With great effort I pried open my stinging eyes, blearily focusing on the figure walking toward me.

"Not bad, Cassie," said Helen Strepp.

6

I LAY ON THE COLD sand feeling like a dying seal while Ms. Strepp made some notes about my death-defying feats. My days of caring about what she thought were over.

"Leaders have to make hard choices," she said. "Leaders sacrifice the comfort of their souls in order to save others from having to make hard choices. You *finally* made the right choice, and just in time. If you'd failed again, you'd be on your way back to Cell B-whatever it was."

"Killing my sister was the right choice?" I mumbled against the sand.

"Yes," she said crisply. "Obviously."

A voice came toward me, floating out of the line of trees circling our compound. "Yeah. And I plan to hold it against you for the rest of your life," Becca said.

I blinked and turned my head slightly to see her. Her white snowsuit was splotched with bright-red blood. More of our fellow soldiers of the Resistance came behind her, a bunch of underfed, overtrained kids in white camo, their arms and faces marred by scars old and new. Many held heavy weapons with ease, showing it was second nature.

I let out a breath, flattening more onto the hard sand. If I'd failed this time, I would've never seen them again. Slowly my brain thawed out and started generating coherent thoughts. I was a soldier, just like them. A year ago I'd been a senior in high school in a tidy farming cell that produced feed corn, beef, and smaller amounts of vegetables for the Co-op.

Then Becca had disappeared and I'd set off to find her. We'd ended up at the Crazy House. Months there had broken down everything we had known or believed about our cell, our lives, ourselves. All truths had been dismantled and remade. Among the lessons in survival, killing, surveillance, and endurance, I'd been conditioned not to cry—never to cry.

When we'd gotten out, we were soldiers.

Inhaling deeply, I brushed sand off my face and sat up, feeling about a hundred years old. Now that feeling was coming back, every muscle burned, and I felt sick. Becca knelt by me, her bloody snowsuit inches from my face. Our eyes met and it was both like looking into a mirror and looking *past* a mirror, *through* it to another me, another universe.

I started crying silently.

7

WIPING MY NOSE ON MY wet sleeve, I stood up, ignoring Becca's helping hand. She gave a wry smile of understanding and passed me a flask of something warm and laced with alcohol: moonshine. It acted like antifreeze, making veins open and blood flow again.

"Finally," said Sasha, a soldier maybe a year older than me. I handed her the flask and she drank and then said, "Jeez, I was getting so sick of watching you screw up."

I shivered, my sodden hair dripping down my back, starting to freeze into a hard lump.

"I know it was superhard." That was Mouse. She was so small and young that she shouldn't be training as a soldier, but we needed every able body, even skinny twelve-year-olds. Anyone able to hold a weapon was being conscripted into the Resistance Army.

A guy came over and took a drink from the flask. "I was sure you were going to bail on killing Becca," he said.

I almost had. "Me? No. No way," I said, trying to inject some strength into my voice. "I knew I had to kill Becca."

"If you had forsaken your duty, it would have been the wrong choice," Ms. Strepp said coldly. "And it would have cost you—cost *us*—everything. These training scenarios are to prepare you for the realities of war."

Someone moved toward me through the circle of soldiers—Nate. Nate Allen, my...*boyfriend* is such a stupid word. I don't know what to call him. Anyway, he got to me and hugged me long enough that the heat from his dry body penetrated through my cold, wet clothes. I almost sighed with relief. When I finally looked up I saw Ms. Strepp's eyes on me.

"Everyone head back to camp," she ordered. "The show is over. You have time to run sprints before eating."

We all groaned and headed back through the woods, automatically taking different paths so as to leave a more confusing trail for outsiders.

"I can't believe it took you this many tries. There was a time back home on the farm you would've gladly killed me for borrowing your truck," Becca said, walking beside me.

I knocked her shoulder with mine. "Smothering you in your sleep and ordering your bloody death by sniper are two very different things."

Just then a couple of kids ran out of the compound, screaming, their hands clamped over their mouths and noses.

It hit all of us at the same time, stopping us in our tracks and making us scowl at the couple of rough outhouses that served the camp. Instinctively I quit breathing and pinched my nose shut.

Our pal Diego from the Crazy House came out of one, saw us, and waved, adjusting his pants.

"What'd I miss?" he asked. "Did you kill Becca this time?"

8

HERE'S WHAT YOU HAVE A lot of in training camp: Pain. Injury. Grit. Adrenaline. Anger.

Here's what you don't have a lot of: Softness. Gentleness. Patience. Lightheartedness. Cute clothes.

So when Ms. Strepp announced that we would have a celebration that evening, it took me a few moments to process that concept.

"Our last leadership member has finally passed a crucial test," Ms. Strepp announced without looking at me. "You've all been working hard. Tonight you'll be rewarded."

Warm, recognizable food? Check. Sweet, fruity, punchlike substance? Check. Dressing up in fun, sparkly party wear? No. But I did shower.

Recent rains had left the middle of our camp full of frozen, churned-up mud, but we threw down a layer of dried pine needles and danced there anyway. Someone rigged a portable sound system and it hung from a tree, blasting music we hadn't heard in forever.

A cold, full winter's moon hung low in the sky, casting long, silvery shadows, disguising bruises and dirt, highlighting scars with fine white lines.

The whole camp was dancing in one writhing, disorganized clump, but Nate and I and Becca and Tim tried to stay together as much as possible. The music was too loud, its bass reverberating in my chest and making my ears ring. Someone had spiked the punch—more moonshine—and all of my aches and pains and injuries melted away into the night air. I felt exhilarated and intensely alive. And despite the differences that Ridiculous Rebecca and I had, have had, and will have—in this new, post-cell life of battle and secrecy, violence and fear, there was no one I loved or trusted more. I guess she wasn't really "Ridiculous Rebecca" anymore—not after the Crazy House. "Reckless Rebecca" on the other hand…

Nate grabbed my arm and spun me around, pressing close so our bellies touched. He smelled like harsh camp soap and I saw he'd worn his least-destroyed camo pants. After Becca, Nate was the person I was closest to. He and Becca's boyfriend, Tim, had both easily passed leadership training, making hard, life-or-death choices with no hesitation. I was thankful they were with the Resistance rather than the United. Nate looked down at me, his eyes shining despite a darkening bruise on his left cheek, and I smiled up at him and looped my arms around his neck.

"Attention!" Ms. Strepp had to raise her voice three times before someone shut off the music. She climbed on top of a wooden crate and looked at us, these hundreds of kids she'd mercilessly trained and beaten into some sort of a military force.

"Some of you have been here a year or more," she began. "Some of you have been here only weeks." A kid got a flashlight and aimed it up at her, giving her a weird, statuelike appearance. "Some of you have a grasp on the broader picture of what we're facing, and some of you have simply learned to shoot." Her eyes, always frosty, raked over us. "But enjoy yourselves tonight. Feel young, feel free, feel hopeful. It's perhaps the last time you'll feel any of those things."

I frowned—this wasn't the cheerful, "Go get 'em!" speech I was expecting.

"Tomorrow, and every tomorrow after that, will be uncertain," she said. "Starting tomorrow, we will officially be at war with the United. We will be on the path to overthrow them, to seize their power, to topple their leaders. It will be the only path we know, and we'll stay on it until we succeed—or die."

My buzz was wearing off and my dance-fever warmth had ebbed, leaving me chilly.

"My troops, my comrades-in-arms, my soldiers—we will be free!" She punched her fist in the air and shouted it again. "We will be free!"

The rest of us took up the chant, punching the air and yelling, "We will be free! We will be free! We! Will! Be! Free!"

9

BECCA

NODDING AT US IN SATISFACTION, Ms. Strepp jumped down from her box. Within minutes we were dancing wildly again, throwing off our coats, putting our hands in the air, and letting every instinct of life move us to the rhythm of the pounding songs. While we'd been in training, every moment had been controlled, focused, dedicated. This was the one night to let loose.

Thank *God* Careful Cassie had finally passed the last leadership test. I mean, *good lord,* what was so hard about it? After the last three months of training, she should have been like, *Kill Becca? Sure! No prob.* The last three months had made our stint at the Crazy House look like a goddamn *spa.*

"Here." Tim handed me a cup and I took a sip, then smiled.

"Spiked!" I said, draining it. We headed back to the dance area and leaned together, arms wrapped tightly around each other, and swayed slowly to some sappy song about how love was like a walk in the rain.

"You feel good," he murmured against my hair. I rested my head on his shoulder, glad I'd taken the time earlier to get most of the tangles out of my hair. A lot of girls here had gone the crew cut route: easier to care for, keep clean, and gave enemies nothing to grab. So far Cassie and I had both resisted, but I was weakening.

"You know what?" I said into his muscled chest. "I hope when we're out fighting, we'll find one of those non-cell towns Strepp told us about. The ones with the big houses and fancy cars."

"Yeah," he agreed. "Take it over, raid their food. Medical supplies."

"Do you believe all that stuff she told us?" I asked. "All those pictures and videos of people with so much... stuff. And everyone in the cells with barely enough to scrape by? It just seems crazy. Not real life."

"I guess I believe it," he said slowly. "I want to think we're fighting for *something*."

For seventeen years, Cassie and I had lived in a regular ag cell, going to school, helping on our parents' farm. It had been boring as hell. Now, with the whole United ahead of us, our army rushing out to meet whatever, I was too excited to feel fear.

Tomorrow, everything—*my life*—would really begin. This party, this celebration, felt like the last night on earth as we knew it. Slowly I edged us over to the food table, where I refilled our cups. He threw his back and I finished mine in three gulps. Grinning at each other, we rejoined and clung together, barely moving our feet.

"Tomorrow we're getting our assignments," he said. "Strepp has been dropping hints for weeks."

I nodded. "Fingers crossed that the four of us end up on one team. She *has* to keep us together." Cassie, Tim, and Nate had my back, without question. We would fight more effectively as a unit. A unit of trust.

"I can't believe it's finally happening," he said, stroking my back. "All the shit we've gone through, the pain, the injuries—it's all been leading up to tomorrow."

"I know," I said. "Strepp better make it worthwhile, that's all I'm gonna say." Reaching up, I wound my arms around his neck.

"Let's sneak away," I whispered, going on tiptoe to reach his ear.

He looked down at me, his fair eyebrows—one split in half—raising. "Out into the snow?"

I grinned. "You can keep me warm."

He smiled back, doing a decent wolf impression, and we slipped past the trees and out into the darkness. The world—our world—might end tomorrow. But tonight I was going to live.

10

CASSIE

ANOTHER SLOW SONG CAME ON and we all groaned at its corny lyrics. Nate pressed me closer, and I loved the way he felt.

If only it could be like this forever, I thought dreamily. Not just me and Nate, but Becca and Tim, too. Sticking together. Living next door to each other. The four of us just seemed...*right*. Like we were linked. *Supposed* to be together. It was trust, I decided. We all had the ultimate trust in each other.

"Let's go out where it's dark," he whispered in my ear.

"Why?" I asked, not wanting to move. "It'll be cold out there." I snuggled closer to him and let my eyes drift shut.

"I'll keep you warm," he promised, and took my arms from around his neck.

After the warm crush of bodies on the dance ground, the woods were *super* dark, oddly quiet, and, as I predicted, freezing. The cold caught my breath.

"I need my coat," I said.

"Come here," he said, and wrapped his coat around both of us. His chest was lean and hard, and his arms around me felt like steel bands. Had it been just this morning that I'd almost frozen to death, almost drowned?

Lowering his head, he kissed me. I tilted my head and opened my mouth, deepening our kiss, wanting this to never stop. A flame of happiness sparked into life in my heart and grew steadily. When was the last time I'd felt happy?

Maybe…maybe the last time had been before my dad had shot himself? That was more than a year ago. That was a long time to go between feelings of joy.

We ended up on the snowy ground, with Nate bearing the discomfort of the cold earth and me on top of him. I held his face in my hands and kissed him over and over, feeling his thick hair in my fingers, a ridged line of scar tissue on his skull from some fight.

Finally he pulled away, holding my face, looking at me. A thin shaft of moonlight wove through the dense trees and lit the side of his face, showing his beauty, the movie-star looks I'd always sneered at in high school.

"Tomorrow we're going to get our assignments," he said quietly, an intense expression on his face. "We don't know where we're going or what we're gonna face. We don't know if we're coming back."

I sat back, straddling his hips, keeping my hands on his chest, aware of his breathing. "We've been on this road for a year," I said. "We've always known we might die. I mean, if there's one thing the Crazy House taught us, it was that we were gonna die, and probably die young. But we're prepared, and we're alive and together now."

He stroked his hands along my cheekbones, as if memorizing the feel of my face.

"Yeah," he said, and then, "Cassie—I want to marry you. If we die tomorrow or the next day or the day after that, I want to know that we were married, that we belonged together. Forever."

As soon as he said the M-word, I was shocked into stillness, my pre-kiss mouth open like a croaking frog. My brain had jammed, then whirled into frenzied activity as it processed this bizarre notion.

I hadn't expected this. Slowly I let my gaze slide over his face until I could search his eyes, see if he was serious or just, you know, like, brain-damaged or something. Sure, people got married young in our cell, but...

My mind cleared. I leaned down and kissed him again. "Ask me later, on the other side."

"I'm asking you now," he said, a note of irritation in his voice.

"Then I'll ask *you* later," I told him.

"I want to feel connected," he insisted.

I squirmed on his hips, seeing his eyes glaze for a second, and I grinned. "We can feel connected...if you want," I said.

Much later, we stood up and brushed twigs and dirt and leaves off our clothes. I had an idea and took out the knife that was always with me. I flicked it open—it was seven inches of razor-sharp blade that I cleaned and honed almost every day.

Slowly, carefully, I made a small, stinging cut across the pad of my palm, then handed him the knife. Knowing what I wanted, he made a cut on his palm. Then we pressed our hands together, making sure the blood mixed.

"I love you forever," Nate said solemnly.

"I love you forever, too," I promised. "And we will get married. Someday."

We sealed our pact with another kiss, then headed back to camp.

11

BECCA

MY MIDDLE NAME IS NOT "Patience." I was about to come out of my skin, waiting here in the hallway outside Strepp's office with a couple hundred of my closest friends. This was what we'd been waiting for, working toward, for months. This was why we'd left our cells, our friends, everything we knew behind. It had all come down to this: our assignments. What each of us would do to fight the United.

Since dawn, Strepp had been calling soldiers in—sometimes one alone, sometimes small groups. Cassie, Tim, Nate, and I stuck together and waited.

The door opened and three soldiers older than us came out looking grimly satisfied. When the door closed they gave each other high fives and sauntered out.

"They got a good assignment," Tim said in a low voice. "Hope we're as lucky."

"I can't believe this is it," Cassie said. "This is why we were taken, why we went through the Crazy House, why we've been trained." She shook her head and leaned against the concrete wall, looking still and thoughtful—two words that had never been applied to me.

"It's our chance to strike back at the United," Nate said. I'd noticed he and Cassie giving each other lovebird looks all morning, and I'd been grossed out until I caught myself gazing adoringly at Tim. In return his eyes glittered knowingly at me, and while I'm not a blushing-type person, I did feel a little thrill race down my spine.

I nodded and said, "This is for Ma and Pa and everyone back at the cell. The United won't be keeping us on a leash anymore."

"Never again," Tim said, and we all repeated it: "Never again."

Two more kids came out of Strepp's office looking sad. One of them wiped tears away from his cheek.

"Bad assignment," Nate muttered.

It went on, everyone but the four of us getting called, everyone then trooping out and down the hall. Some soldiers looked thrilled, some looked terrified, some looked kind of sick to their stomachs.

We were last. More than three hundred freaking soldiers were given their jobs ahead of us. What was gonna be left? KP duty? I could already feel my blood rising. I hadn't trained like an effing dog all this time just so I could stay here and man the shortwave radio or some shit.

It was almost noon when we finally entered Strepp's camp office.

We were Strepp's best fighters. I knew that. I was hoping that meant she'd held on to the toughest assignment, saving it for the A-team. Squaring my shoulders, I strode in and stood at attention in front of her desk.

"Your childhood is over," Strepp said, standing up. "Your childhood has been over for a while now."

Well, there's a news flash, I thought.

"You're adults now, with adult power . . . and adult responsibility."

Cassie's pinkie reached out slightly and touched mine. I didn't dare look at her—we would both burst into laughter if I did.

"You think you're hotshots," Strepp said, her voice cold. She walked around us, raking us with her gaze as if she were watching a worm fry on a hot sidewalk. "Kids, you ain't done nothing yet. Talk to me when you've saved lives, when you've stopped evil, when you've actually made *one* goddamn difference in this world!"

This was Strepp at her worst. She'd always been able to change her persona in an instant—there were times I'd swear I'd seen warmth or caring in her eyes. It was hard to imagine right now.

"This isn't training," she went on, pacing. "This isn't just some *battle*, and we're not trying to claim a *cell*. This is an all-out *war*. You're fighting not for *one* cell, but for *all* cells. You're fighting not just for *your* future, but for *everyone's* future. The future of *humankind*. Do you understand? Do you fully grasp that concept?"

We all muttered, "Yes, ma'am." What else could we say?

"Becca," she said, whirling to look at me. "You'll be a squad leader, commanding five soldiers. You'll be advance scouts, covering a great deal of ground. Your squad's job is to make maps, neutralize any United outposts, and make contact with undercover Resistance agents in the Outerlands."

I clenched my fist at my side so I wouldn't give a victory punch in the air. *Yes!* Oh, yes! This was going to be *awesome!* High risk, high reward—the way I liked it! I almost laughed out loud, picturing me, Cassie, Nate, and Tim crawling through underbrush, peering through binoculars—and best of all, *I* was *in charge!* I almost bounced on my heels with excitement and couldn't wait to get out of here so we could all talk about it.

Then Strepp turned to my sister. "Cassie, your assignment is to stay here."

12

CASSIE

MY WHAT WAS TO WHO now??

Hadn't I just gotten my assignment? To go with Becca and be awesome?

"What?" I blurted.

Ms. Strepp walked around her desk and sat back down. She tapped a pile of papers into a tidy stack and went on coolly. "Everything that we know about the Outerlands, everything I've shown you, is just a tiny bit of what we need to battle the United, to overthrow its power," she said. "We need more *facts*. I need you to head up the research department, integrating info that scouts bring back, as well as trying to hack into the information pathways of the United. Believe me, this job is every bit as important as Becca's."

I was speechless, like I'd just been thrown back into that damn cold river. Heat rose in my face and I knew I was turning pink. Maybe smoke was actually coming out of my ears. It felt possible.

This was a shit assignment. My fingers itched for my rifle—I'd been trained to be a *soldier*, not a paper-pusher. I wanted to scream, refuse, and throttle Ms. Strepp. It took everything in me to simply stand still without reacting, like a soldier. But my face tightened and my breath came fast.

After a moment she spoke again, her voice one tiny degree softer. "Look," she said. "Things weren't always like this. Something *happened* to change our world, to divide it into cells and non-cells, and people into cellfolk and Outerlanders. What happened? We don't know! Your job is to find out. While you've been training, Resistance soldiers have been hunting down and collecting this information. It's time for you to get to work."

Still seemed like a shit assignment, though part of me could see how that info might be useful. But goddamnit! What was wrong with me that I couldn't be a scout with Becca? Had it been about the leadership test?

I was humiliated and furious. The only good thing was that at least Tim and Nate would have Becca's back.

13

BECCA

THIS WHOLE TIME, NATE AND Tim had been standing at attention. Without even seeing their faces, I could tell they'd both been excited to be on the scout squad, and been dumbfounded at Cassie's assignment. I was crushed about leaving Cassie behind, but was glad I would still have Nate and Tim to back me up.

"Continuing," Strepp said, looking up at us, "I've noticed that you four have paired up into couples. I think the *whole camp* knows that you've paired up into couples."

I hadn't expected this. *So what?* I thought. There wasn't a law against it.

"It's like you haven't learned *anything*," she said, suddenly enraged. "Like you haven't learned that death is *imminent*, that the future is *uncertain!*" She slammed a paperweight down on her desk, angry spots showing in her thin cheeks. *"Ties are lethal.* You *saw* how Cassie's tie to Becca almost cost her *everything.* It's a *weakness."* She practically spat the words. "It's normal and useful to bond with your fellow soldiers—your lives depend on it. But what you've done is more than that, and it's dangerous. It makes you *vulnerable."*

I kept my face blank, sure that the other three were doing the same.

"And if you're *vulnerable,"* she said, "then you're risking *all* of us. Do you see that?"

Well, maybe. I guess. A little. But she was way overreacting.

Suddenly she slammed both hands on her desk, making me jump. *"Do you see that?"* she roared.

From me she got a sullen nod.

"My job is to keep you from putting all of us at risk," she said. "Which is why *Tim* is going to stay here and help *Cassie.* He's a strong fighter, but that's his *only* strength. Helping with research will make him more rounded."

"What?" Tim said, stepping forward. "No way! I'm going with Becca!"

Strepp emitted wafts of frigid air as she narrowed her eyes at him. When she spoke, her voice was very quiet and rigidly controlled, each word like a bullet. "You will stay here and help Cassie, or you will leave camp now, this minute, alone. Are we clear?"

I felt Tim's anger, his indecision. Knowing that I wouldn't have him on my team was a huge blow. No one else would have my back like he or Cassie would.

"Nate? You will be going with Becca."

Nate opened his mouth to speak but Strepp held up her hand.

"The only answer I'm looking for here is 'Yes, ma'am'!" she snapped. "This is not up for *debate*. These are not *suggestions*. These are your *orders* and you will carry them out as commanded or you will leave *now*, with only your self-righteous sense of *entitlement* to protect you!"

My jaw hurt from clenching my teeth. I had nothing against Nate, but he wasn't Tim in a firefight. I had to get out of here right now before my head exploded.

"Are we *clear*?" she demanded again.

We nodded and mumbled affirmatively.

"Then you are dismissed," she said, and turned her back on us.

14

AS SOON AS WE WERE out of Strepp's hearing, Cassie burst out, "This is bullshit!"

"You got that right," Tim said grimly.

The four of us ducked behind the mess tent, then stood and stared at each other. I was still happy about my assignment, but felt sick at losing Cassie and Tim. My sister's face was flushed pink, and I knew how she felt.

"Is this another test from Ms. Strepp?" Cassie asked. "Is everything still a test, all the time?"

"We should have been more careful," Nate said bitterly. "We should have hidden our feelings, our relationships."

"If we have to hide our relationships, then what are we fighting for?" Cassie exclaimed. "I mean, 'we will be free' means *we will be free*, right?"

"Yeah," Tim agreed bleakly. "Like, I just can't do the whole research thing."

I didn't know what to say. Tim was from a manufacturing cell, where kids left school and started working when they were twelve. He was smart but hadn't had the same schooling the three of us had had.

Cassie covered her face with her hands, obviously embarrassed, like she wasn't good enough for the Resistance Army. I put my arms around her, touching her forehead with mine. She tried to pull away but I held her more tightly.

"Hey," I said. "I want you on my team. I don't know what Strepp is doing, but I'd give anything to have you with me. No one's as kickass as a Greenfield, am I right?"

Cassie shrugged angrily. "Easy for you to say."

"Look, Strepp is separating us," I said. "*This war* will separate us. *Death* might separate us! But don't *you* ever separate us, you got that? I'm sorry you're mad, I wish like hell you were going with me, but don't you *dare* pull away from me. Not *ever*. You hear me? No matter *what*!"

Slowly, my twin raised her eyes, met mine. After a minute, she nodded. She put her arms around me and we hugged each other as if we would never come apart.

15

CASSIE

BECCA, NATE, AND A FEW dozen other troops had been ordered to leave the next morning before dawn. Tim and I were there to say goodbye. We weren't the only ones staying behind—most of the kid soldiers were assigned to the camp for additional training and to keep things running. Only the lucky few got to go out on assignment. All of us getting left behind looked miserable and angry. I know I did.

I saw Becca's squad off to one side as they put finishing touches on their gear. Their team was Becca, Nate, a girl called Bunny, and three kids I didn't know. Bunny was taller and heavier than Becca, with a black Afro crew cut and a scar on her face at the corner of her mouth. She was a good fighter and I was glad she was on my sister's team.

I tried to smile when Becca broke rank and came over to me.

"Stop that," Becca said briskly. "You look like a dying cow."

"You guys are loaded for bear," I observed, trying to sound casual.

"Yeah," Becca said, hoisting a backpack onto her shoulders. "I didn't even know we had all this stuff." She got her backpack situated and looked at me, then made a circle with her thumb and her index finger. After a moment, I made one, too, and joined it with Becca's to make a connected link. I was overwhelmed with love for my exasperating, reckless sister, and this goodbye might be our last one. My chest felt like a horse was sitting on it and it was hard to breathe.

"You and me forever," Becca said softly.

I could hardly speak, but I needed to show Becca that I wouldn't be the one to split us apart.

"You and me forever." We hugged goodbye, breaking off too soon so we wouldn't start bawling.

Then Becca hugged Tim, whispering stuff to him, and I faced Nate, who looked deeply unhappy. He was my first real boyfriend. My first real love. He might also be my last. Just realizing that made me want to shriek like a banshee. Us fighting side by side hadn't bothered me. Now we were getting split up. We might never hold hands again, never kiss again, and it felt like my heart was getting ripped out of my chest.

As if he could tell what I was feeling, Nate smiled bravely but it didn't reach his eyes. "I'll be back," he said firmly.

I couldn't even pretend to believe that, be sure of that. I wanted to say so many things, tell him I loved him, assure him that we would get married someday, but all I could come up with was, "Don't—don't do anything stupid. You and Becca stick together, got it?"

A pompous look came over his handsome face and he put on his most annoying son-of-a-Provost voice. "I'm incapable of doing anything stupid." Then he grinned at me, a bit wobbly, and crushed me to his chest. "I'm going to come back to you," he whispered.

I nodded, but inside I thought, *We're all going to die. And I'm never going to see you again.*

Over Nate's shoulder I saw Strepp looking at us, her eyes narrowed. What an inhuman bitch. Didn't she know that separating Becca and me weakened us *both*? Didn't she know that Becca would fight better with Tim at her side?

Maybe Ms. Strepp wasn't human. Maybe she was a cyborg.

It was the only explanation that made sense.

16

TIM AND I SILENTLY WATCHED the various groups head out of the compound, knowing they would split up to head in different directions. My chest ached with wanting to be with them. My biggest fear wasn't that Becca or I would die—but that one of us would die *without the other*. My throat hurt and I knew if I tried to speak it would come out in a bitter croak.

I barely noticed that other soldiers, armed with clipboards instead of weapons, had started hustling some of us remaining losers off to our new jobs—KP duty, watchtower shift, maybe advanced weapons training. In case we might ever actually need to use weapons.

"You," a voice said, and I looked up to see a tall, wiry girl with red hair and freckles standing in front of me. She held a rifle and wore a thin purple armband—she was a guard, as opposed to a soldier. Guards were enforcers, answerable only to Ms. Strepp.

"What," I said, matching her narrow-eyed gaze.

"You two come with me," she said. "Ms. Strepp is waiting for you."

Right then I could have cheerfully told Strepp to go screw herself, but Tim fell into line behind the guard, his large hands curled into fists. Sighing, I followed him, my jaw clenched with fury and my neck stiff from tension.

Once inside the main building, the guard led us to a door and rapped it firmly.

"Come in," said that horrible voice.

The guard opened the door and motioned us through, then stood behind us at attention.

"Thank you, Havers," Ms. Strepp said, and the guard turned smartly and marched out the door, closing it behind her.

Once the three of us were alone, Ms. Strepp looked us up and down, nodding to herself. Suddenly she caught my eyes with a sharp, knowing look.

"Still pissed?" she asked.

"Yep," I said, deliberately looking away.

"You bet," Tim said, his voice hard.

"Sorry about that," she said briskly, not sounding sorry at all. "But I need you here. I made the right decision."

It took all my willpower not to say, "Whatever."

Quickly she crossed to her office door and locked it, very quietly. Then, motioning at us, she led us to another door and opened it, revealing a short, dark hallway. It led to a crummy, old-fashioned bathroom, apparently just for her personal use.

Oh, my God, I thought in despair. *I am here to* literally *scrub toilets.*

40

My contribution to the Resistance would be sparkling toilets. My heart sank and I wanted to both shriek in rage and break down crying.

We stood in silence, looking at the bathroom. It was small and rough with a chipped, rust-stained sink and an old-fashioned pull-chain toilet. The walls were crumbling brick, their layers of paint showing tan, blue, then institution green.

I refused to be the first one to speak. Tim, beside me, was practically vibrating with anger and disappointment.

With the three of us crowding in, Ms. Strepp closed and locked this door, too. For the first time, a flicker of fear edged into my anger. This was not a good situation. If Tim and I suddenly *disappeared,* not a single person would notice or care. Shit. What was happening?

Suddenly she leaned down and pressed one of the caps on the toilet's base that covered the screw holding it to the floor. Tim and I shot each other lightning glances as Ms. Strepp stepped back quickly...and the painted brick wall opened smoothly and turned, revealing a perfectly hidden narrow hallway.

"What I had been expecting" had taken a left turn back when she locked us in the bathroom. Now, as she stepped through the doorway into an inky darkness, I had no idea what to think. Cooler air wafted toward us from the opening, and her calloused white hand motioned us to follow her. Maybe she was taking us to be eliminated. Maybe we'd been left behind because we had no value. Maybe we were going back to prison, like the Crazy House.

There was no way I'd be the fraidy-cat and make Tim go first, so I stepped boldly into the darkness, praying that nothing would spring out at me. I was glad when I felt Tim's warmth close to my back.

She pushed the fake wall closed and we were in darkness. Absolute, utter, creepy, no doubt spider-filled darkness.

17

AUTOMATICALLY I BLINKED AND OPENED my eyes wide but couldn't see a damn thing, not even my hand two inches from my face. I heard a click and one dim, bare bulb cast a completely inadequate fuzzy corona of light that illuminated precisely nothing. But my eyes adjusted rapidly, and I could make out...a worn rope ladder hanging against a dank brick wall. It led up maybe ten feet, maybe a hundred. No way to tell.

Ms. Strepp took hold of one side of the rope ladder, jerked her head at me, and said, "Up!"

Yes, *climb up to hell, Cassie,* I thought, but made my face blank, refusing to show fear. Grabbing hold of the dirty ladder, I cautiously put one foot on the bottom rung, testing to see if it would hold my weight. It did.

Rung by rung, I climbed up into nothingness. Once I glanced down and saw Tim holding the other side of the rope ladder, looking up at me. Though he wasn't Nate, he was a friend, and I was glad we were together. The air grew warmer the higher I climbed and then suddenly as I pulled myself up another rung my head banged hard on a ceiling.

My breath hissed in as I swallowed a cry of pain. What had been the point of this? My anger rekindled and I glared down the ladder, knowing they couldn't see me.

"Are you okay?" Tim asked, having obviously heard the dull *thunk* of my skull.

"Yes," I said, tight-lipped.

"Push upward," Ms. Strepp ordered.

I lifted one hand and pushed. Nothing happened. Gritting my teeth, I lowered my head and pressed against the ceiling with my back. Something moved a bit, so I gathered my strength and pushed again. It was a trapdoor leading into...yes, that would be more utter darkness. A musty smell floated down and surrounded me like smoky gray fingers. I climbed to the next rung and gave a big shove, and the trapdoor rose and flopped over with a loud *bang*! Instantly, fine dust roiled out of the opening, making me gag. I closed my mouth and held my nose shut.

I didn't have to be told: I climbed up the last few rungs and pulled myself through the trapdoor, which was about three feet square. I uncoiled myself slowly, not knowing if I would hit my head again, but finally I was standing upright. Tim's head and broad shoulders were barely visible, coming through the trapdoor. Ms. Strepp followed him and once she was up I heard another click and a single lightbulb hanging down on its cord cast a circle of light around us.

Blasé resentment faded as I stared around, stunned. One by one, more bare lightbulbs flickered on. *Click, click, click.*

"Jeez," Tim said. "What the hell is this stuff?"

"Where are we?" I blurted at almost the same time.

"In a place no one in the world knows about except me, and now you two," Ms. Strepp said, barely above a whisper.

18

BECCA

THE SUN ROSE AS WE, Squad Six, reached the top of the hill east of the camp. We made our way through the trees, avoiding stepping on branches, not touching anything, trying to leave as few marks in the snow as possible.

We were an hour in and I'd already learned some important things. Like, when you're the *advance scout,* no one has gone before you to tell you about the dangers. You find out by surprise! Word to the wise: Always look up, because mountain lions apparently like to lurk in trees.

Another thing I'd learned was that kids could be trained to be tough, fearless, grade-A soldiers and still manage to be a bunch of little shits.

By mid-morning I was convinced that Strepp had given me the

THE FALL OF CRAZY HOUSE

Squad Least Likely to Survive. This was probably yet another of her incessant tests—testing my leadership skills. Leadership is basically being able to convince people to do what you want. I'd been great at that since I was a little kid. But these guys were, so far, resistant to my charm.

One boy, Mills, seemed to resent the fact that I was younger than he was, and female. I figured I would have to take him down, hard, in the very near future. So there *were* perks to being a leader.

Another boy, Levi, was a sweet fourteen-year-old who shouldn't be here or allowed around weapons. He seemed to live in his own world—sort of loping along, talking or singing quietly to himself, occasionally pointing out a pretty bird or a beaver or something. Of course I'd taken him aside and had the "Be silent or we all die" talk, but its effect was already wearing off.

Bunny was tall, tough, and strong, and I was happy to have her. But she had a hair-trigger temper and saw danger everywhere. More than once I'd had to knock her rifle down because she'd been about to shoot at, like, a woodpecker or something. "Guns are *loud*, Bunny," I'd hissed, and she'd nodded curtly at me like, *Yeah, but, woodpecker!*

To top it off, there was Jolie, and I only knew her name because she had spelled it into my hand. Jolie was deaf. I hadn't realized it for a while because she *looked* totally badass. Her head was shaved except for a long blue Mohawk running from her forehead to the nape of her neck. Her ears, nose, and one eyebrow were pierced, and her collar covered most of a tattoo on her neck. It was only after she had ignored my whispered commands a couple times that

I had grabbed her shoulder. She'd whirled on me, knife in hand, black eyes blazing.

"Oh, she's deaf," said Levi cheerfully, and I'd stared at him. Then at her.

"What?" I said.

"She's deaf," Levi repeated. "She can't hear anything."

"Then why is she an em-effing *soldier*?" I exclaimed.

Angrily, Jolie grabbed my hand, palm up, and spelled into it, B-E-C-A-U-S-E-I-C-A-N-K-I-C-K-Y-O-U-R-A-S-S.

Which was how I found out that she could read lips. Then she spelled her name into my palm, and I nodded, trying not to worry that she could be a liability for the team.

Finally there was Nate. He'd been the leader of the kids' resistance long before Cassie had gotten involved with him. I knew he was loyal, brave, and a good fighter. But he was no Tim. At least he wasn't actively trying to get us all killed. So, yay?

19

IT WAS A HUGE RELIEF to reach hard, rocky ground on the other side of the hill. Snow makes it impossible to leave no trace; it provides an extremely clear map of where you've been and where you're going. We'd tried to obliterate our trail as much as possible, so instead of six soldiers carefully picking their way through the woods, it looked like a large drunken bear had careened his way down to a lower altitude.

When we reached an outcropping, I agreed to a fifteen-minute rest. Catching Jolie's eye, I mimicked sitting down, then flashed my five fingers three times. She nodded and swung her rifle off her shoulder. I felt a little bitter about being saddled with someone I had to take care of.

Nate scanned the area ahead of us with his binoculars. The trees at this altitude hid us well. Soon we'd have only tall valley grass with the occasional woody copse to camouflage us.

Silently Nate handed me the binoculars and pointed. I looked.

"That's a cell," I whispered. "In that valley, between those two little mountains."

"Maybe five, six miles away?" Nate said softly.

I calculated the distance. "Yeah," I said. "We can get there by sundown if there's a way through to the valley."

I felt a tap on my shoulder. Jolie pointed downward. "Yes, we have to go down," I said. She shook her head, then took my hand, pointed my finger, and aimed it. I squinted, seeing nothing and feeling impatient. Jolie lifted the binoculars to my eyes and guided them.

As I peered through the lenses, Jolie took my hand and spelled, R-O-A-D.

"Road?" I moved the binoculars in tiny increments, and suddenly it came into view. I looked up. "An old road!" I said, and she nodded without smiling.

"Nate, look. There's a road and it looks like it isn't used anymore. If we stick to one side it'll speed us up without too much risk."

"Let's do it," he said, and I turned and held up my hand for a high five. Jolie smacked it maybe a little too hard.

As we headed single file down the rocky face, I wondered if Jolie being deaf meant her other senses were better—like better vision because she relied on it, or maybe she was really sensitive to vibrations or something.

Occasionally we slid downward when we lost our foothold, leaving a fairly visible path, but at least no one could tell there were six of us.

Hiking along the road was a thousand times easier than going up or coming down the mountain, and though we felt a bit exposed, someone would have to be almost directly overhead before they saw us. I turned around and saw Jolie looking at me. I gave her a thumbs-up and motioned at the road, and again she nodded without smiling.

After a few minutes we saw some old, rusted train tracks that ran by the side of the road. From back when cells were connected? Had cells ever been connected? Is this something I should report back to Strepp? It's hard to know what was important enough to relay back to camp. Mostly, our mission was to scout east and report back on any and all United troops, resources, movements, blah, blah, blah. Know your enemy, I guess.

"Oh, whoa," Bunny said, and I almost bumped into her when she slowed. We'd just come around a bend and now saw an opening in the side of the mountain. The train tracks disappeared into a dark so black it's like where light went to die.

Cautiously we walked toward it, our hands on our guns. As we approached, bats flew out of the dense darkness, and my skin crawled when several small shapes raced out of the tunnel along the metal tracks: rats.

Oh, God, I thought, looking around. To our left the road wound uphill, probably curling around the mountain on one side and then weaving down on the other side. I'd assumed there was a direct route to the cell we'd seen. I'd been wrong.

"If this is a tunnel going all the way through the mountain," I said, making sure that Jolie could see me, "it will save us several hours of hiking."

"If it's a mine shaft, we could all die," said Mills flatly.

"Yes, thank you, Mills," I said.

"I vote no," Mills said.

"You seem to be laboring under the impression that this squad is a democracy," I said icily. "It isn't. I'm in charge, I make the decisions, and when I want your opinion, I'll ask for it. Don't hold your breath."

Mills's face colored; he was pissed and I knew we'd have to have a showdown soon. But not yet.

Instead, I gritted my teeth, all leaderly, and said, "Weapons ready!" Then I went first into the deep blackness. 'Cause that's what a leader does.

20

CASSIE

WE WERE IN AN...ATTIC? A huge attic that went on and on, though it was hard to tell because of all the stuff everywhere. I couldn't see any windows. In the middle where the room came to a peak it was maybe six feet high. Tim couldn't stand up straight.

Ms. Strepp was silent as Tim and I tried to understand what we were looking at. The whole place was just *full*. Full of stacks of dusty cardboard boxes, some of them split and spilling their contents. There were old beat-up trunks, with boxes and sacks of paper piled on them. I saw a table covered with maybe thirty small, weird machines. Suitcases were stacked sideways against the knee-high wall. Old newspapers, bundled and tied with string, were layered high enough to make a maze barely wide enough to walk through. All of it was covered with a thick layer of dust.

"This is what's left of the world," Ms. Strepp said, sounding sad and angry at the same time.

"What do you mean?" I asked, trying to read a headline on a newspaper.

"The world still exists," she clarified. "But not its history. People have forgotten. People have buried it. People have lost themselves." She turned to Tim and me and said, "You two are going to help them find it again."

"How?" I asked.

Ms. Strepp moved through the attic, weaving between stacks and piles, almost disappearing behind mounds of paper. "Something happened that made our country like it is today," she said as I followed her. "Today with the cells and separation and Provosts. The rumor is that it wasn't always like that—but no one knows why it changed, or how or by whom. Or no one admits to what happened pre-System. These bags"—she gestured at this stunning amount of crap—"are full of . . . artifacts. Things from the past. Forbidden things, things that would get us all killed if anyone knew they were here. Forbidden *knowledge*."

That sounded a little interesting. Sure, I could spend an hour or two every day looking through this stuff.

"You two are going to sift through all of this," Ms. Strepp went on. "Make notes. Put together the pieces of the puzzle. You two are going to come up with *the lesson that will save the world*. Save *humanity*. Save *all of us*. Before it's too late."

So, no pressure, I thought. "Okay," I said. "But what should we do with the rest of our time?"

Ms. Strepp made the dreaded face—the frown, the narrowed eyes. "You won't have any other time," she told me coldly. "This is your job, your *only* job. And it's every bit as important—perhaps more important—than being in battle."

Tim made an incoherent grunt. She ignored him. "You will report here every day," she said. "You will make sure the hidden door is completely shut. When you're up here, you will pull up the rope ladder and keep the trapdoor shut and bolted." She pointed to a large, rusty hasp bolted to the floor. "And every day, I want a progress report. What you've done. Every single item catalogued. Each piece of everything examined. We need answers, and you're going to provide them."

Giving us each a final glare, she nodded and began going down the rope ladder. When she got to the bottom she called, "Pull up the ladder!"

Tim pulled it up and I closed the trapdoor, struggling to get the bolt through the old hasp.

Thinking that she might still be able to hear us, might still be listening, I whispered, "Holy shit," and he nodded.

He was hunched over, looking incredibly uncomfortable, and I pushed a desk chair over to him. He sat down and put his chin in his hands. "Yeah," he agreed. "Shit."

21

BECCA

BEING A LEADER DOESN'T MEAN you have to like bats. Or rats. Or pitch-darkness. It means you have to keep going *even if* you're afraid of that stuff. Within a few minutes of entering the tunnel we'd lost any light coming in from outside. All of us had miniature flashlights on one shoulder. Their light was small, but at least we could see each other.

"Single file," I ordered quietly, shining my light on my face so Jolie could see me. "This place looks empty, but we don't know. Be on guard, keep your weapons ready, and pay attention to your surroundings."

My team mumbled and nodded. I put a hand to one ear and whispered, "Excuse me?"

That got me a chorus of whispered *Yes, ma'am*s.

I led slowly, trailing my left hand along the dirt wall, trying to see what was in front of me. Thick wooden beams braced against the dirt of the sides and ceiling. They looked way too puny to hold up a mountain. This tunnel had never been used by cars—solely for trains. A few withered weeds grew unenthusiastically between the rotting wooden railroad ties, and every so often we disturbed more bats or rats that squeaked and hurried past us.

How big was this mountain? A mile across? Two? Three? Did this tunnel even go all the way through? Maybe it had only been for trams to come in, get ore, and carry it out. How long should I go before giving up?

Lost in thought, I put my foot down and took a split second to realize it hadn't *landed on anything*. Suddenly I was sliding downward into a bottomless hole.

A yelp of surprise escaped my mouth as I fell, scrabbling wildly at the dirt wall. *No no no no* my brain screamed as my fingers clawed for something, *anything* to hold on to. My right hand instinctively closed around...a root! I threw my left hand up to grab it and hung there for a moment, my mouth dry with terror and my brain firing incoherently. The root was already giving, pulling out of the dirt. Slowly I tilted my head downward—the narrow beam of light couldn't pierce the darkness enough for me to see if there was any bottom.

I looked up and blinked as several flashlights shone in my face. I could see my team clustered around the opening above.

Nate began feeding a rope down to me—he'd already tied a loop in the end to make it easier to hold on to. Letting go of my root felt like risking death. My heart pounded and a clammy sweat beaded my forehead.

"Do it!" Nate said firmly.

It was what I needed to break the vise of fear holding me. I grabbed the rope with one hand, then the other, letting go of the root that had saved my life. Then Nate, Bunny, and Jolie began to pull me up.

By the time I clambered gracelessly out of the pit, I'd had time to be less afraid and more embarrassed. Some leader I was. I crawled over to the wall and sat against it for a minute, my chest heaving.

"You okay?" Nate asked.

I nodded and stood up. Unclipping my canteen from my pack, I took a long swig, then wiped my mouth on my sleeve and said, "Okay, everyone. Avoid that hole."

How's that for good leaderly advice?

22

WE WENT AROUND THE PIT on the other side and headed deeper into the mountain's guts. I decided to give it five more minutes and if no end was in sight then, I would call it quits.

But after five minutes, I just couldn't give up. We went on for six minutes, seven, eight...

"Look!" Levi said. "Light!"

I sighed with relief once we were out of that damn tunnel. It was nearly dusk—not much daylight left. The train tracks curved off into the woods and I decided to stick with the road.

"This is stupid," Mills said. "We should be up high somewhere, hiding and watching."

"Yeah?" Bunny said. With her smooth dark skin and her kinky hair cut close to her head, she looked beautiful—and deadly. I was glad she hadn't been at the Crazy House; I wouldn't have wanted to fight her. "How long should we stay hidden, somewhere up high? Days? I'd rather be a moving target than a sitting target."

Thank you, Bunny, I thought.

This abandoned road led to an abandoned...cell? But there was no boundary fence around it, and no signs saying B-25-600 or whatever—no designation at all.

We just walked right into it. The buildings were empty, with broken windows and some doors hanging open. We walked past a doctor's office, its sign dangling by one chain: DR. ELIZABETH MARKS, GENERAL AND FAMILY MEDICINE. Then a grocery co-op, its windows broken and its shelves bare: MCDUFF'S GROCERY.

"Where's...where's all the United signs?" I asked, looking around. "How come it's Dr. Marks, and not the United Health Center? And McDuff's Grocery, not the United Food Co-op?"

"That *is* weird," Bunny said.

"At home it was United everything," Levi agreed.

It was like that all the way down the empty, overgrown street. Only people's names. Like this place had never been a cell at all.

Turning to Jolie, I made the gesture of taking a picture.

Jolie nodded and took out her camera. She was aiming it at one of the weird signs when *ping*! It got shot out of her hand!

"Take cover!" I yelled, and the team scattered instantly, their training making them obey without thinking. Five seconds later I couldn't see any of them. Nate and I dove over a broken windowsill into a "café." I tapped the comm on my collar. "Report?" I asked. "Anyone see the sniper? Anyone hurt?"

"I'm with Jolie, and we're fine," Levi answered. "Her hand is okay."

"I'm good," said Mills. "But I can't see shit."

"Why is there a sniper protecting this old cell?" Bunny asked the obvious question.

"No idea," I said. After a moment I tapped my comm again. "Bunny? Peek out a bit."

"Roger that." Seconds later we heard gunfire.

I tapped my comm again. "Bunny?" I asked urgently. There was no answer.

23

"THAT SUCKED," BUNNY FINALLY SAID, sounding breathless.

Mills radioed in. "I'm gonna see if I can spot the bastard."

"Copy," I said.

More gunshots. "Goddamnit." Mills sounded mad.

"Jolie's going to take a look," Levi radioed.

"Copy," I said again, tensely.

And...gunshots.

"She's okay," Levi reported a few seconds later. "But we can't tell where the guy is, or if there's more than one."

I looked at Nate. "We need to get out of here. We're advance scouts. We need to keep *advancing*." I was the leader; I needed to fix this. *Make a decision, Becca,* I told myself.

"You know—" Nate started.

"Shut up," I said. "Let me think."

I pinched my lip, trying to work through different scenarios. In one of them, only three of us died. God.

"Look," Nate said, and I glanced up, narrowing my eyes at him in a way that made most people back down. Nate being Nate, he barreled on. "We can triangulate where the sniper is. Or figure out if there's more than one. With geometry."

Oh, good. One of my favorite words.

Still, a good leader has to listen—sometimes.

Nate took my lack of glare to be a sign to continue, and he explained what he meant. He explained it twice before I understood.

"Okay. Is that going to work?" I asked.

Nate shrugged. "Sitting here *isn't* going to work," he said. "We know that much." Keeping out of sight, Nate and I talked very quietly, coming up with a plan that I sketched out in the dirt. Not for the first time I wished Tim was here. He would have figured this out by now with no stinking geometry.

The sun had gone down, which made this weird cell even creepier. But it would help us. I tapped my comm for a group chat. "Okay, guys," I said. "We're calling this plan 'Fun with Geometry.'"

There were groans.

"We're gonna make a hypotenuse triangle."

"The *triangle* isn't a hypotenuse," Nate said, sounding irritatingly patient. "The hypotenuse is a *part* of the tri—"

"Shut *up*," I said.

24

CASSIE

"HOO, BOY," I SAID, LOOKING around. "Where should we begin? Where did she get this stuff?"

"It's a mystery, all right," Tim said glumly.

An old-fashioned computer sat on one table, its light blinking. I opened it and clicked on the spreadsheet program, making a new template. I made columns for what each item was, what year it was from, and a space for a brief description of its contents. I'd used this program when I worked at the All-Ways Grocery Co-op, back home. But instead of tracking carrots, feed sacks, and five-pound bags of flour, I was tracking...history? Truth? Crap?

Turning the computer to face him, I explained, "We can fill this in as we go, and send it to Ms. Strepp at the end of every day."

He nodded, looking unimpressed.

"Should we each start on a pile and log it in ourselves, or maybe one of us go through stuff and one of us logs?"

He shrugged and I felt a hot stab of irritation. I mean, I didn't want to be here, either! I would rather be with Becca, too!

Sighing, he stood, keeping his six-foot-three height hunched beneath the six-foot ceiling. "How about I move stuff for you?" he said. "Stack things up better? Bring boxes to you or whatever?"

"Oh, no!" I exclaimed, glad that I, at least, could stand up straight. "You don't get out of the shit work! If I have to slog through this horrible haystack looking for one stupid needle, you do, too!"

"I don't know what to look for," he said, sounding bored.

"Neither do I! I guess Ms. Strepp thinks we'll know it when we see it." I pointed to a stack of magazines, most of them missing their covers. "You start there! Find out what cell those are from and what year. See if they're farming manuals or something else."

He frowned. "You're not the boss. You don't tell me what to do."

I crossed my arms over my chest. "You don't get to do *nothing*! I can tell you *that* right now!"

"I just don't want to go through all this dumb shit!" He waved his hands to encompass the entire enormous space, the tons of who knew what.

"Here's a thought," I said acidly. "I don't want to, either! But this is what we've been assigned! And we might find out something, something important that will help the Resistance!"

He looked mulish, and I was ready to punch him. Knowing that he had eight inches and more than fifty pounds on me wasn't a deterrent. Finally I realized that this was weird, that Tim wasn't acting like himself.

"Tim. What's going on?" I asked more calmly. "What're you doing?"

He looked away. "My cell made things," he said. "Like out of wood. Furniture and windows and houses."

"So?"

"So...I don't know how to read," he said.

25

I KNEW I SHOULDN'T STARE at him or gape like a fish. But I was shocked. I mean, education, at least to a point, is mandatory in the United.

"Oh," I said carefully, making my voice casual.

"Like, I can read a *blueprint*," he clarified. "I can recognize some words. But not actually *read* them, you know?"

"Ah," I said, nodding as my mind raced. "Okay, well—time to learn."

"Nah," he said, still looking embarrassed. "It's too late to bother now."

Maybe he was afraid he wasn't smart enough? Maybe he was just lazy. Either way, I wasn't buying it.

"Tim," I said, gesturing to this hockey field of an attic, "we might be up here for a decade. I will not be doing all the work by myself."

"I can move things for you."

"You will be moving your eyeballs across all the words," I said firmly, and picked up a pen. On a stack of four cardboard boxes I wrote the alphabet, capitals and lowercases. "Okay, this is how everyone learns." Pointing to each letter, I sang him the alphabet song.

I did it again. And again. Then I fished out letters to build words he might recognize: L U M B E R. N A I L S. W I N D O W.

"Huh," he said.

I wrote out his name, my name, and Becca's name. I wrote out CELL and UNITED.

"Huh," he said. I handed him the pen.

"You practice," I said. "Sound out words. Practice writing the letters. Copy down words you don't know."

"Okay," he said, sounding more enthusiastic. Maybe he was much smarter than he realized. I left him to it and started to wade through this bizarre collection.

MCDONALD'S FRENCH FRIES, I typed into the log. The small white box was flattened and oil-stained. There was no way to tell what year it was from, or where. Or who McDonald was.

I found a small plastic rectangle with BANK OF AMERICA written on it, and a name: MIKAYLAH WISDOM. There was a string of embossed numbers and EXP: 10/22. I had no idea what any of it meant, but I logged it, plus hundreds of other items. I hoped it would be dinnertime soon. Would someone come get us? My stomach rumbled. Tired of sitting at the desk, I got up and wandered around. He had covered many boxes with writing and he was now looking at an old street sign.

"This doesn't make sense," he said. "Ped Xing. What's a ped? What's an Xing?"

" 'Ped' is short for 'pedestrian,' " I explained. "And the X stands for 'cross.' So this sign means 'pedestrian crossing.' "

He frowned. "Like they were trying to trick people."

"They're trying to save space on the sign," I said. He looked like he wanted to argue about it, so I pointed to a block of color nearby. "Hey, what's that?"

It was a suitcase covered in pink flowers. He popped the lock and I felt a tingle of excitement. The first thing I saw was a green journal labeled SECRET! KEEP OUT!

26

BECCA

"**EVERYONE CLEAR ON THEIR ROLE?**" I whispered into my comm. I got a chorus of *yeah*s and *uh-huh*s and *roger*s. "Watches synced? Okay, I'm going to count to five. Move on FIVE—not four and not six, got it?"

They assured me that they got it.

"One, two, three, four, FIVE!" I said, and Nate, Bunny, Mills, Jolie, Levi, and I each popped up from our hiding places like groundhogs.

Pying! Pying! Pying! Pying! Almost as quickly, the sniper shot at us. On cue we all dropped down again. More bullets sprayed the buildings around us, splintering wood, breaking windows, making signs swing precariously.

Lying flat on the café's tile floor, I looked over at Nate. Of all of us, he hadn't been trying to dodge bullets. He'd been watching and listening, seeing who'd been shot at first, where the bullets landed the quickest, and a bunch of other nitpicky details I'd never be able to pay attention to in a gunfight.

Nate crawled over to the patch of dirt where we'd sketched out his plan. He pointed his stick to one of the buildings not on the main street, but on the next street over.

"This is the only place he can be," Nate said. "It's a church with a steeple. I bet he's up in the bell tower. It's the only place that makes sense."

"Okay," I agreed. "We need to defuse him."

"We could—" Nate started, but I held up my hand.

"Let me think."

If our sniper was in the bell tower, and he probably was, then he was well protected. It would be almost impossible to get a shot at him unless we were almost as high. Our other option was to lure him out somehow...

I hit my comm. "Who wants to set something on fire?"

27

NATE LOOKED AT ME ANGRILY. "That's what I was going to say ten minutes ago! Burn down the bell tower! Jeez!"

"I guess you're just brilliant," I said, the snark dripping heavily. "But *my* plan sets the bell tower on fire and *then* waits for him to escape, followed by picking him off like a corn rat."

"I want to set a fire!" said Mills, followed closely by Bunny, also volunteering.

"Okay, it's dark, so you should have some cover," I told them. "Both of you, light opposite sides of the bell tower, and pay attention to where the wind is coming from. Got your matches?"

"Yeah," Mills said. I could hear the rustling as he got his stuff organized.

"Got it," said Bunny. "Mills, you ready?"

"Yeah. Meet you in twenty seconds."

I clicked my comm off and told Nate, "I'm heading across the street—I'll be on the second floor of the mercantile building."

"Okay. I'll raid the doctor's office for medical supplies—if there's any left."

"Good thinking," I said. Then I peeked out into the street, found the deepest shadow, and slid soundlessly into it. Praying the sniper didn't have night-vision goggles, I nipped across the street as fast and lightly as I could.

Just as I dove through the broken door of the mercantile, gunfire peppered the street behind me, and then I heard shots off to the right. Crap. Had he seen Mills and Bunny?

At the rear of the store I found the ladder to the storage loft. As soon as my head poked through the top I froze—the moonlight illuminated a horrible scene: several skeletons, still clothed, grouped around the eave's window. There was a woman, two kids, and two men. One of the men held an old-fashioned hunting rifle.

"Gross," I whispered, and forced myself up. What had happened here? It looked like these people, this family, had holed up here to fight some enemy. Why hadn't their bodies been burned afterward? This was the most horrible not-cell I'd ever seen. This was the *only* not-cell I'd ever seen.

Gritting my teeth, I gently pulled one of the kids' skeletons away from the window. The shoulder bones came apart so I was pulling an empty shirt. The kid's skull rolled off to one side and I saw the one neat bullet hole in the small forehead. Who would do that?

I crawled between the woman and one of the men, trying not to dislodge them. Their silhouettes were visible through the window—surely the sniper had already seen and discounted them. Carefully I rose just enough to see the street below...and yes! A small flame flickered on one side of the bell tower! Immediately I saw the sniper's shadow as he leaned out and aimed straight down.

I quickly skipped parts two and three of the plan, raised my rifle silently and aimed. The sniper was moving fast from one side to another, shooting.

Wait . . . wait, I told myself, curling my finger around the trigger. I didn't move my rifle, just waited for the shadow to flit across the crosshairs. Then, in between breaths, in the millisecond that the sniper filled my sight, I gently squeezed the trigger.

The rifle kicked against my shoulder but I'd expected it and didn't move. The sniper staggered, then fell out the bell tower archway and landed two stories below with a thud. The flames licked at the old wood more eagerly, lighting up the night.

28

"THERE'S A SURPRISE," NATE SAID as we gathered around the sniper's body. He wore a United Army uniform but had no identification on him.

"Jolie," I said, looking at her. "Go up in the bell tower and see if he left any equipment we could use. Be careful—there might be another gunner we don't know about."

Jolie watched my lips, then nodded and took off, her gun ready.

Bunny unbuckled the army guy's gun belt, adding it to the one she already wore. Mills took his rifle and the ammo from his jacket.

"Why was he here?" Nate asked. "Why protect this abandoned town?"

"There's got to be something here," I said. "Maybe he has to check in every so often? When he doesn't, they'll send a replacement. So let's split up and scour this place as fast as we can, and be out of here by midnight."

Mills snapped me a sharp salute and I rolled my eyes at him. Bunny waited for Jolie, but the rest of us scattered.

We were back on the road by midnight, having found absolutely nothing of value, nothing mysterious. We'd left the sniper's radio with him, since it probably had a GPS in it to track him.

Slowly we worked our way east, picking carefully through the woods and then hunkering down through tall prairie grass. I went first, whistling quietly and pushing the grass aside with my rifle.

Jolie tapped my arm. She traced a question mark onto my palm.

"Snakes," I told her, and she nodded and was even more alert after that.

We'd been on the move for six hours since we left the not-cell, when the long march caught up to us. We dropped where we stood and I was lying in the chilly, damp, hay-smelling grass, my eyelids weighted by exhaustion, when it occurred to me.

I propped myself on one elbow. "I think—I think that town was guarded not because of what was there, but because *it* was there. It was being guarded because it was a *not-cell*. Maybe the United doesn't want anyone to know that not-cells ever existed, or still exist, anywhere."

Bunny nodded slowly. "Yeah—I bet you're right. There sure wasn't anything else there."

"It makes sense," Nate said.

I lay back down and looked up at the clouds turning orange from the rising sun. This same sun shone down on the camp where my sister was, where Tim was. It shone down on the Crazy House. It shone on Cell B-97-4275, where my dad's ashes were. I wondered if I would ever see home again.

29

CASSIE

I SET THE JOURNAL ASIDE for later and took more things out of the suitcase. Tim sat beside me as I unfolded a wall poster. It wasn't for seeds or tractors; it was a photograph of a pretty teenage boy holding a microphone. He was lit by spotlights and had the words PETEY SALVEZ LIVE SAN FRANCISCO, AUGUST 11, 2027 printed on him.

"A musician? A singer?" I guessed. "But who's San Francisco? Oh, look—schoolbooks!"

They looked like they were for maybe grade five? There was a science text, a math text, and a book on reading comprehension. "See what you can make of this," I said, handing him the reading book.

Finally I rested my back against a stack of boxes and broke the tiny lock on the journal. The first page said, *Do not read! None of your business!*

The page after that said, *For my eyes only! Stay out! This means you!*

"No way to keep me out now," I told Tim, and he smirked. The following pages were covered in childish, loopy handwriting, and I dove in, hoping that this kid's journal would somehow hold the key to the past. But it wasn't exciting—just weird. It was all fantasy stuff or some kind of pretend life. Like, Julie said she was going to see her aunt in New York on a *plane*, which clearly would never happen, a regular person on a plane. And what was New York, anyway? What happened to Old York?

"This kid has a wild imagination," I told him. "She says that she and her family went to the beach, which, okay, maybe their cell is on a coast. But she says it took seven hours to drive there!"

"No cell is that big," he agreed. "They're all pretty much alike. You could get across ours in half an hour."

"Exactly," I said. "She made up some crazy stuff, like her mom quit work to stay home with the kids. Quit *work*. To stay *home*."

"Was she sick?"

"She doesn't say." I let out a deep breath, frustrated. I was bored, he was bored, he was actually bo*ring,* and most likely none of this stuff was going to give us one single useful bit of information. I threw the journal back into the suitcase and replaced the other things. I was making room for the schoolbooks when my hand brushed the suitcase lining and I heard a crinkle.

I ran my fingers over the lining, then peered closely at it. "Tim! This has been resewn!"

I grabbed my knife and slit through the tiny stitches holding the pink satin in place. "There's something in here!" Soon I reached the edges of some paper, which I fished out.

He watched over my shoulder. I drew in a breath—it was a map.

"I bet that's the whole United," he said.

I looked at all the markings. "It says…United States. United *States*? What states? States of what?"

"The boundary lines are wrong," he said as I smoothed it out on the floor. "I bet she made all this up—part of her make-believe life."

The map had big lines crisscrossing everything, separating the United into six large sections: A, B, C, D, E, and F. But they were clearly handwritten.

"What do those other words say?" he asked, pointing.

I read, unsure of the pronunciation, "Cal-i-forn-ya. Or-ah-gon. Mon-tan-a. Flor-i-da, down here." Tracing the map with my finger, I found where my cell probably was, in an area called Neb-rask-a. I had no idea where we were now, relative to home or this map.

On the margin a note was scrawled in pencil—the writing was recognizable as an older version of the journal's script.

"What's that say?" he asked, and I turned the map to see better.

"It says, 'It's not just rumors—the deportations have started. Tell Murtaugh to mobilize!—JW,'" I made out. Deportations? Rumors?

I looked up. "Go get Ms. Strepp."

30

BECCA

IN THE BRIGHT HARSH LIGHT of early afternoon, we left the high grass and came across another road. I looked at Nate.

"Road, with no tracks *and* no cover, or grass *with* tracks and cover?"

"Oh, now you want my opinion?" he asked coolly.

Oh, brother. "Yes."

"Are you sure?"

My fingers flattened out, the better to bitch-slap his handsome face. Resisting the urge to mention the words "Provost's son," instead I just repeated, "yes."

He looked up and down the road, then up in the sky.

"If they use drones or helicopters, they'll see us either way," he said, and I tried not to look startled. I'd forgotten about drones or anything from above.

I nodded, like, *of course.* "Yeah. So I'm thinking road. We can always dive into the grass if we hear anything."

"Yeah," he said.

Walking on the edge of the road, heading east, I could tell it hadn't been used in a long time. It was cracked and unrepaired, with weeds growing up through the cracks. Tall grass and other plants, shrubs, and small trees were creeping onto it from both sides. It was being taken back by nature.

"Becca?" said Levi after a couple of hours.

"Yeah, Levi?"

"Jolie says there's no birds and no little animals," he said.

I turned and Jolie nodded, making a zero with her thumb and index finger.

We stopped to listen and look.

"It's true," I said, frowning. "I don't hear a single bird. And it's almost dusk—that's when they all go apeshit."

"Have you thought about becoming a poet?" Nate asked mildly. I gave him a sour look, then motioned for everyone to keep going.

For an hour into the evening, we didn't see any living creature except ourselves. It was unbearably unnerving—the animals clearly knew something we didn't. We came across three abandoned cars, rusted and silent with open doors, missing windows. None of us recognized their makes. They were bigger than cell cars, with more complicated dashboards and seats like sofas. For some reason they made my skin crawl.

"Something really bad happened here," Mills said.

"Yeah," said Bunny, looking hyper alert and wary. "This whole place feels dead."

81

"Bunny!" Levi cried.

"What?" she said, spinning.

"No, *bunny*," Levi repeated, pointing.

Down the road, a small, shadowy creature hopped across the road and disappeared into the scrub.

"That's a good sign," said Mills.

A moment later we got another sign of life: the long, low howling of wolves as they bayed at the rising moon.

"Crap," I muttered to Nate.

"Wait, I see something else," he said, squinting in the darkness. "Lights!"

As we crested a small hill, we saw an extremely recognizable circle, enclosed with a fence and well lit. A cell.

31

EVEN KNOWING WHAT I KNEW about the United, I was so freaking glad to see a cell, something familiar. Still, I forced us to wait and watch until after midnight before we belly-crawled closer.

It had the familiar boundary fence, the unmanned guard towers, the open gate. A sign hung on the right side of the gate: E-07-20. It was so homey that my chest hurt. We saw no police, no guards, no nothing, so finally we walked through, two at a time, waiting five minutes in between to see if we triggered something.

When we were all through and walking past large manufacturing buildings, Nate said, "Look for a sign of a cat."

"Like poop?" Bunny asked, confused. "Scratches or something?"

Nate grinned at her and for a moment I remembered that my sister loved him. I guess he grinned at her a lot. Changed his whole face.

"No," he said. "Like, the outline of a cat's face, or a drawing of a cat. Painted small on something or scratched into a wooden post. Maybe carved on a rock."

"Why?" Levi asked, so I didn't have to.

"It's the sign of a Resistance-friendly house. I was the leader of the Youth Resistance back in my home cell, and that kind of stuff is passed through the network—ways to find each other, help each other."

Another thing I hadn't known. I guess Nate had his uses.

We reached the first row of houses, all pretty much the same, mostly dark, mostly quiet. A few dogs barked. It was like home but not like home, and my throat tightened. I wondered if they had a curfew, like we had.

"Everyone, stay in the shadows," I reminded them softly. "Don't walk through streetlights. If a car comes, scatter and disappear."

That was when it really hit me: this was a cell, but who knew what had been going on in the outside? Maybe they'd found the bell tower guy. Maybe we were being tracked right now, the United Army circling us in the dark. I kept my hand on my rifle, ready to swing it up if necessary.

House after house had no cat sign.

"Maybe there isn't one here," Nate said, sounding exhausted.

"I'm starving," Bunny said.

"I'm really tired," Levi said.

"Let's check out the next row of houses," I said. "If we don't see one there, we'll leave the cell and camp in the woods."

"Maybe there just isn't one here," Mills said.

Very possible, I thought wearily. My stomach growled and I felt like if I lay down I would sleep for a week. The next house had a garden in front, still bare from winter. A gnome stood in front of a small windmill, laughing. There was a stone frog next to him, a stone squirrel, and . . . a stone cat.

32

"NATE?" I WHISPERED. "COULD IT be a whole cat, not just a symbol?"

He looked at the statue, thinking. "Yeah, I guess. You guys stay back—let me go up." Quietly he went around to the house's back door and we followed. Nate tapped on the door, three raps, then two, then three again.

Please don't be a trap, I thought, or a sound sleeper.

After a couple moments the door opened, spilling light onto the cold brown grass. A white-haired man in pajamas stood there with a shotgun, which he pointed at Nate.

"You're pretty heavily armed, eh, son?" the man said.

"I thought I smelled a pie cooling," Nate said quickly, and the man squinted at him.

"We got a cherry one, just come out of the oven," the man said.

"Cherry's my favorite," Nate said, and the man lowered his gun and opened the door wider.

One by one we appeared from behind shrubs, cars, and a broken wooden fence. The man blinked, but let us all in.

"Why didn't you tell me the code?" I hissed at Nate when we were inside and following the man down his cellar steps.

"I didn't have to," Nate said in surprise. "I'm here."

Making a mental note to destroy that lame argument later, I watched as the man knelt before a cabinet and opened its bottom door. It was full of home-canned peaches, green beans, peppers, and so on, the jars clean and shining, labeled carefully.

The man did something inside the cabinet and it swung open slowly. He went through first and clicked on a light to reveal a small room, maybe ten by eight, with two rough wooden bunk beds, a small table and chairs, and a big map on the wall showing all of section E. There was a dot at the very top of the map showing where we were, and other dots labeled as cells.

"You all wait here, and I'll get some food," the man said, leaving us and shutting the cabinet door.

"Look," I said. "These cells are connected by lines."

"Roads. Trucks have to ship stuff," Nate said.

Mills looked closer at it. "No—roads are marked differently. These lines don't connect every cell—just a small number of them."

"Maybe they're cells who are friendly to the Resistance," Levi said.

"Huh," Bunny said, and nodded. "It's nice to know we're not alone."

And that seemed like the most profound thing anyone had ever said.

33

"SO IS IT MOSTLY TRACTORS you build here, or combines, or what?" I asked. It was early afternoon—the six of us had basically eaten and then crashed last night, and it had been almost noon when we woke today. I felt amazing—clean, fed, and rested. I couldn't remember the last time I'd had all three things going for me at one time.

Nate and I were wearing typical cell clothes—T-shirts that said UNITED MANUFACTURING, and basic blue coveralls over that. The other four members of my squad had been content to stay back at the house, watching Cell News and eating again.

"Tractors and some attachments, like disk harrows," the man said proudly. We hadn't exchanged names or anything else, nothing we could be questioned about. "Plus we rolled out cotton pickers last year, and word is we're going to add a silage machine next year."

"I saw some of these tractors at an ag cell," I said. My parents had had an ancient model. When that broke down, we'd used oxen—Ed and Ned. When my dad killed himself, Cassie and I let the farming go.

"Yeah?" The man looked pleased. "I never knew what happened to them after they leave here. I figured they probably all went east to the big city."

"What big city?" I asked. Nate touched my hand with his as if to say, *Be careful.*

"I don't know," the man admitted, looking truthful. "It's just an idea I had. I don't know if anything like that exists. You know, you hear rumors."

"Yeah," I said.

I'd never had a tour like this of another cell, and it was interesting and infuriating. Interesting because they had schools and grocery co-ops and other familiar things, and because everything was manufacturing oriented instead of farming oriented. Infuriating because I'd somehow forgotten how the United stuck their name all over everything and took all the credit.

THE UNITED NEEDS YOU TO DO YOUR BEST! was one of the most common factory signs. DON'T MAKE EXTRA WORK FOR YOUR NEIGHBOR! said another. HEALTHY UNITED WANTS TO SERVE YOU! They really stuck out after we'd seen the signs at the not-cell. This place had United Eyewear, United Shoes 'n' Boots, and United Car Repair.

All I wanted to do was run through the cell, ripping down sign after sign—which would be a dead giveaway that the Resistance existed. So I *imagined* ripping them down and stomping on them, and that was almost as fun.

"For ten bucks I'll rip these signs down and run over them," Nate had murmured, and I'd blinked in surprise at how similar our thoughts were.

The three of us stood and watched as a shiny new yellow tractor rolled onto a big shipping container. The man glanced at us and said, "We've…we've built some flaws into the tractors."

I stared at him. He was taking a huge chance by telling us this. If we were captured and tortured, I might offer this up to protect my friends. My sister. Tim.

Nate gave him a sharp glance. "Won't they be traced back to this cell?"

The man shook his head. "It will look like a flaw in the metal. When they trace that, it will look like a flaw in the actual ore."

My mind raced. If tractors broke down, most people couldn't plant or harvest crops. No crops meant nothing to take to the collective. This one link of the chain breaking would cause the System problems everywhere. My mind reeled when I thought about the enormous implications of this. The Resistance was much bigger and more widespread than I'd thought. But it also showed how huge the United was that we were up against.

I squared my shoulders, refusing to think about it. If I really let myself understand what we were doing, I'd try to sit out the rest of the war. Probably.

"We better get back," I said. "We're taking off at sundown."

34

CASSIE

"VERY GOOD, CASSIE."

I tried not to glance at Tim, standing behind Ms. Strepp, because he was making an "Oh, my God she said something nice" face, and I would crack up if I looked at him. But yes, it was stunning to hear. In fact, it was pretty much the most unbelievable thing I'd ever heard out of her mouth.

"So this is the kind of thing you're looking for?" I asked.

She nodded. "Yes. This is a tiny piece of a huge puzzle, but it is a piece. Look at the date: 2034. The note says the deportations have started."

"What deportations is she talking about?" I asked.

"We don't know," she said. "But do you appreciate the value of being able to ask that? To even know about the deportations?"

"Yeah?" I said. It came out sounding like a question.

"And this map," she went on. "This shows one of the first divisions of the United into the sections. How did this happen? Who was Murtaugh? Were these some of the first resisters? What happened?"

I'd never seen her look so excited. Her eyes shone and her hands trembled, holding the map. Then she seemed to remember herself, and in a second the same old Ms. Strepp was standing there: cold, forbidding, unyielding.

"We need the rest of the puzzle. Speed it up."

Late that night I lay in my bunk, listening to the breathing of the soldiers left behind, not looking at Becca's empty bunk next to mine or the dozens of other empty bunks of soldiers not condemned to office work.

Someone came and lay down in Becca's bunk—it was Tim. He pressed his face into her pillow and breathed. "Still smells like her," he said.

"How can you tell? Most of us take maybe one shower a week," I said.

"I can tell." He got under her covers. "I can't believe we have to go back to that goddamn attic tomorrow."

"I know," I groaned. "And it's kind of creepy, finding out about this stuff. Like, a hundred or two hundred years ago, everything was totally different. Ms. Strepp thinks people were forced to change, forced to go into cells. So was there a war? Were there resisters even then?"

"Well, if there were," he said, looking up at the empty bunk above him, "we know one thing: The resisters lost."

35

AFTER OUR ONE BREAKTHROUGH, TIM and I spent the day being *slightly* more motivated. But whoever had collected this stuff had simply gathered everything they could find without stopping to think if it was a crucial clue to the past or, like, a piece of useless crap.

He held up a shirt that said ATLANTA BRAVES. "I've seen this word before," he said, pointing to "Atlanta." He went to the map that we'd tacked on the wall and started searching.

I'd made an executive decision of what to do with useless items we'd gone through: The trash bags were piling up. Printed pieces of paper called "coupons" showed that food had been super, super expensive but they also had a lot of things I'd never heard of, like SpaghettiOs and "sports drink."

"Found it!" he said. "It's a cell, here!" He pointed to an area in section F. "A cell called At-lan-ta," he clarified, sounding out the word. "Maybe they were famous for their extra-brave people."

"Cool," I said. "What do you make of this?" I threw another

T-shirt at him and saved him the trouble of sounding the words out. "It says 'Grateful Dead.'"

He frowned. "That's a weird name for a cell. I'll see if I can find it."

I smoothed out Crumbling Yellow Newspaper #1647 and wrote down its date: March 18, 2029. CHINA LAUNCHES MISSILES AT JAPAN! IS THIS THE START OF WORLD WAR III?

"World War Three?" I read. "So…there were two others? Two other whole world wars? Tim, put this on the timeline."

We'd drawn a long, long timeline across one of the solid walls, and when we found something interesting that had a date on it, we wrote it in.

He came over to get the newspaper and I showed him which words to copy. He had all his numbers down, so that was good. "I couldn't find the Grateful Dead cell anywhere," he said.

"Put that paper in the Ms. Strepp stack when you're done, okay?"

"Look—what's this?" He held out a flat silver disk about as wide as his hand. "It says 'Adele' on it."

"I don't know," I said. "Is it part of some machine? Hey, like one of those little machines on that table? See if it fits any of them."

While he looked at the machines, I tossed a menu for Popeyes fried chicken, business cards for a tax service, an ad for a haircut salon, and an ad for something called a tarot card reader into a garbage bag.

"It fits in this one!" he said, pressing a button. The blast of music startled both of us and for a minute we just stared at each other in surprise. "I like it," he decided.

"I like it, too," I said. Soon we were both singing along, and I was tapping my fingers on the pile I was working on. "Send my love to your new luh-uh-ver, treat her be-eh-ehter, we gotta let go of all of our ghosts..."

This was definitely a solid link to the past.

36

BUT EVEN WITH THE MUSIC and the challenge of figuring out the past, this was a boring, dirty job. We were hunched over for hours, shaking dust and cobwebs off everything, reading every last slip of paper or artifact. For each possible clue, we weeded out thousands and thousands of valueless garbage.

One day after lunch I was on the floor leafing through a magazine called *The New Yorker*, reading its cartoons. I remembered Julie's diary entry about going to visit her aunt in New York—maybe it wasn't fantasy after all.

I jumped when Tim tossed an empty plastic cup at me. "We're falling asleep, because we have the stupidest job ever," he said. "But we're not gonna let it make us soft! Drop and give me twenty!"

"What?"

"Thirty!" he commanded.

A week ago, thirty push-ups wouldn't have winded me. This

time I was panting and sweating, my arms shaking when I finished. Then he surprised me by also doing thirty push-ups.

"New plan," he panted when he was done. "We work for two hours, then work out for twenty minutes. If we get invaded we need to stay in top fighting condition!"

It was a good plan. Maybe his reading was on a kindergarten level, but he had practical smarts.

During our next twenty-minute break he leaped on me and we wrestled hard, using the tricks we'd learned at the Crazy House. Our sweat mixed with the dust and we looked like we'd come from a mining cell.

My moment of pride was when I slammed his head against the floor and he grunted, but my victory was immediately wiped out by him pinning me for the third time. His arm across my neck, one leg holding my body to the floor, he panted, "I miss Becca so bad."

I went slack immediately, and he let me go.

"I do, too. I know she's alive, wherever she is," I said. "I would feel it if she weren't."

He met my eyes. "I would, too."

Later he found another silver disk, but instead of audio, it was video. He messed with it until he got it to play on a blank wall.

It was a biography about a guy who was in a war and then ran a lot and then had a fishing boat. We were so engrossed in the pre-System world that we forgot to bolt the trapdoor after lunch, and of course that was when Ms. Strepp came up with no warning.

"I assume this is you two, working hard?" she asked frostily, her lips turning white from being pressed together.

"Yeah…it's…showing that some things from the past are the same today," he said.

"Such as?" she asked.

I met her eyes bravely. "'Shit happens.'"

37

BECCA

AFTER FOOD, SLEEP, AND RELATIVE safety for twenty-four hours, I was much closer to being human. My squad and I set out when it turned dusk, and I was relieved when we were out in the wild. Maybe I couldn't live in a cell again. Maybe the only people who can stand it are people who don't know there's a choice.

Again we stuck to the edge of the abandoned road. I was more patient, able to explain to Levi that we were going single file because it would hide our numbers, and so on, and other leadery teachable moments.

Still, this night-silent road was creepy, keeping all of us alert and on guard, scanning the woods and the tall grass for anything that might burst out at us. United soldiers? Crazy locals? Killer robots? Anything felt possible. We hadn't heard wolves lately, but that didn't mean that they—or something worse—weren't there.

A chilly wind picked up, making wisps of hair fly around my face. Then I held up my hand—Stop. My squad froze and I squinted at the trees, listening.

"Are those bugs?" I breathed quietly to Nate. "Cicadas or something?"

Nate shook his head slowly. "At this time of year?"

I opened my mouth to tell the squad to scatter but a blinding light flooded the area, so bright we winced and shielded our eyes.

"Run!" I yelled, just as a spray of bullets strafed the leaves around us, shredding them and splintering bark. I dove into the tall grass and lay still, looking upward. I shaded my eyes and saw that it was a United military drone, about eight feet across, loaded with cameras, lights, and weapons. It continued to lay down round after round of gunfire, slicing grass in half, leaving pockmarks in the old road surface. Was there only one of them?

Slowly I raised to one knee and put my rifle to my shoulder. I adjusted the gunsight, looking through one eye. I didn't know how well protected the drone was, but I had to stop it, and damn fast.

Blood pounding in my ears, I aimed. The drone flitted around like a big, ungainly dragonfly, darting high and low, left and right, tilting. I followed it for a minute, adjusting for its movements, and when it skimmed through my crosshairs, I fired. Once, twice, three times, *pop pop pop.*

It exploded, raining shards of hot metal and tough plastic down on us. Someone drew in breath with a hiss as if they'd been hurt, and I leaped to my feet. Overhead, the fractured drone whirled crazily like an injured animal, its smooth artificial sound now hiccupping and raspy. It crashed into some low trees across the road, and almost immediately small tongues of flame started curling through the leaves.

"Freeze!" The voice was loud and mean, shouted through a bullhorn. Suddenly, dark-uniformed soldiers pounded down the road.

"Sic 'em!" I bellowed, springing out of my hiding place. The rest of the team materialized, weapons raised, assessing the threat like professionals.

"You're illegals!" a soldier shouted at me, billy club raised.

"I don't recognize your law!" I yelled back, and launched myself at him.

38

I ALMOST SMILED WHEN I saw the United soldiers wearing tactical gear—all foolishly brave and overconfident like it was a magical shield. Ooh, body armor! Guess we'll give up!

Guess again! I took Billy Club Guy out with a flying tackle and choke hold. Of course Strepp had trained us on tactical gear. She'd trained us on every single thing she could possibly think of. If an irate farmer came at me waving barbecue tongs wrapped with a spitting cobra, I had a plan in place.

Running up behind one guy, I smashed his knee from the side, and he buckled. One hard blow from the butt of my rifle and he was out. Nate used his knife to slice through the straps of the soldier's holster, then yanked it free, seizing the pistol. He pistol-whipped the soldier in the temple. Three down, a dozen more to go.

The smell of fire was strong and thick; coiling smoke had started to weave among the frenzied action. I caught a glimpse of Jolie, her eyes wide and determined, as she shoved her rifle under a helmet, popping its straps. Then it was easy to deliver a knockout kick to the head.

Mills leaned over a prone body, his fist raised. Bunny was everywhere at once, showing herself a graduate of the Crazy House by her combination of mixed martial arts, street-fighting tricks, and random violence.

Still the soldiers kept coming. Between the dark of night and the smoke, it was impossible to sweep the area with cover fire from my rifle. I couldn't avoid hitting my team if I spewed bullets everywhere.

Someone grabbed my arm and without hesitation I swept my other arm over and brought it down on his wrist, breaking his grip. I had a second's view of his surprised eyes and then my balled fist hit his throat and my hard, flat palm shot up into his nose, easily breaking it. He went down without a sound.

I took down two others, wrenching their weapons out of their hands, stomping on their radios, knocking down the ones starting to come around. As I was punching one of the barely conscious soldiers, another got the drop on me, tackling me to the dirt. I heard a crunch and a sharp pain flared in my hip. I flipped to my back and locked my legs around his neck, squeezing until he passed out.

The fire had spread and was now huge, flames slicing twenty, thirty feet into the air. It had jumped across the road and I realized with a pang of fear that we were surrounded.

Finally, all I saw was my squad standing among bodies as the heat got closer and the smoke got thicker. It felt like the fight had lasted an hour but it had probably been maybe six to eight minutes.

"Grab their gear!" I yelled, and we loaded up with as much as we could carry without slowing ourselves down. I snagged an automatic rifle off one soldier that was much nicer than the gun the Resistance had given me. Finally, exhausted and bloody, I found a tiny break in the flames that got closer to us with every second.

"We just gotta go through," I said. They nodded grimly.

I took a breath, then shielded my face with one arm. Of course, I had to go first—I was squad leader. Ducking my head, I plunged into the fire and ran through as fast as I could, wincing at the scorching heat that felt like it would peel my skin off. In seconds I was on the other side and Bunny was close behind me.

"Drop and roll!" she shouted. "You're on fire!"

I dropped and rolled. Nate tore off his jacket and smothered the embers in my hair as the others ran through in my wake. My face felt sunburned and there was a horrible smell of scorched hair, but no one had anything worse than that. We'd been lucky.

A minute later we were back on the road, sticking tightly to the line of trees, fairly invisible from above.

"No one's following us," Nate reported.

"All those guys we left there," Mills said, coming up beside me. "Do you think the fire will get them?

"I'm counting on it," I said grimly, and hitched up my new rifle.

39

CASSIE

"YOU'RE SLACKING OFF!" MS. STREPP yelled, and threw my latest reports on the floor. "You should be getting through *thousands* of items every day! Yesterday was what, three hundred? Today only two-eighty? What is *wrong* with you?"

"Nothing," I said tersely. "Every single thing needs to be looked at and a decision made about it. Then we have to log it, maybe put it on the time—"

"Excuses!" she shouted. "You losers are just wasting time! Are you *napping* up here?" Her eyes narrowed. "Are you *fooling around* up here?"

"Oh, God, no!" Tim said.

My face flushed with heat. Did she think the four of us were just interchangeable?

"No. It just takes time." I didn't mention that Tim was still pretty slow at reading and I was doing 98 percent of the logging work.

Her face was hard and suspicious. "Speed. It. Up." She kept the glare going all the way down the rope ladder.

Tim quickly closed the hatch and this time didn't forget to lock it.

"I'll try to get faster at the preliminary sorting," he said, looking embarrassed.

"It would help if we had something specific to look for," I said, settling next to some stuffed garbage bags, thinking I should probably just take crap out of this bag and transfer it right into a new one. "It's impossible deciding whether a *menu* is crucial or a *postcard* some important clue."

"Yeah," he said, sitting on the floor several yards away. The attic had four low windows that began at the floor and came up to his knees. Some of their panes were cracked and all of them were caked with ancient dust and dirt. He rubbed a spot clean and gazed out.

I bet he was wishing he was out there with Becca. *Well, so am I, pal.*

Precious Treasure Bag #702 held crocheted doilies that were stained and fraying, a broken china shepherdess statue, dried-out tins of shoe polish, some half-burned candles, and a cracked jar of candy all melted together and disgusting. I did in fact simply transfer all this to a new garbage bag.

Last, I pulled out a box of small frosted cakes. By God, yes! Let's squirrel *this* away forever! This, *this* will hold the key to United civilization! I was getting bitter.

He looked over, saw the box in my hands. "Twuh—" he sounded out, scooching closer. "Tweennn-kye?"

"I think Twink-ee," I said, and ripped open the box. Inside, each cake was individually wrapped. I'd never seen anything like this and tossed one to him. "Here, try it," I joked.

He held the package up and looked at it from all angles. After a long examination, he tore open the cake package.

"Not really!" I shrieked. "Don't eat that!" I stared in horror as he took a bite and chewed thoughtfully. "You are gonna die," I predicted.

He turned it to show me that it was full of whipped cream. Whipped cream a hundred years old. Older. He took another bite. "It's not bad." He finished it and crumpled up the wrapper. "So how old do you think it was?"

I picked up the torn box. "Best by August 18, 2036," I read.

"Whoa. That's old," he admitted.

I picked up Yellowed Newspaper #1,000,000 and skimmed it, wondering when he would suddenly double over and start barfing. Some words caught my eyes and I went back and reread them.

"Oh, my God," I said, looking up. *"Oh, my God."*

40

"WHAT?" HE ASKED, LEANING OVER to see. "What is it?"

Wordlessly, I held up the paper to show him the headline. His forehead wrinkled as he tried to decipher it, and I took it back.

"'CDC Scientists Confirm Use of Biological Weapons,'" I read.

"What's the CDC?" he asked.

"I don't know," I said. "But this sounds bad." I read on: "'The New World party has released a biological weapon into the water supplies of cities across the US'!"

"US," I said. "The United States! What the United used to be, right?" I went on: "'The vaporized particles, based on organophosphates, dissolve readily in water and are quickly absorbed by plants, animals, and humans.'"

The cold feeling in my gut told me we'd finally found a real clue.

"Oh, crap," he said. "So, don't drink the water, or eat, or breathe. This must have killed ... a ton of people."

My heart pounded and adrenaline-fueled alertness woke my

brain cells. "Who did this?" I asked out loud. "Who was the New World party? Tim! Look for more newspapers!"

We tore open boxes, cut bags apart, rifled through piles, but for a good hour we found only more useless junk—grocery store receipts, stacks of paper called Tax Returns, a cookbook that I set to one side to look at later.

"Here, newspapers!" he said, hauling out a stack from an old trunk.

He scanned the dates. "This one's from…1926," he said. "It's pretty much dust." He tossed it in my lap and I gave it a quick look.

"'Ederle Swims the English Channel,'" I read. "That makes no sense—oh, Ederle is a person." It was from too long ago and I tossed it.

"Hey, look! A dartboard!" he said, holding up a round target. "The bars in my home cell always had dartboards." He smiled at it and leaned it against one wall. "Just gotta find some darts," he muttered.

I was on fire now, pawing impatiently through stacks as fast as I could, getting filthy. I refused to take a twenty-minute workout break and worked right through lunch, though he put a sandwich on the floor next to me. My arms actually ached toward the end of the day and I'd almost given up when I pried open an old foot-locker and found more newspapers.

"Bingo!" I said, "2037!" I spread one on the ground and skimmed headlines—disturbing headlines. I read slower. This couldn't be true. It couldn't be true…I flipped to the next paper and the more I read, the colder my skin got and the more my stomach hurt.

"You've gone white," he said. "You're making me nervous."

I'd almost forgotten he was here, and now I looked at him as if I'd never seen him before. I blinked a couple times and drew in a breath, feeling like I was about to throw up.

"How...how much of this stuff do you think is from after 2037?" I asked him weakly.

He glanced around. "Probably...maybe most of it? Like, it can't all be ancient. Why?"

I could hardly say the words. "Because everything, *everything* after 2037 was infected with a...plague," I said, looking at all the bags and papers we'd handled. "A fatal plague."

41

BECCA

WE WALKED MOST OF THE night, taking a couple hours before dawn to rest. It was those cold half-sleeps when I was curled in a shivering ball that made me miss Tim the most. I thought about him, his big, warm body, his strong arms, the scent of his skin, and hot tears came to my eyes. I tried to put him out of my mind.

Now, close to dawn, I sat up, shivering, and reached for the mobile phone tucked away in a hip pouch. Strepp had given me the precious piece of technology before we left the camp so I could report back to her. I figured the skirmish with the United soldiers last night counted as important enough to risk using an unsecured cell signal. But when I pulled the phone from its holder, pieces of plastic rained from my hand.

Shit! The phone had been smashed when that United asshole

tackled me. Strepp was going to kill me—if I survived long enough to see her again.

We had to get on the move again. I woke the team and we broke camp, removing all signs that we'd been there. As we walked, I did constant sweeps, remembering to look up as well as all around. Didn't want any more drones to sneak up on us. I froze suddenly when I saw—in the trees—

I held up my hand, and the footsteps behind me stopped. They'd seen it, too—I heard gasps from my squad and whirled to give them a silent "shut the eff up" gesture.

Nate stood next to me.

"Shit," I breathed almost soundlessly. Nate nodded.

The woods were full of...skeletons? Skeletons. Hanging from the trees. Fraying ropes were still looped around the small bones of their necks. I looked around, my eyes peering through the gray half-light of the coming sunrise. Under some trees were small piles of bones—the ones whose ropes had finally given way. Carved into the bark, almost grown over, were the letters O W.

"Ow?" I said softly.

"A warning," Nate whispered. "But an old one. How old? Why? Who?"

I nodded, triply on alert, and advanced silently, gun drawn. Despite the grisly remains, there seemed to be no other dangers.

We stayed in the woods for more than an hour, picking our way east. Finally the filtered light got brighter and we could see ten, twenty feet ahead. I was thrilled to see the approaching end of the woods—my skin had crawled the whole time we were in here.

There had been no birds, no insects, no animals, just like a couple days ago.

Near the edge of the woods I surveyed the field we were approaching and I almost jumped when Levi whispered, "Weird."

"What?"

Levi pointed up and I took a step back in surprise. Above us were... *boats*. Boats stuck in trees.

42

CRANING MY NECK, I WANDERED in a circle, staring at the treetops. There were actually *boats* above us, maybe twenty feet up. One was old and wooden, with the name *Jack of All Trades* barely visible, painted on the side.

Jolie took my hand and spelled F-I-S-H-I-N-G. The only fishing boats I'd ever seen were much smaller, used only on Cattail Pond.

Another boat was much fancier than the fishing boat but had been broken in half, its rear end missing. Its once-white sides were stained gray-green with lichen and age. And right at the edge of the woods was a long, long gray metal thing, like a boat turned on its side and almost completely buried.

Without speaking, we walked the length of it, unable to believe that there had ever been a ship this big. Toward its pointed bow was painted US NAVY.

"US?" Nate said. "Like, United Sea something?"

I shook my head. "No idea." I wish we still had Jolie's camera to document the weirdness. Strepp would want to know about this.

I turned and looked back at the woods. Boats in trees. The woods were growing up around the boats, through them, eating them. Why would someone put boats in a forest? How long had they been here?

"Maybe this used to be a lake or something?" Bunny suggested, her dark face lit by morning's first sun.

"In the middle of dry land?" Mills scoffed.

"You got a better idea?" she challenged him.

"Basically, we have no freaking clue," I said, settling it. "Let's just file it under Crazy Shit We Saw, along with everything else."

Before us was a high, sloping plain of tall grass, but different, more like grain. It reminded me of wheat or oats but I didn't recognize it.

"Let's cross this slowly, guys," I directed. "Watch out for trip wires and snakes."

"I'll take point," Nate said, moving into the grass slowly, tapping a long, thin branch ahead of him.

Mills followed him, then Levi and Bunny. Jolie went next, and I took up the rear, scanning the grass with my binoculars. Nothing.

"Ulp!"

"What?" I demanded, snapping back to look at the team.

"Nate's gone," Mills said, sounding freaked.

43

"WHAT THE HELL?" BUNNY SAID, then she, too, disappeared.

I dropped to my knees and clicked off my rifle's safety. Then I tapped my comm and hissed, "Nate! Report!"

Nate's voice came back, angry and embarrassed. "I tripped on a rock." The grass ahead rustled and he stood up.

"It was a big rock," Bunny said, standing up, brushing dried grass off herself.

"A *rock*?" I said, standing up and clicking my safety back on. My heart pounded and my brain swirled with now-unneeded rescue plans.

"They're everywhere," Mills said, pushing his boot through the grass and almost immediately hitting a tall stone.

It turned out that the field was littered with hundreds and hundreds of these big weird stones. Some were maybe knee-high, some almost to the top of the grass. They were rounded, and weathered. We threaded our way through agonizingly slowly—sometimes there was barely room enough to walk between them.

Ahead of me, Jolie followed Bunny but she paused and pulled some grass away from a stone. Her quick blue eyes met mine as her sensitive fingers rubbed the stone, left and right. She held up a hand.

"Wait," I said, and the team stopped and turned.

Jolie rubbed the rock harder and once the lichen was mostly gone she pointed to words cut deeply into the worn stone.

I leaned closer to look. It said ANNA-LEIGH WESTON, BORN JANUARY 26, 2025, DIED MARCH 7, 2037.

"These are all tombstones!" I said, staring at the huge field.

Now everyone pushed grass aside and rubbed lichen and dirt off the weathered stones. They weren't like cell gravestones—those were flat slabs. These stood upright and went on as far as we could see—waves of golden grass with thousands of stones barely peeking through like mountains through clouds.

I looked up to see Nate watching me.

"This was from some catastrophe," he said. "Every person died the same year—2037. And there are thousands of stones."

"What the hell happened?" I exclaimed. "I mean, the skeletons, the tree-boats, and now this. It's like one huge mystery—are they connected? None of it makes sense!"

44

CASSIE

"**WHAT DO YOU MEAN**, *PLAGUE*?" Tim demanded.

I drew in a deep breath. "Okay—so the other paper said that the New World party had released organophosphates into everything, right? It's some kind of poison. Almost a year later, this paper says that the organophosphates killed about sixty million people, right off the bat."

"Sixty mill—that can't be true," he said.

"But I guess sixty million wasn't enough," I said, feeling my hands tremble. "This paper says that there's also some kind of plague infecting people." Again I looked around at the stacks of papers, food wrappers, and magazines lining the walls of the attic.

A sharp rapping on the trapdoor made us both jump.

"Open this door!" Ms. Strepp said.

Slowly I got up and walked over to it, then knelt so I could speak through its cracks. "I don't know if that's a good idea," I said.

There was a pause and I could imagine exactly what her face looked like—outraged.

"Open. This. Door."

"Well—we might ... be ... sick."

Silence. Then, "What? Why would you think that?"

I explained what I'd read in the newspapers. "After the first wave, the New World party wanted ... survival of the fittest for the future. So they infected everything, *everything* with an ... aerosolized virus. At least, that's what this paper says. So everything in here after 2037 could have come in contact with the virus."

My chest felt tight and I hoped that she would tell me to quit being stupid, open the door, of course there was no plague.

She didn't. Instead there was an even longer pause, then: "What kind of plague? From where?"

Her words turned my heart to ice. They showed that she accepted this *insane premise* as a real possibility.

My soldier's brain went on autopilot and I turned the page of the crumbling newspaper. "A virus," I reported, running my finger down the page. "They spliced a virus with ... like, yeast?" I read quickly, aware that Tim was taut with tension next to me. "The yeast allowed the virus to be dormant for a long time and then reactivate again in the right conditions."

I thought of her, holding on to the rope ladder below the trapdoor, in the dark, thinking hard.

"What kind of conditions?" she asked.

"Like ... in people," I said shakily. "In other mammals. If that's true and the virus came into contact with newspapers and clothes and stuff—then maybe Tim and I have breathed it in. Touched it. It could be reactivating. Inside us."

She was silent for once.

I tried not to panic. "So, Tim and I should probably be quarantined in sick bay," I said. "Just in case. And you might want to, you know, keep back a good distance."

"No," she said. "No, don't come down."

Tim and I looked at each other.

"We feel fine," I clarified. "This paper is from a long, long time ago. I'm probably worried for nothing." I clenched my fists, mentally begging her to tell me I was worried for nothing.

"You two will stay there," she said. "I'll have supplies brought to you. You are to stay up there until we know for sure it's safe for you to come down." Her voice already sounded farther away, as if she was climbing down the ladder.

"What?" Tim said loudly, pounding the trapdoor. "I'm not staying here! I can't even stand up straight!"

"You'll stay there!" she shouted from down below. "I'll post guards, so don't try anything. We can't risk you infecting the entire camp."

This plague was so dangerous, Ms. Strepp was willing to reveal the secret room? My mouth dropped open as I pictured Tim and me *dying* in this filthy attic, surrounded by junk.

"The things you're discovering are hugely important, Cassie and Tim," she called up, sounding just a touch softer. "You're providing crucial pieces of the puzzle. It's exactly what I need you to do."

I looked at Tim: We were thinking the same thing. She meant, *even if we died doing it.*

45

BECCA

AFTER THE FIELD OF GRAVES, we started climbing some rocky hills, still headed east. Mills, scouting ahead, found a cave barely big enough to hold all of us. After some tense discussion, Nate and I agreed that we could light a fire near the mouth of the cave.

"Use only the driest wood you can find," I instructed my squad. "The drier it is, the less smoke it puts off."

We sat around the small fire, our hands and feet stretched out to it as we ate our dried rations.

"What could have killed so many people all at once?" Bunny asked. "A bomb? A disease?"

"War?" Nate suggested, moodily poking at the fire.

"The skeletons don't make sense if a bomb wiped everything

out," Levi said, his small face thoughtful. "No one would have time to string them up. But if they were a warning about a war..."

Jolie spelled into Bunny's hand and Bunny translated.

"Jolie says they might have been a warning about a disease—like, don't come any closer because people die here."

"That's true," I said tiredly. "That would explain why they didn't burn the bodies, like normal people." All I wanted was to check in with Cassie and Tim back at camp, but all I had left of the cell phone Strepp gave me was the SIM card. Stupid plastic piece of crap.

"The map at the underground stop showed we should keep going in this direction," Nate said.

His words were interrupted by a low growl coming from overhead.

I gave Levi and Mills narrow-eyed looks. "Cut that out—it's creepy."

"That wasn't me," Mills protested, and Levi echoed him.

Nate moved around the fire to the cave entrance and looked around. Our night vision was shot because of the fire. Before he could say anything, another growl made my blood run cold. I jumped up as a huge animal leaped onto Nate, knocking him down.

"Wolf!" Bunny screamed, scrambling to her feet. I heard a *thunk* as her head hit the cave roof and she gasped.

"Cassie!" Nate screamed in a voice I'd never heard before. I grabbed my pistol and ran out to see a tsunami of wolves jumping down from the outcropping above the cave entrance, one after the other. Everywhere were lunging, snapping jaws, deep-throated snarls, and panicked screams of terror.

I threw myself on top of the wolf pinning Nate, stuck my gun in its side, and pulled the trigger. It howled and drew back. I had a second of seeing blood-red rage in its eyes before it fell sideways. A glance at Nate showed him lying still, his eyes open, looking upward.

46

"HELP!" BUNNY SHOUTED. ARMS BLOODY, she was straining against an enormous black-pelted wolf, trying to keep its sharp teeth from her throat. Crouching by Nate's side, I aimed and shot the animal in its head. It dropped like a sack of wheat, and Bunny staggered back.

Jolie had taken a burning branch from our fire and was swiping it at three animals circling her. They backed away from the flame when it was close and lunged for her when they could.

"Shoot them!" Mills screamed, unholstering his own pistol and firing at a hulking black wolf. I took a split second to gauge angles. I shot five times and dropped three wolves. Instantly another animal lunged. Jolie swung her burning branch like a baseball bat, and the wolf yelped and ran off, its fur lit with fire.

Still they kept coming, more than I could count. I'd been chased by a mean dog once, and had been terrified as I hopped a fence, its yellowish teeth snagging the hem of my jeans. This was infinitely worse.

"I'm out of bullets!" I shouted, reaching for the hunting knife in my shin sheath. It would have to do until I could grab my rifle; there was no time to reload. An enormous silver-streaked beast leaped at me, its paws as big as my hands. Its weight knocked my breath away and I made no noise as I hit the ground. I felt its sharp fangs pierce my jacket, then my skin and muscle, time spinning out as I lay there in shock. Somehow I still held my knife and sank it into the wolf's side as hard as I could. The blade scraped a rib; I pulled it out and angled it upward, pushing to the hilt. The wolf yelped and jerked but came down on me again, its hot breath in my face. Again I pulled the knife out and stabbed, over and over until the heavy weight sank on me, smelling of heat and fur and blood. I heard gunshots and shouting. They sounded very far away.

With a hard shove, I pushed most of the heavy animal off me, its sticky blood running onto my jeans. "Team! Report!" I gasped. I looked around but didn't see any more wolves.

Mills said, "I'm okay," in a strained voice.

Shakily I got to my feet and staggered over to Nate. He lay on his back beneath the wolf, his open eyes still staring skyward. His throat was a mess and his limp hands were covered in blood.

"I'm okay!" Bunny called. "So is Jolie."

"Levi?" I said, still kneeling by Nate.

There was no answer.

"Oh, God," Bunny said, sinking down next to a small form on the ground.

"I'm okay." Nate's voice was a hoarse whisper. I was shocked that he was alive, and could speak. In fact, I was shaking all over, my shoulder was killing me, and I was covered in blood. It had hap-pened so damn fast.

"Becca!" Bunny said. Quickly I knelt by Levi and searched for a nonexistent pulse.

"Oh, Levi," I breathed, looking at him, little fourteen-year-old Levi who never should have been a soldier in the first place. His sweet face was untouched, but his torso was a raggedy mess of hor-rific gore. I put my hand over my mouth, wanting to scream or cry or fall to pieces.

Every one of us bore the effects of the wolf attack. Nate might be dying. Levi was dead. Some leader I was, huh?

47

THE WHOLE THING HAD TAKEN maybe three minutes. Three minutes, and Levi was gone. Nate was trying to sit up, one hand pressed to his neck. I felt sick at how much dark blood ran through his fingers. But if the wolf had hit his carotid artery or jugular, he'd already be dead.

I gathered whatever inner strength I had. "Okay, let me see," I said, prying his fingers away. I angled him to see better and tried to keep an "Oh, shit!" expression off my face. "It's deep, but not torn, and he didn't hit an artery. A couple staples and you'll be all set."

Nate's bloodless face turned even paler but I pretended not to notice. Jolie, on the alert as always, dropped the med kit next to me and I grimaced my thanks. I took out what I needed, but first things first.

Standing up, I went to the rest of the squad. "Guys, take everything of Levi's that we can use, as long as it won't slow you down. Then we need to hide his body—we should burn it, but that would take too long, make too much smoke. This ground is probably too hard to dig into, so maybe put him at the back of the cave and cover him with rocks."

Everyone looked at me, horrified. The thought horrified me, too, but it was necessary. "Do you want to leave his body here for the wolves?" I asked acidly. "Or for trackers to find?"

Mills swallowed and shook his head *no*.

"Right. Do it as fast as you can and scatter any blood into the dirt and leaves. I'm going to patch Nate up and then we need to hit it."

Working quickly, I swabbed Nate's gory neck with antiseptic wipes, which was like putting a Band-Aid on an arm that had been caught in a combine.

"Levi's dead?" Nate asked quietly, and I nodded.

"Yeah. Be still. When you talk I can see your muscles move, and it's gross."

I'd helped Pa patch up our horses when we had them, and Ed and Ned, our gentle oxen. Sometimes they'd wander into a barbed-wire fence or something. After a fast, completely inadequate local anesthetic, I put my fingers in Nate's neck, squeezed the muscle together but not too tightly, and shot a staple into it. He yelped and reared back.

"Come back here," I said.

Nate's face was green with pain, but he crawled closer and tilted his head. I sprayed some more anesthetic on his skin and repeated the process, shooting in two staples and making tears come to his eyes. We'd all had the bejesus kicked out of us at the Crazy House, and this wasn't too much worse. But I was glad it wasn't me.

It took half an hour to gather enough rocks to cover Levi's small, thin body. My throat ached and Jolie was crying, making odd snuffling noises that she herself couldn't hear. I forced Nate to lie down quietly while we worked and also made him drink a bunch of water. He'd lost a lot of blood.

Finally we were ready to go. The night felt like it had lasted a week. Bunny took point, followed by Jolie, then Mills, then Nate, then me. The adrenaline from the attack had drained out of me, leaving a cold, hollow feeling in the pit of my stomach.

I was glad that Nate wasn't dead—Cassie would have killed me—but he wasn't out of danger yet. His wounds could get infected, either killing him or making him so sick that I'd be forced to leave him somewhere. And there was a chance that the wolves had been rabid. So for the next week I had to keep an eagle eye on all of us—anyone who had gotten scratched, bitten, or drooled on. Because if any of us had rabies, I'd have to kill them myself. No exceptions.

48

CASSIE

AT LEAST HE DOESN'T SNORE, I thought, looking at Tim's sleeping form in the dim light. There was so little floor space up here that our sleeping mats were only a few feet apart. We were used to sharing rooms and dorms with others, but this was the first time I'd ever slept in the same room with just one guy. Too bad it was Tim. If it were Nate...this could almost be romantic.

Oh, my God. *Romantic?* I must be going cow-brained. I was in a filthy, dark, yucky attic with *my sister's boyfriend* and the *plague*! *Could you set the romance bar* any lower, *Cassie?*

I rolled onto my back and pulled my sleeping bag up higher. Speaking of plague, I did a swift self-check, as I'd done every five minutes I was awake. With nothing else to do last night, I'd read all the newspaper reports out loud to Tim. They'd listed the warning signs: sore throat, fever, swollen glands, bruises. These would rapidly devolve into bleeding from…everywhere. Then high fever, blackened pustules, bloody stool…awesome. Gosh, Cassie, that would be even *more* romantic!

Come to think of it, I was glad Nate wasn't here. Groaning, I wiggled out of my sleeping bag and rolled it and the mat up, stowing them out of the way. High fever? *Nope.* Bloody stool? *Not yet!* Excellent.

I opened the trapdoor and felt for the new rope we'd tied to a hook. It was heavy and I pulled it up, wondering what Strepp had sent us for food today. I pawed through the contents, looked at sleeping Tim again, and decided not to let him eat anything he couldn't spell.

Peanut butter sandwiches. I remembered when Becca and I made waffles or pancakes, drenching them with syrup from our own maple trees. We'd drunk fresh apple juice and real coffee with real milk from our cows. Suddenly I missed my cell so much that my chest hurt and tears came to my eyes. If I could go back just one year, back when things were normal and I was usually mad at Becca…

The horrible thing was that now I knew what a crock it had been. I'd thought my life was normal, but I'd been living a lie. This life, as much as it *totally sucked* right now, was *real.* I mean, you know, horrible and filled with probable plague, but still. It was real. And bad real is better than good fake.

49

HOLDING MY SANDWICH IN ONE hand, I went to a table where I'd cleared a space. Every relevant newspaper account that I'd been able to find was lined up in order.

Ms. Strepp had given us a phone so we could report without having to see anyone face-to-face. I jumped when it rang loudly and grabbed it. "Hello?"

"Report," Ms. Strepp said.

"We're not dead," I said, and took a bite of sandwich.

"Any symptoms?" she asked.

I looked over to see Tim starting to sit up. "Nope."

"I hope your theory is wrong," she said. "It's quite possible that any plague spores are long dead. Tell me what you've found out."

"Well, weirdly, reports about the plague stop abruptly," I said. "It was plague, plague, plague for about three months, then no papers at all, and then suddenly the papers were back, looking different, with no mention of any plague."

"Are there any numbers anywhere of how many people died?" she asked.

"Between October 2037 and March 2038—I mean, this sounds crazy," I said. "But everything added up, it's about two hundred million people, dead."

There was a long silence and finally I said, "Hello?"

"I'm here." Her voice sounded flat, quiet. "Then the newspapers suddenly stopped?"

"Yeah. They start again in May 2038. But get this—in the early stacks I've got newspapers from all over, all these weird places: New York, Chicago, Los Angeles, Washington, DC. And they're all separate, like different companies or whatever. After May, all the newspapers say *New World News*, New York edition, or Chicago edition, or whatever. The news got centralized by one company."

"This is amazing information, Cassie," Ms. Strepp said. "You've done remarkably well in putting clues together and forming theories."

"But what does it mean?"

"I'm not sure," Ms. Strepp said. "It looks like the New World party killed vast numbers of people to be able to control the relative few who were left. To divide them up into cells."

"So the New World party became the United?"

"I don't know. Keep digging," she said, and hung up.

I finished my sandwich and glumly looked around the attic. We still had untold piles of crap to wade through. Piles of possible clues. We had to sift through it all, as long as we were able.

He shook his head and rubbed his neck, scowling at me. "Wish you were Becca," he said out of the blue, sounding mean.

"Wish you were Nate," I snapped back.

As if realizing he'd been a jerk, he muttered, "I have a head-ache." Like that was an excuse.

I realized I had a headache, too. "Eat something," I said, point-ing to the basket.

We had to keep going—I didn't know how much time we had.

50

BECCA

WE DIDN'T STOP AFTER THE sun came up. We needed to leave wolf country and get to a cell or safer place to rest. The last fifteen miles had been one horror show after another, with the sea of tombstones, the skeletons hanging from trees, and rabid wolves.

The land had changed to small, flattened hills and then to rocky, thickly forested woods. We hadn't seen anything of note since four a.m., which was how I liked it.

I kept Nate ahead of me so I could watch him. He was matching our pace, but it was costing him. He moved stiffly in his torn, bloody coat, and his face was grim and pale, his lips pressed together so hard they were surrounded by white. Every so often I noticed him putting a hand up to the bandage at his neck, which was becoming splotched with blood. Maybe I should have added more staples.

The rest of the team was unusually silent and subdued, but more alert. We each jumped with every cracking twig, every odd bird-call, every rustle in the undergrowth. I was remembering to scan up as well as all around, and Bunny and Jolie had been ordered to look out for traps, trip wires, and sudden pits of doom. Anything was possible.

It was on one of my three-sixty sweeps that I noticed an old, rusted metal rung stuck into a tree trunk—almost entirely grown over. I stopped and peered upward. The rung was about a third of the way up the tree, maybe twenty feet in the air.

"Hang on," I said softly, and the team stopped. I pointed at the rung, then peeled off my backpack and rummaged in it for my rope. I tossed the rope over a branch and climbed up while Mills and Jolie belayed me. There were more rungs, some of them only slightly visible, deeply embedded in the tree's bark. But they were climbable. After twelve feet I saw a small platform way at the top of the tree's crown. Now the branches were thinner and closer together, which was good because the rungs had either stopped or been swallowed completely.

I had to squirm through a narrow spot to get up to the actual metal platform, which had been bolted to the tree who knew how long ago. A rotted canvas tarp was thrown over something lumpy. I gritted my teeth, sure this would be some horrible dead body, maybe more than one. Holding my breath, I yanked the tarp off to reveal...

"What the hell is that?" Bunny asked, pulling herself up onto the platform.

"It's an anti-aircraft gun," I said slowly, brushing a pile of dried leaves off the metal seat. We'd all been drilled on every kind of weapon Strepp could find out about, everything from nunchucks to the big tank-mounted 150-millimeter war cannons. So I'd seen pictures of things like this.

I sat down on the metal seat and looked at the scope. It was crusted with dirt and rusted into place but I scrubbed the gunk off and peered through it. With effort I turned various dials and finally fuzzy blobs in the distance merged into focus. I sat up and looked at Bunny.

"What?" she asked.

"It's pointed right at a cell," I said, looking again. I scanned along the boundary until I spotted a sign near the road. "Cell B-24-23."

"Huh," Bunny said. "How far away? Likely to be friendly?"

"Can't tell about the friendly part—maybe...four miles?" I sat back, somewhat relieved. They'd have real medical facilities— maybe we could get Nate patched up better. Plus, it felt good to have a concrete destination instead of just *heading east*.

"Can I see?" Bunny asked.

"Yeah, just a sec," I said, moving the gun's barrel with effort. It showed more wooded plains, more hills, more...

"What the almighty hell?" I muttered in shock.

"What? What?" Bunny asked.

"Holy shit," I said, feeling like I couldn't take a breath. "It's a... I think that's *a city*."

51

"A CITY?" BUNNY SAID. "YOU mean a cell?"

"No," I murmured, unable to believe what I was seeing. "It's so much bigger than a cell." I moved the barrel back and forth, my mouth hanging open. *The city never seemed to end.*

"Get *up*, goddamnit," Bunny said, hitting my shoulder.

I stood, my brain reeling. Bunny sat down, put her eye to the scope, and I was gratified to see her mouth drop open, too.

"Oh, my freaking God," she said. "Those buildings are way too big! Like fifty, sixty stories tall. *There are lights on.* How could there be that many people in one place?"

I tapped my comm so I wouldn't have to yell. "Guys, come up here and see this. Not you, Nate. Don't you dare."

"I'm fi—" he started, but I cut him off.

"You. Will. Stay. There," I spit out. "Keep watch or something." I clicked my comm off as he started to swear.

Jolie and Mills joined us on the small platform. Bunny got up, looking shocked, and Jolie sat down and focused the scope. Her blue eyes widened and she stared at me. I nodded. She reached for my hand and spelled out B-I-G-C-I-T-Y-T-H-A-T-G-U-Y-T-O-L-D-U-S-A-B-O-U-T-?

"Yeah," I said. "I won't lie—I am freaking."

Mills nudged Jolie and she got up.

"It *can't* be that big," Mills said, moving the barrel back and forth like I had. "It's like…twenty-five, thirty miles *across*? That's impossible!"

"But you see lights, right?" I asked. "It's inhabited."

"So are we headed there?" Bunny demanded.

"Yep," I said, then thought about Nate. "I think the city is about twelve to fifteen miles away. We're all fried. So first we'll head to the cell, which is much closer. Rest up there for a night, then make a line for the city."

I knew they wanted to argue—we were all dying to see it up close. But yeah, we were all fried. One more time I sat down and put my eye to the scope. From this distance the city was a huge, lit-up blob compared to the tidy, ordinary outlines of the cell. What kind of cell, I wondered, moving the scope back and forth. And what…what is that other thing?

"Momento," I said, holding up one finger. The others had climbed down, but Bunny was still halfway on the platform.

"What," she said.

"There's something else," I said. "Closer. Something this gun could have hit even with its sights covered."

Bunny climbed back up and took my seat. I helped her point the rusted metal in the right direction. "Gol' dang," she breathed.

"It's a United outpost," I said, stating the obvious.

"It's small," Bunny said, her eyes narrowing as she thought.

"We need to go there," I said, lowering my voice.

Bunny nodded, then pointed downward and mouthed, "Nate."

I nodded. He was a problem.

We climbed down, hitched up our gear, and I told Nate about the freakishly huge city.

"Are we headed there now?" he asked.

"No. We're headed toward Cell B-24-23," I said, and explained why. He was silent for a while, amazingly enough.

Then he said, "Who was the gun aimed at? The cell or the city?"

I'd wondered that. Had this been self-protection for the Resistance? Or a tool for the United to help squelch troublemakers?

"I don't know," I said.

We walked on in silence—we had four miles to cover before we could rest or eat. Nate kept up, despite still being pale, despite being in obvious pain. *Hm*, I thought. Not bad for a Provost's son.

52

CASSIE

TIM LAY ON HIS STOMACH on the floor, looking out one of our four small windows. Neither of us felt like working or doing twenty-minute workout breaks or anything productive. It was more like we just sat there and tried to turn our brains off.

I lay next to him, pushing him to move over. Once again I was reminded of the differences between him and Nate. Tim was bigger, heavier, more physical. Nate was muscular—after Crazy House, everyone was. But he was more finely built, less bulky. He felt just right when I held him close. Tim would feel like I was hugging a statue. Not that I would be hugging him.

Below us in Regular Land, we saw recruits in training, marching up and down or running past us in formation. I heard Ms. Strepp barking at them through a bullhorn, telling them to move their lazy asses, etc. I sighed. Good times.

Out of sight we heard gunfire and shouting but we were used to that. One way to make recruits pay extra attention is to use live ammunition. It has a distinctive sound.

"I feel stupid, being up here like this," he said. "I should be down there, where I could do some good. Up here, I'm just—"

I got to my feet, resigned to working my way through one more box, one more bag, one more pile. "You're my manly brawn," I said.

He gave me a look. "You can lift and move anything up here."

I tried again. "You're my entertainment."

"That's awesome. That's what I want to be. That's what I trained so hard for."

His voice was bitter. I was saying all the wrong things.

"I don't mean *entertainment*," I said, thinking quickly. "I mean...look. I'm stuck up here because I got good grades in school. I assume. Basically Ms. Strepp looks at me and thinks 'librarian.' That's not what I want, either. You might not be doing all the writing or cataloguing, but I mean it, Tim. If I can't be with Becca and Nate, then I'm really glad I'm with you. You...make me feel less scared."

I hadn't meant to get all gushy, and I didn't want him to get the wrong idea.

I looked up to see him gazing at me thoughtfully. "Yeah?" he said.

"Yeah." I nodded. "You don't get hysterical. You don't take it all personally. You're not an asshole."

His eyebrows went up. "Okay, I feel better now. Thanks for the pep talk." His face was sardonic but his voice let me know he was

141

kidding. He stood up, hunched over, and came to see what I was working on.

I'd opened an old suitcase, but instead of the usual clothes and personal things, it was full of books. They were mostly for kids, and some of them were really, really old, like from the 1990s. There was one about a kid who lives on a farm. It showed them harvesting their wheat, which was totally normal, but then they just sold it themselves to another company, which was crazy. They didn't turn it over to the United for the collective or the Co-op. It was beyond weird to think there was a pre-System time when the United didn't exist.

There was one about a bunny and how much his bunny mom loved him. For some reason it made my throat hurt, but it passed. I logged the books' titles and the date they were published, handed them to Tim, and he stowed them in the Keep Because It Might Be Important But Sure Doesn't Seem Like It pile.

"I like seeing the old-fashioned clothes and cars and everything," I said.

"Yeah, it's weird," he said, then coughed. He coughed more and I watched him solemnly. Was this the first sign of illness?

He saw me looking at him and frowned. "We're surrounded by hundreds of years of dust," he pointed out.

Yeah, okay. I'd give him that.

At the very bottom of the suitcase, I found a thin book wrapped in stained and faded tissue paper. The paper disintegrated when I opened it. Inside was another book, but this one had been partly burned. Across its singed back someone had scrawled, *Lies! Destroy!*

Is that why someone had tried to burn it? It had been saved so carefully.

Trying to keep the covers from falling off, I opened the book.

Its title was *Adam and the Plague,* and it had been published in 2037.

53

ADAM AND THE PLAGUE WAS obviously meant for kids—it was short, not too many words, and had pictures on almost every page. But it was incredibly dark and depressing. Like, if you wanted to make a kid cry themselves to sleep every night for a week, give 'em this book.

"Geez, Tim, look at this," I said, and read out loud: "'One day Adam's sister, Amy, came home from school early. She felt terrible. Her throat hurt. Her eyes were red. She had a fever.'"

Tim made a face and coughed again.

For Tim's sake I skipped the whole middle part, with the illustrations showing exactly how Amy's symptoms progressed. I mean, the kid died in three days, and by the end of the third day Amy barely looked human.

I put it into a Keep pile and wandered casually to the dinky, inadequate bathroom. As soon as I shut the door I peered at my face in the mirror, feeling my neck for swollen glands. They felt fine. Then I looked at my skin everywhere to see if I had weird blisters or pustules. I didn't. So far.

When I came out, he was working his way through what looked like a homemade pamphlet—printed poorly, stapled together. Its title was FIGHT BACK NOW!

"It says that the New World party infected everyone in the United States with the plague on purpose," he said, looking disgusted.

"Yeah, we knew that," I reminded him, then leaned over so we could read the pamphlet together.

```
Here are the facts!
  • The plague has been disseminated by
    the New World party.
  • Their goal is to reduce the
    population to a "manageable" number
    of people with strong immune systems.
  • Their final goal is to restructure
    society. Everything is run by them,
    and the rest of the people provide
    for them.
```

I frowned. Like, in cells? Farming cells, manufacturing cells? The final paragraph of the pamphlet said:

```
People! Fight Back! Drop off the grid!
Build self-sufficient homes and hide
them! Live on your own, don't connect
```

```
with anyone! Never let anyone know where
you are! Don't depend on the government
for anything! Self-sufficiency is your
only chance.
```

"I'm getting such a bad feeling about this," he said.

"A bad feeling like, oh, God, this is the truth?" I asked him. He nodded.

I thought about the different cells I'd seen and the big expanses of empty land between them. Could some people still be hiding away, self-sufficient, after all this time? What would happen if we found some?

54

BECCA

"OKAY," I SAID, PUTTING ON my best leader voice. "Let's stop and rest for a minute."

Nate's determined trudging came to a slow halt. His face was damp with sweat and he looked a bit greenish. But that wasn't why I had stopped.

"We must be just a mile or so from the cell," Mills said.

"Yep," I said, checking my rifle and slinging extra ammo around my shoulder. "But this is a nice acre or so of winter wheat, perfect to hide and rest in. Just watch out for snakes. Probably too cold for them, anyway," I added as an afterthought.

"Okay, so we're resting," Mills said, "in this nice field of wheat. But why? Just because he's dead on his feet?" He pointed his gun at

Nate and I knocked it down so hard that its barrel tip jammed into the dirt.

"I wasn't gonna shoot him," Mills protested.

"Don't point your weapon at anyone in the squad," Bunny said, leaving the "idiot" silent.

"We're resting because Jolie and I have to make a little side trip," I said, motioning to Jolie to arm up. She nodded, watching my face.

Mills and Nate looked surprised, so I quickly explained about the United outpost we'd seen.

"We should all go!" Nate protested, and I just looked him in the eyes until his cheeks reddened and he sat down, furious.

"Jolie and I are just going to run over and check things out. You three will stay here and protect each other. I have my comm if you need anything, and we'll be back before dark. Most likely."

Leaving Mills and Nate both pouting in the field of winter wheat, Jolie and I trekked toward the trees, where there'd be some cover. As we walked, I told her what was going on, just moving my mouth, not making any sound. She nodded her understanding.

When we were within shooting distance of the outpost, I looked through my field glasses and saw that really, it was damn small. Weirdly small. The bunkhouse was barely bigger than an outhouse and could hold no more than six soldiers. Maybe eight. There was a ten-foot chain-link fence topped with razor wire, but we could get through that. The most interesting thing was that between the small bunkhouse and the other building that I assumed was an office of some kind, there was an old-fashioned whipping post. No one in our cell ever used one anymore but there was one here and it had a man tied to it.

I turned to Jolie and mouthed, "He's not in a United uniform."
She spelled into my hand, R-E-S-C-U-E-?

I grinned and nodded my agreement. We sat very still, hidden by trees, and watched the place for more than an hour. There seemed to be no more than six United soldiers—one in the office, one on guard, one yelling at the tied-up man, and one in the back, peeling potatoes. I assumed two were sleeping in the bunkhouse, waiting for their turn to be on guard.

We timed our attack well, taking out the guard and the cook quietly with a choke hold and rifle butt to the head. I searched the guard, but he didn't have ID or any useful intelligence. He *did* have a pistol with a sound suppressor, which I liberated. From there we used wire cutters on the fence, glad it wasn't electrified, and crept in. My shoulder hurt from where the wolf had bitten me, and in the back of my mind was the knowledge I had to get food and help for my team ASAP.

Right now the only thing keeping me going was adrenaline, and that would wear off soon enough. Jolie and I headed to the bunkhouse, using signals.

The door to the bunkhouse was unlocked, and those two guys never felt a thing. This was starting to feel too easy. We opened a bunkhouse window just a slit and gave each other a "ready" nod. Then I picked off the guy yelling at the man on the whipping post, dropping him mid-rant. The last United soldier ran out of the office, gun raised, but Jolie was ready and shot him before he had time to get a shot off.

From there we went to the office and shot up their communication equipment, screens, computers, etc. Only then did we approach the man.

He wearily looked up, his face lined with pain, and then we were all surprised.

"You're kids," he said hoarsely.

"So are you," I pointed out.

55

HE WAS A BIG KID, the way Tim was, over six feet and with the muscles of a farm boy. We got him out of there as fast as we could, weaving ourselves through the trees and making our way back to the others. A few times we had to catch him before he fell over, but we gave him water and the last of my protein bars, and he stumbled through the woods much like Nate had: almost silently.

So he had some training.

"Please tell me you're part of the Resistance," he said at last.

I rolled my eyes at Jolie. "No, we're just a couple of crazy kids with some TX-97s and a dream," I said, patting my weapon. "*Of course* we're part of the Resistance."

"So am I," he said. "My name is Ansel. I'm from B-97-250."

"How did you get there?" I asked, nodding my head back at the outpost.

His face grew ashen. "We're—we were advance scouts under our soccer coach, Mr. Tsu. Those guys took my whole team and tried to get us to talk. I was the last one." His voice choked and he scrubbed a dirty, sweaty hand over his eyes.

Jolie took his hand. I-M-S-O-R-R-Y, she wrote. He looked mystified.

"Concentrate on what letters she's writing in your palm," I told him, and she wrote it again.

. "Thanks," he told her.

"Where's the rest of your team?" I asked.

"At the bottom of a gully about a quarter-mile away," he said, his voice sounding thick. "Not even burned."

"Okay, Ansel, we're about to come up to the rest of our team, who are waiting for us," I told him.

"There's a cell, B-24-23, not far from here," he said. "We were headed to it."

"That's where we're headed, too," I said. "Gotta patch up one of our team."

"Do you know about the city?" he asked.

I stopped and looked at him. "Yeah, we know about it. What do *you* know?"

"I know it's the capital of the United," he said, and my stomach turned over. "And they call it Chi-ca-go."

I schooled my expression, trying not to look shocked.

"And," he added grimly, "I know how to get in."

56

WE INTRODUCED ANSEL TO BUNNY, Mills, and Nate, and the six of us agreed to make for Cell B-24-23 as fast as we could.

Its gate was closed, which was unusual. We'd have to take a chance that there was a friendly house here. In one of the deepest shadows of the boundary fence's perimeter I crouched and took the wire cutters out of my pack. Soon we could bend back enough of the fence to crawl through.

Our field rations were just about gone, and there were now six of us again. Nate and Ansel both looked like they were running on empty, like they might fall over if they stopped plodding forward. The rest of us were hungry, thirsty, and exhausted. I knew if we weren't, we'd be racing toward the humongous city we'd seen. It was just so hard to believe something like that existed.

Unlike at home, this cell wasn't ringed by farms, acres of wheat and corn, fenced-in pastures with softly breathing horses or cattle. Instead, right after the traditional thicket of conifers blocking the sight of the boundary fence, we were immediately in a neighborhood.

"Fancy," Mills said under his breath.

It *was* fancy, like the nicest part of downtown back home. But this wasn't the downtown—it should be the boondocks. It was strange for everything to be this nice: houses painted, gardens manicured, no laundry forgotten in the chilly night.

"What's that?" Bunny whispered, pointing.

Mills scoffed. "It's a car, duh. Like a Provost's car."

"But it's not," I said. "Look—this can't be a whole street of Provosts. Every one of these cars is super fancy."

"It's weird," Nate said. "Keep looking for a sign, guys."

Back home, our house had needed painting. Lots of people's had. It all depended on how good your harvest had been. This place was just . . . really nice. We walked quietly down street after street, looking for a sign. The farther we got from the perimeter fence, the edgier I felt. As tired as I was, a cold drip of adrenaline trickled into my veins, making me alert and jumpy.

We were a good mile in and I was about to suggest we get out of there when Jolie finally spotted it: a small cat's head made with pebbles in a garden. Silently we headed around to the back of the house and tapped softly on a window. There was no answer. Bunny tapped again a bit louder. Finally the door opened a crack.

"Who's there?" The woman sounded suspicious, or scared.

"I thought I smelled a pie baking," Ansel said.

There was a pause. "I've got a cherry one just come out of the oven."

"Cherry's my favorite," Ansel said. He knew the code, and that was the final thing that convinced me he was one of us. Now I just had to get him to tell me the secret of getting into the city—the *capital*.

"Go to the back garage," the woman whispered. "The door is open. Go upstairs. Pull the drapes before you turn on any lights. I'll be over in a few minutes."

Just to be out of the cold seemed amazing. We went upstairs silently despite our weariness and found that the space over the garage had beds and a kitchenette and a shower. I was concerned about Nate—he'd been flagging more and more all day, despite keeping up. Now he looked gray-skinned and clammy.

I hoped rest and food would give him the strength to carry on. I hoped I wouldn't have to leave him here.

Cassie would kill me.

57

IT WAS MAYBE TEN MINUTES before the woman appeared with food.

We fell on the hot stew like starving pigs, then shoveled in bread and butter and cider and fruit as fast as we could while the woman watched us with equal amounts of amusement and horror. Even Ansel, exhausted as he was, was able to put away a good amount, and he looked much better afterward. The open wounds around his wrists and ankles needed tending, but he was going to be okay.

Only Nate ate slowly, as if each bite took too much effort, as if swallowing was difficult. I could tell the woman noticed it, and she said there was first-aid stuff in the bathroom.

"What kind of cell is this?" I asked when I couldn't inhale any more anything.

"Manufacturing," she said. "We make luxury cars. I can give you a tour tomorrow—this cell is big and you won't stand out."

"What's a luxury car?" Mills asked. "Like for a Provost?" He shot a glance at Nate. "Some of them," said the woman. "Not all of them. Get some sleep."

My squad of tough, kickass soldiers was soon splayed across bunks like puppies, shoes still on, rifles cradled like stuffed animals. Except for Nate.

"Come on," I said, gesturing him to the bathroom. He sat on the toilet while I carefully unwound his bandages, wetting them with warm water when they stuck.

"How does it look?" Nate asked.

Like you're about to go septic, I thought, but said, "Okay." His wounds were ugly, raw, and red. I cleaned them really well, then slathered them with antibiotic cream and rebandaged them. Tomorrow I would ask the woman if she could get her hands on stronger antibiotics.

"Okay, here," I said, giving him three generic pain pills. "Go to sleep."

Nate staggered to an empty bunk and collapsed on it in slow motion.

I climbed into the last empty one, thinking about tomorrow, about Nate, about Ansel, about my sister and how she was doing, and most of all about Tim, who I missed so much that my arms ached.

I closed my eyes for just a second.

58

IT WAS DARK WHEN SOMETHING woke me—I'd been a super light sleeper since the Crazy House. Frowning, I listened again and heard the same sound. Instantly I was out of bed, on my feet, and reaching for my weapon.

Moments later I realized that it was Nate. He was still asleep but moaning in pain. I put my gun down and felt his forehead. He was burning up, hot and dry-skinned, but also shaking with cold. *Crap.*

I padded to the bathroom, got more pain meds, and managed to help him sit up a bit to get them down with some water. Then he curled up again, his chills wracking his body so hard that his bed shook.

God, what to do? Everything in me just wanted to hit my own bed and sleep for three days. But I was the squad leader. I was responsible for everyone in it. I'd already lost Levi. Was I going to lose Nate, too?

Tiredly I grabbed the blanket off my bed and threw it over him, then climbed into his single bunk. I wrapped my arms around him and pressed against his back, trying to warm him. The shivering was annoying, but his fever was like a little furnace, keeping me warm. I wished he were Tim. Tim was okay, wasn't he? He and Cassie were keeping each other safe, right? Surely I would be able to tell if something happened to either one of them? I was glad they were back at camp and together, out of harm's way.

I fought against the growing daylight as long as I could, snuggling deeper into the delicious warmth and the comfort of the not-a-rock mattress. Very gradually I became aware of something odd—the heat was coming from one side...there was a person next to me.

My eyes flew open to see Nate's pale, concerned face looking down at me.

"Hi?" he said. He still had circles under his eyes, but his fever seemed to have broken, at least for now.

I cleared my throat and sat up abruptly. "You had fever and chills," I said matter-of-factly, swinging my legs out of bed. "I didn't know how else to warm you up."

Ansel and the rest of the team were still sleeping, thank God. What I had done had made sense, was practical, and I would have done it for anyone in my squad. The fact that Nate was Cassie's boyfriend made it weird.

Nate nodded. "Seems to have worked. I actually feel hungry."

Ansel's injuries also needed rebandaging, but they weren't nearly as bad as Nate's. I was wondering about the best time to question him about the capital. Now, in front of everyone? Later, when we were alone? Leader-type choices. I hated 'em.

Before I let Nate eat, I checked his injuries again. They were maybe 1 percent better—still swollen, still red, still ugly. Dammit. Nothing to do but wait. I put on more ointment and rebandaged him. It was bizarre, taking care of someone like this. I don't do stuff like that—Cassie does. She always has. She should be doing this.

The sooner Nate got better, the better. For everyone.

59

CASSIE

THE NEXT MORNING I WOKE up hungry, which I took to be an encouraging sign of health. Still in my sleeping bag, I did a self-check. Everything seemed okay: No sore throat. A headache that would go away when I had coffee. I punched the air quietly. Yay for not-plague-having! At least not yet.

Tim was still sleeping. He'd stayed up later than I had last night, working his way through some of the easier books we'd found. For someone learning to read when he was eighteen years old, he was catching on fast. I almost never had to help him with long words anymore.

By the time he got up and shuffled to the small table we ate at, I'd made coffee and was on my second cup. He sat down, wrapped in a blanket, and I realized his beard was growing out. I tried to remember what he was like in the Crazy House, how he had looked and acted, how scared of him I'd been. We used to call him Bruiser! That seemed like a lifetime ago. Two lifetimes.

"Found this," Tim said, and pushed a book across the table. "It's not about the plague, but it's important." He flipped through some pages and pointed to the copyright: 2039, by the New World Party.

I picked it up as he poured himself some coffee. It was called *The Rights and Responsibilities of Every Citizen*. Chapter one was an old-fashioned map of the United States, showing all the little lines dividing up the fifty named territories. On the next page was the same map, wiped clean except for several big lines that cut the land in half, and then into sixths.

"Oh, my God," I said slowly, staring at it. "This is the beginning of *the United*. This is when they were *creating cells*. See the six chunks labeled A through F? My cell was B-97-4275. So we were in the B section." This was amazing to me, actually. I knew other people came from other cells, but I'd never been able to… like, *place* them. I'd never known whether our B stood for Beef or Building or Best or whatever. Now I knew that it meant its location on a *map*.

"Those years must have been a total nightmare," he said. "Like, first you have a zillion people dying. Your family. Almost everyone you know. Then the New World party comes in, carves up the land, and tells you where you're going to live and what you're going to do. I bet people were freaked out. Like, *way freaked the hell out*."

I nodded, going through the book.

"Have you checked for breakfast?" he asked, looking around.

"Not yet," I said, reading.

Tim opened the trapdoor and felt for the rope where our food basket was hung.

"Dammit, nothing," he said. "Someone's late."

"It'll be here soon," I said. "This book is amazing—it's *propaganda*, like what Ms. Strepp told us about."

"But it's just—*life*, now," he said. "I mean, all those rules—that's just how we live. Used to live. Nothing weird about it."

"Yeah," I said. "We didn't know any different. But how did they get everyone to agree to do it? To move into cells? How did they decide who went where?"

"Maybe we'll find more info in that same stack. But this is stupid," he said, picking up our phone. "I'm starving." A minute later he put down the phone. "Strepp's not answering."

"That's weird," I said, looking up. "Give it a couple minutes and try again."

He did. And a few minutes after that. Then every five minutes for an hour. We even tried calling Havers. No one answered, no one brought breakfast. No one brought lunch, either. When we looked through our windows, the grounds outside were empty. No marching recruits, no shouts, no vehicles rumbling by.

By evening, we weren't even pretending to work, just kept looking at each other with wide eyes.

Finally I said what we were both thinking.

"Something's wrong. Something's really, really wrong."

60

BECCA

NOW THAT IT WAS DAYLIGHT, I peeked through the window blinds to see that this garage was surrounded by trees, large shrubs, and ivy climbing up a fence. Good camouflage. As each member of the team woke up, I directed them to take showers and inspect any wounds they'd gotten. Was it only two days ago? Less than. Levi had died *two nights ago*. We'd rescued Ansel just *yesterday*.

There was a well-stocked first-aid kit in a cupboard, and as I slathered on ointment and bandages, I felt about a hundred years old.

All of us had suffered in the wolf attack. I didn't want to admit it, but my shoulder was killing me. When it was my turn to shower, I looked at the angry punctures with dismay. I was just as likely as Nate to get rabies—any of us were. I'd known people and animals both who'd died of the disease, and it was not a good way to go. I had a quick image of my squad out in the middle of nowhere, killing ourselves one by one.

I didn't want to die without seeing Tim one more time. I didn't want to die, period.

After breakfast Nate was listless, dull-eyed, but trying his damnedest not to show it. Silently I prayed to a god I didn't believe in that the food and rest would pull Nate through. Ansel and the others were patched up and almost back to normal, but I knew my squad was remembering the wolves, remembering little Levi.

Our host told us her name was Kelly, but we knew it was fake, just as she knew the names we gave her were fake.

"How come there're so many fancy cars here?" Mills asked her.

Kelly laughed, her Afro sparkling with tiny raindrops from the drizzle outside. "This is a manufacturing cell," she said. "We make cars. There are five different factories here—each one has thousands of employees."

"In our cell, the fanciest car was the Movolo," Nate said quietly. "That was for the Provost."

The Provost, his father.

Kelly made a face. "The Movolo is the lowest level we build."

I couldn't speak for a moment. Back home, most people drove little electric Hoppers or maybe a Daisy, if they had more than two kids. Seeing the Provost's fancy Movolo showed everyone how important he was, how he got the best of everything.

"If a Movolo is the lowest kind of car you make," I asked, "who drives the others?"

"What could be nicer than a Movolo?" Mills asked.

Kelly laughed again. "I'll show you nice!" she said. "We ship ninety-nine percent of our cars out, of course, and I have no idea who drives them." She glanced around the small attic-like room and lowered her voice. "No one's ever said, but I've always thought that they go to the big capital, in the east." She shrugged. "I don't even know if it exists—it's just rumors, really, because we don't know."

"Oh, we sa—" Bunny began, but I kicked her under the table. We'd seen that huge city from the scope of the anti-aircraft gun, and Ansel had confirmed what we thought. But that didn't mean that Kelly had ever seen it or knew for sure that it existed. Bunny coughed and mumbled something, then drank more tea.

Kelly was a foreman at one of the factories, so after breakfast we walked over with her to get a tour. I forced Nate to stay in and rest, and when I say forced, I mean I pinned him down by his shoulders while he struggled uselessly against me. It was pretty fun, actually.

"You will stay here and sleep," I snarled quietly. "Or I will kick your ass."

At the factory, Kelly gave us workers' coveralls and hard hats, then took us to the production lines.

It was...it was...like a dream? Except no dream could have imagined this stuff. My family had had a beat-up, ancient pickup truck and a dinky moped that couldn't go faster than twelve miles an hour. We were totally normal.

These cars belonged in fairy tales, like the big one painted with shiny blue paint flecked with sparkles. *Sparkles.*

"This model has heated and cooled seats," Kelly said. When we looked at her blankly, she explained, "You know, so that on cool days your seat will be warm and on warm days your seat will be cool." More blank looks.

There was a car that could hold seven or eight people, but it wasn't a bus. The floors of all these cars were covered with *carpet*. The steering wheels were wrapped in *padded leather*.

"If someone wants to pay extra, they can have colored lights underneath the car," Kelly said, and flipped a switch. We stared at the blue light making the factory floor glow. All I could think was, when Nate finds out he missed all this, he will kill me.

People, real, actual people, would drive these cars.

It was truly hard to believe that they existed, that this factory existed, that people would own these cars and drive them.

More than ever, I knew that my mission was to head for that city, no matter what.

61

BACK UPSTAIRS AT KELLY'S GARAGE I found Nate sitting up, showered, and cleaning his handgun. But his face was flushed and damp with sweat, and his expression was the kind of resigned misery I'd seen on animals that had to be put down.

I sat down next to him as he wiped lubricant off the barrel, then pushed a clean cloth patch through the barrel itself.

"How you doin'?" I asked, though it was obvious.

"Fine," he said tightly, then met my eyes. "We should move out today, as soon as it's dark."

Yep, I thought. *And I will have to leave your ass here.* I rubbed my forehead, then realized how much it hurt my shoulder to move it. Sighing, I pictured Cassie's face when I told her about what had happened to Nate. She'd be heartbroken and furious. I was glad Cassie wasn't a yeller, or at least, she didn't used to be. Then I pictured Cassie's face full of disappointment. That would be awful, and unfortunately I knew *that* face all too well.

I sighed again and gave him a *very* brief rundown of the factory, omitting all of the most fabulous, outrageous details. He asked enough questions that I could tell his brain had some battery power.

Still, he wouldn't be able to hold his own on the trek east. The big city had been what, fifteen miles away? One by one, I took the others aside and let them know that we'd be moving out tonight, and that he would be staying here. They were all upset, but no one protested. They'd been trained too well.

Right now my plan was vague, involving zip ties and duct tape. I'd work out the details later, but we'd be on the road by midnight.

At dinner that night, Kelly sat with us while we once again ate like starved, socially challenged bears. Nate asked her some questions, nothing too specific. What was he getting at?

If he noticed our squad casually packing their gear, he didn't mention it. But when I was rolling up my clothes in the bunkroom, I looked up and saw him standing there, watching me.

"What's up?" I asked casually, and he came to sit across from me on a bunk.

"I know you're going to leave tonight," he said, "without me."

62

I STOPPED ROLLING SOCKS FOR a second but didn't look up.

"I can't blame you," Nate said. "I'd probably do the same thing. *However.*"

Then I did look up, and for a second hardly recognized him. Yeah, the whole wolf attack had left him looking like shit on a stick. But part of me still expected to see Nathaniel Allen, Provost's son. The last year had changed him, marked him permanently. He was no longer groomed and smoothly good-looking. He looked older than his age, rougher, his face more angular and his muscles more sinewy.

"I've been thinking," he said. "Did you hear Kelly at dinner tonight? Those fancy cars get shipped out every three days, on big tractor-trailers."

"Yeah," I said. "They have to be going to the city we saw through the scope."

"I wouldn't know," he said with exaggerated politeness. "I myself didn't see it."

I put on a face of mock sympathy. "I'm sorry I kept you from bleeding to death, or from fainting halfway up a tree and falling twenty feet down. It was selfish of me."

"Yeah, and you'll pay later," he said. "But the next shipment is *tomorrow night*."

It took .08 seconds for me to see where he was going.

"We could…hitch a ride on those trailers," I said, and he nodded.

"Better yet," he said, "we could maybe help ourselves to one of the *cars*."

It would mean waiting an extra day, but if I was honest with myself, which I hate, I could use a day of rest. We all could. Plus, it would give me time to get information out of Ansel and formulate a real plan to get into the city. Maybe even contact Strepp if I could borrow a mobile phone. My brain flew through the ramifications, pros and cons, and I looked up again.

"I…" I said slowly. "I am not seeing a flaw in this plan."

He grinned.

63

CASSIE

I LEANED OVER TIM ANXIOUSLY. "Can you see anything?"

Tim was peering out the window through a child's ancient toy binoculars. The sun had just come up, and we were hoping to see signs of life. We'd spent a long, hungry night waiting and hoping someone would call us back, bring us food—*anything*. I'd even take Ms. Strepp yelling at us for being slackers.

He shook his head. "Not a goddamn thing. No one's moving or marching or digging or anything."

I took the Captain America binoculars from him and tried to angle out farther. If I craned my neck to its most uncomfortable position, I could see the mess hall.

"The mess hall is dark," I said in wonder, looking up to see the alarm on Tim's face. "Open this stupid window."

The window had been painted over a hundred times and hadn't been opened in forever. Tim got a big wrench and took several hefty whacks at the lock, breaking paint off and finally snapping the lock itself. Then he kicked the small window open and looked out.

"The recruits should be having breakfast," he said. "I can see the edge of the training field—the barbed wire, the climbing wall, the muddy ditches."

"And nothing?" My stomach rumbled as if it was outraged that this was happening. "This is too weird. There are a few lights on, but no shadows of people passing. Let me see the binoculars again."

I leaned out the window so far that Tim held on to my belt. Very slowly, I scanned from left to right, trying to see in every window, looking at every doorway. Then I saw it. Or them.

I tossed the binoculars at Tim. "On the ground, eleven o'clock, right at the corner of dorm five."

"Boots," Tim said, sounding grim. "With legs in them. Not moving."

"What the hell is happening?" I cried. "Maybe they're on an overnight training mission and forgot about us?"

"So whose feet are those?" Tim asked. "Why are they still?"

I looked out the low window again. Once more I scoured the scene for any clue, any sign. Something like a big poster saying, SIT TIGHT, CASSIE AND TIM, for example. And I *did* see a sign. "Oh, crap," I breathed. I pointed, and he didn't need the binoculars to see the clue we had missed before: a hand. A small brown hand, draped over an open doorsill. Completely still.

Tim grabbed an old magazine and rolled it up. "Hey!" he

shouted through his megaphone. "Hey! Anybody!" He really bellowed, almost hurting my ears, and I watched tensely, hoping to
see someone running to us.

"What's going on?" Tim shouted as loud as he could. *"Is anyone
there? Help!"*

The hand didn't twitch, the feet didn't shift.

"We have to go see," Tim said. "Even risking infecting everyone. Some weird shit is going down."

"I...agree," I said. "But we didn't hear a battle, you know? No
alarms or shooting or yelling. *And* we don't have weapons."

"Yeah," Tim said, looking around. "It's not like we can *antique*
them to death. We just have...hand to hand. Like at the Crazy
House."

Yeah, that had been *super* fun. Tim stuffed the book he'd found
in his jacket pocket, but I went first, opening the trapdoor, then
climbing down, all my nerves on high alert. I waited in darkness
until Tim climbed down and joined me. Together, we listened. The
complete silence was bizarre, eerie. I nodded at Tim, and he put his
hand on the lever that opened the secret door.

64

BECCA

IT WAS TRUE. ANOTHER TWENTY-FOUR hours of rest, food, and healing, and we were all in much better shape, even Nate. Kelly had provided antibiotics for the infections, but she couldn't get her hands on rabies meds. So that was still up in the air. I hadn't mentioned that to Ansel. Let it be a surprise.

It was close to midnight and all lights in Kelly's house were off. We hadn't told her about our plan, of course, but left an unsigned note of thanks in the bunkroom.

We went downstairs in the dark and filed silently out of the garage, closing the door with a barely audible click. Sticking to shadows, we headed to the factory. Even in the dim light I saw that Nate was moving better, with more energy. Ansel was blending into the team as if he'd always been one of us. He was especially good with Jolie's deafness, making it no big deal, like we all learned to. I can admit I was wrong about her. She didn't just look like a total badass, she *was* a total badass. My shoulder felt about 40 percent better. Waiting a day had been a good decision.

In the factory's outside lot, three tractor-trailers were waiting, their engines idling, headlights super bright in the night. We hid behind a large stack of empty wooden pallets and watched as those amazing cars were loaded, one by one. Each trailer held ten cars, five on the upper deck and five below. Some were backed on, some were loaded frontways. I peered through my binoculars to see how each car was fastened down by straps through its wheels. There were four straps total, and a worker ratcheted the webbed cables tight.

Two of the trailers loaded up and drove off—it had taken more than an hour. When the third trailer was almost full, I turned to my squad.

"Okay," I whispered. "We split into two groups, each flanking the trailer, out of sight. When the last car is loaded, the factory workers will go back inside. The truck driver will get into the cab. As soon as his door closes, get yourself up on the trailer. We'll reconnect once we're on the road. Got it?" I looked at Jolie's face, and she nodded firmly. Nate, Ansel, and Bunny went to one side, and Mills, Jolie, and I took the other.

The truck driver signed some paperwork, the factory person went inside, and best of all, she shut off the outside lights. The second the driver's cab door closed, I ran over and leaped up onto the trailer. It had no real floor—just the two tracks for the car wheels and a support structure underneath. I slid beneath a car and found some good handholds to cling to. Peering around, I checked to make sure everyone else was on board.

"There's no freaking bottom," Mills whispered, working his way through the supports to me.

"Yeah," I said. "Don't fall."

When the truck lurched into gear, it shook all of us and I clung to my car chassis. The truck driver drove through the cell gates and out onto the unlit highway—not knowing that there were six kids flattened beneath the bellies of five luxury cars.

65

AS SOON AS WE WERE out of sight of the cell, I climbed out of my hiding place and made my way to the first car, the one closest to the road. Or was it the last car? Anyway, I was thrilled to see its key fob in the cup holder, and I climbed in and pushed the Start button.

Mills had climbed up next to me and pointed to what I had already seen: the battery showed almost no charge. I got out and the six of us had an almost soundless meeting, using a lot of hand gestures.

We could just jump off and walk the rest of the way to the city.

We could push that first/last car off the trailer and use the next one in line.

Jolie shook her head and pointed upward, and for a second I thought she was saying that God didn't want us to do that.

She wasn't. She was saying, "Use the first car on the upper level."

Huh. I climbed up and checked it out. Its battery was full, its key fob in the glove compartment. I'd never pushed a car off a twelve-foot height and didn't know if it would just fall apart or its engine drop out or what.

I'd driven Pa's truck, of course, but had never driven a car, much less a fancy car. Nate at least had driven a Movolo. We climbed to the top level and sat in the last car. Nate examined the control panel.

"Can you do this?" I asked him. He definitely looked as if he'd pulled one foot out of the grave, but the walk and the wait and the climb had taken their toll. He was pale and pasty beneath his tan.

"Of course," he said smoothly, but his hand trembled as he adjusted the mirrors. I pressed my lips together tensely. His future was in no way certain. Which meant mine wasn't, either. No one's was—not even Ansel's. If rabies didn't get him, something else probably would.

I took a deep breath, then got out of the car and looked at the team.

"Okay, here's the plan," I said over the road noise.

"There's a plan?" Mills asked, and I made a "screw you" face at him.

"Jolie, Ansel, and Mills will get in the backseat," I said. "Bunny will get in the passenger seat. Nate will drive."

W-H-A-T-A-B-O-U-T-U-? Jolie spelled into my hand.

"Someone has to sever the straps, pretty much at the last second," I explained. I'd thought about this while we'd waited back at the factory, and that sentence didn't *begin* to cover all the certain- or near-death possibilities facing us, and *especially me*. "So everyone get in now, and for God's sake, fasten as many seat belts as you can find."

"But where will you *be*?" Bunny asked.

"In the trunk," I said briefly. "Everyone ready? Nate?"

"Wait," Ansel said, taking a deep breath. "You guys rescued me—the United guys killed the rest of my squad and definitely would have killed me. But you don't need to *keep* saving me. I can head off on my own. You have your hands full."

I thought about it—did I need him?

"Do you know how to get into the city?" I asked abruptly.

He nodded. "I told you so. I know how my squad was going to get in."

I scanned the faces of the team. "What do you guys say? Does Ansel stay or go?"

Jolie pointed at him, then swirled her hand to show "All of us." She wanted him to stay.

"Yeah, sure," Mills said. "If he's a traitor, we'll kill him, but you know."

"Yeah," Bunny said, shrugging.

I looked at Nate in the driver's seat. "Yeah," he said, staring right at Ansel, then repeated what Mills had said. "If he's a traitor, we'll kill him, but you know."

"Okay, that's settled," I said, and leaned in the front window, my feet balanced precariously on a crossbeam. "When I give you the signal," I told Nate, "it means the last strap is cut, and you need to step on the gas."

"Got it," Nate said, and gave me an intense look. "Be careful."

66

"I'M ALWAYS CAREFUL," I SAID, and climbed down. I heard Nate snort above me. The straps were, like, bulletproof fabric about three inches wide. They'd been ratcheted tight and I didn't have a hex wrench on me. I pretty much had to be beneath the car to do this, and I slid sideways, trying to stay out of the way of the wheels, which would be very crushy if they rolled over me.

Pulling my big knife from its sheath, I started sawing away at the first strap. I'd decided to start in the front. The real trick would be when three straps were cut. The last one could pop by itself, severing some part of me, or the trailer could hit a bump, causing the car to slide off sideways, which would not be optimal or even survivable.

If the car started sliding around while I was still working underneath, I could get knocked off the truck, or worse.

The first strap finally gave. It had taken three times the effort that I'd imagined. Holding my breath, I slid sideways to the other front strap. My arms were already tired, having to reach up, and the rest of me was as tightly wound as the straps.

Second one down. I scooched toward the back of the car and angled myself to start cutting on the third. This was where it really got scary, and I could hardly breathe. This was where my whole plan would either work brilliantly... or kill us all.

My arms shook as I sawed at the last strap. I kept my body right in the middle of the chassis so if it rolled off without me, at least it wouldn't smush me. Then the last strap was done. I waited a bit to see if the car moved, but it didn't. The angle it was at was keeping it in place.

Finally I slithered out and stood up. I gave Nate the signal and grabbed the edge of the trunk, which was popped open.

Nate saw me and gunned the engine. I wasn't as ready as I thought and the car jumping forward almost dislocated my shoulder. Without thinking, I threw myself into the trunk right as the car left the trailer. Time slowed as we sailed through the air, and I grabbed the trunk lid and slammed it shut. Immediately I was in tiny, total darkness. In the next second the car *slammed* down on the road with all of its ton of weight. I cried out as my head hit the roof of the trunk with a jaw-crunching bounce. It made me bite my tongue and my mouth filled with blood.

Had the fall broken the car? Were we moving?

As I swallowed blood, my head ringing, I felt the minimal vibration of the car's electric engine. I braced myself against the trunk's walls as the car reversed quickly, then made a sharp turn that threw me against the side wall.

It felt like a long time before the car stopped and someone opened the trunk lid. It was Nate, and he stared at me, hyped up by the plan's success.

"You alive?" he asked.

"Almost," I said, feeling the huge lump on my head. I climbed out shakily, cradling my wrist. My mouth was still full of blood and I spit it out on the road. Nate automatically kicked dust over it.

I pushed in next to Bunny in the front seat. The team was shaken, their necks hurt, but nothing too serious. It didn't matter, anyway—we had wheels.

"Where to?" Nate asked, looking at me.

"East," I said. "The big city in the east."

67

CASSIE

THE DOOR SWUNG OPEN EASILY and then we were in the small, run-down bathroom. We slipped out into Ms. Strepp's office, every muscle tensed.

It was empty and dark with the shades drawn; we didn't dare turn on the light. Tim did a quick perimeter check while I looked for some kind of clue. Her desk had papers on it, things needing her signature, a full in-box. It was a little messy but didn't look like it had been ransacked.

Without speaking we headed to the door to the outside and I reached for his hand. At the last second I remembered he wasn't Nate and pulled my hand back. Outside, we pressed ourselves against the building, moving soundlessly toward the booted feet, ready to flee if this was a trap. Ms. Strepp was famous for her gut-wrenching tests.

We peeked around the corner and I clapped my hand over my mouth. If this was a test, it was a really, really bad one. The girl was obviously dead, on her back, open eyes staring glassily at the sky. Her face had large open sores on it, her hands were covered with blackened bumps. What skin we could see was pale and greenish, and a thin trickle of blood marked one ear.

"What the hell?" he whispered.

Leaving the victim we couldn't help, we went to find the hand we'd seen. It belonged to Yui, a kid we both knew, a good fighter. He, too, was covered with awful, bloody pustules and sores.

As I stared at him, it came to me. "Tim—it's the *plague*. *They* died of the plague. We were the ones supposedly infected, but *they* all got sick instead."

Yui had been the guard to one of the arsenals, so we weaponed up and moved cautiously through the rest of the compound, stretching the necks of our shirts up over our mouth and nose. There wasn't a living soul. Every single person in the camp was dead, covered with the telltale sores of plague. Everyone except me and Tim.

And Ms. Strepp. We couldn't find her anywhere.

68

OUR TRAINING HAD PREPARED US for everything. We knew how to fight in a hundred different ways, and to the death, if necessary. We could survive in the wild, besiege enemy camps, and easily march fifteen miles in one night.

All of this flew through my head like mosquitos while I processed the situation.

"Shit," I said. "Shit, shit, shitty, shittiest shit!"

Tim rested his automatic rifle on the ground, his eyes bleak. "Yeah."

Still on high alert, we checked the entire training compound again. We counted dozens and dozens of bodies in various stages of decomposition; kids we'd hung out with, drank with, danced with, trained with.

"Thank God Becca and Nate aren't here," I said, and Tim nodded.

"We have to load up and bug out," he said, his voice muffled by his T-shirt. "Gather food, weapons, whatever, grab one of the transports and go!"

"Yeah," I agreed quickly. "Maybe you could load up while I search Ms. Strepp's office for answers?"

"Got it," Tim said, "but don't take too long. I want us out of here ASAP."

I ran to Ms. Strepp's office and opened her computer. To my shock, it wasn't locked. I started scrolling rapidly through files, not even knowing what I was looking for. Making a quick decision, I printed every file that had certain key words in it: my name, Tim's name, the word *plague,* and the word *plan.* The machine was still spitting out pages when Tim burst through the door.

"Let's go," he said urgently. "I don't want to be breathing this air!"

"Okay, okay," I said, grabbing handfuls of printouts. I scrolled through the last files and saw one with Becca's name on it. I hit Print, snatched it up, and ran outside. Tim was already in the driver's seat of one of our All-Terrain Transports.

I threw my stuff in the back, then leaped into the passenger seat. Tim punched the gas and we roared off, watching the compound of death get smaller in the rearview mirror.

69

BECCA

"I GOTTA PEE," BUNNY SAID.

We hadn't driven that far. I was silently cataloguing my various injuries and bruises now that the extreme adrenaline of the car theft was waning. Other than where my body hurt (everywhere), my only thought was getting Ansel to explain the secret of how to get into the city. The capital of the United was a high-value target, and I knew that Strepp would want us to scout it at all costs. Who knows what we could learn. What damage we could do.

Jolie wrote, I-P-2 in my hand.

"Nate, find a place for a pit stop," I directed him.

It took a few minutes, but Nate found a dirt road that was almost totally overgrown. He turned in and we crunched through the woods until we couldn't be seen from the highway. Each of us wandered a couple yards off and took care of business, and then I heard Mills say, "Hey, guys, come look at this!"

When we joined him, he was pointing to a natural shelter, flicking his flashlight around its opening.

"Oh good, a cave," Nate said flatly. "Probably a popular wolf takeout place. I'm going back to the car. Try not to get eaten."

I couldn't blame him—other than poor Levi, he'd suffered the most in the wolf attack. "I'll be there in a second," I called after him as he stalked off.

Jolie clicked her flashlight and the first thing it shone on was a grinning skull. She made an odd noise, not really human-sounding, and dropped her flashlight. The rest of us shone our lights around and saw that this cave was deep, going into its rocky hill about a hundred feet. Besides the skull, still attached to its body, there were eight other skeletons, and they reminded me of the ones I'd found in the ghost town—dressed, sort of a matching group, apparently living here. They were lying on the ground, and two of them still had their skeletal hands entwined.

"So gross," Ansel said with a shiver. He hung out by the cave's entrance while Bunny went farther back.

"Look at this," she said, showing us some ancient, pathetically small food stores and a pile of plastic water jugs, some still full.

Had these people been hiding? From what? Everything we'd found so far had pointed to a war of some kind, but these people weren't set up for a siege.

A sudden crack of thunder made us jump, and then the cave was sealed off by torrents of rain that looked like a waterfall.

"Crap. Let's make a run for the car," I said.

Mills sighed.

"Is there a problem?" I asked, putting a bit of ice into my voice.

"I'm just beat, man," he said. "It's almost one in the morning. I say we just stay here, rest for a couple of hours, then hit the road toward dawn."

"If they're searching for us, they'll assume that we went away from them," Bunny pointed out. "Backward. But the truck went south; we're going east."

I mulled it over. "Yeah, okay. We can crash in the car for a couple hours."

"I'm crashing right here." Mills dropped to his knees and shut off his flashlight. "Car will be too crowded."

"Ready to be a wolf snack?" I asked tartly.

"Not in this rain," Bunny said, also sinking onto the dirt cave floor. "And we have our guns. We won't be surprised this time."

Jolie nodded, looking at me sympathetically, then lay down close to Bunny.

I jerked my head at Ansel, motioning toward the car, but he made an apologetic face and lay down also, as close to the entrance of the cave as he could.

I considered joining them rather than tramping through pouring rain to a fancy car full of legitimately paranoid Nate. With a sigh I pulled my hood over my head and left the cave.

The bastard had locked the car doors, and I smacked on his window to wake him up. I was soaked and shivering as I slid into the backseat. Nate rubbed his eyes and peered through the windshield.

"Where's everyone else?"

"They're crashing in the cave for a couple hours," I said, snuggling down into the leather seat that was like the cushioned desk chair in the Provost's office.

"Take off your coat," Nate said. "It's wet." He got out of his own coat, clumsily because of the steering wheel, and then climbed in the back with me. "Press that button there." He pointed, and I pressed the button on the center console in front of me. Seat warmers! Nate grinned at my wonder as he draped his dry coat over me.

We smiled at each other in the dark as we listened to the rain pounding on the car's roof. It felt cozy and...almost safe.

70

I WOKE BEFORE FIRST LIGHT and found that I was coiled around Nate like a pea vine on a string. I must have been cold, I told myself. I must have thought he was Tim.

Or maybe I was just *crazy*. That was becoming more and more a likely possibility as the stress of our mission weighed on my shoulders.

Quietly I got out of the car and walked on sodden leaves to the cave. The squad was already awake and I prayed heartily that none of them had come to the car and seen me with Nate.

"Hey," Bunny said, looking up. "We've been opening these supplies, and really there's nothing worth taking."

"Any idea how old they are?" I asked, kneeling down to see the split cans of beans, the dried-out jerky.

"This label says it's good until 2041," Mills reported.

"Okay, so we're well past that date," I said drily.

Jolie hadn't made any gestures toward me—I was starting to

recognize certain words and sometimes sentences without her spelling it out. Now I looked at her and saw that she was standing quietly toward the back of the cave, facing the wall.

I walked over to her and made the sign for "What's up?"

She pointed to the wall. I shook my head and shrugged, so she took my hand and rubbed my fingers against the wall.

I brushed away dirt and dust to see the words scratched into the rock:

BEWARE THE PLAGUE!
TOUCH NOTHING HERE!
SAVE YOURSELVES!

I read the words several times, then looked at Jolie's solemn face. Her glance moved to where Mills and Bunny were still opening packages, sniffing ancient food.

TOUCH NOTHING HERE!

I read the dire message again, then looked over at the skeletons. None of them had bullet holes. Had they been ill, and died where they lay?

I made sure Jolie could see my face but spoke softly. "They died a long, long time ago. There's no way there could still be germs here, no way this could be contagious."

Jolie didn't nod, just looked at me with her big, expressive blue eyes.

"Okay, people!" I called, clapping my hands. "Time to go! Make sure you have all your gear! And...where's Ansel?"

Bunny looked up. "He went to take a leak," she said, then frowned. "Been gone a long time."

"No one...went with him?" I asked quietly.

No one answered me, but we all left the cave and spread out into the woods as silently as possible. Without calling his name, we searched beneath shrubs and up in branches till we realized it was pointless. The only person I was mad at was me. I'd made the decision to bring him with us, I'd let him off all this time without forcing him to tell me how to get into the capital, I hadn't bothered to tell anyone in the squad to, hey, keep an eye on him. Which they should have known, of course.

But I was at fault. Because I was the leader.

My jaw set and I was about to start internally screaming at myself when I noticed Jolie scratching at her neck. I stopped her hand and looked closely.

"You have words written on your neck," I told her, pulling her sweater collar aside. Jolie made a surprised face and wrote "?" on my hand. "To the," I read, and looked in her eyes. "What is this?"

She shrugged and shook her head, convincingly mystified. She rubbed at the words again and they began to flake off. They were written in blood.

71

CASSIE

I HAD NEVER SAT IN a vehicle's passenger seat and tried to read anything, so I had no way of knowing that it would make me barfy. After the second time I puked out the window, Tim slammed the All-Terrain Transport to a halt, grabbed my sheaf of papers, and got out to shove them into a box in the back. Then something caught his gaze—he frowned and read a couple sheets.

"This is about Becca," he said, getting back in the ATT. I reached for the pages but he held them out of my reach, like an asshole. Fine. Be like that. He read them while I rinsed my mouth with a bottle of water and spit out the window.

"Oh, my God," Tim said. "Oh, my God."

"What? What?" I cried, lunging for the file.

Again he held it out of my reach. "Becca was sent to *the capital,*" he said. "She's on a special, secret mission that *not even she* knows about—she'll be told when it's time." Tim was a pretty stoic guy—I'd seen him take punches without flinching and hear bad news without flicking an eyelid. But right now he looked like someone had just slammed his head with a baseball bat.

"Sounds...real Strepplike," I said carefully.

Tim let out a breath, his face pale. He swallowed. "Strepp... Strepp doesn't expect Becca or anyone on her squad to come back."

I stared at him, trying to understand.

His voice rough, he said, "Becca's on a suicide mission—and doesn't know it."

"No. No way," I said, shaking my head. "Even Ms. Strepp—"

Tim tossed the file at me, cranked the starter, and gunned the engine so hard we spit rocks twenty yards behind us. "Look at the part right below that," Tim directed, wrenching the wheel of the ATT.

I skimmed down a bit, my head swimming with thoughts of Becca. "What?" I said.

"Right below the part about Becca," Tim said. "Where Strepp says that she's heading to the capital to carry out the Revolution. Look—there are directions. Don't you see that little map?"

"I'm trying not to cry or throw up," I said, dizzily locating the map. "Uh, yeah, um, it says she's going to meet the Loner. The Loner? Who the hell is the Loner?"

"I don't know," Tim said grimly. "But we're going to take that page with us, and we're going to find him."

"Wait—what do you mean, we're going to find him?" I asked. "Where are we going?"

"To find Becca," he said. "We're going to the capital, and we're going to see what the Loner has to say."

72

IT WAS MY TURN TO drive. My years of driving Pa's combine made me okay with a vehicle this big, but right now I was so freaked about Becca that I'd have trouble driving a Hopper.

Becca. My *twin.* She'd been so proud and happy to be chosen squad leader, scouting out the unknown. I'd been so bummed to be separated from her and condemned to a freaking attic. Now I knew that Ms. Strepp had deliberately sent Becca *to her death,* and *I'd* been the lucky one with Tim, somehow avoiding the plague the rest of the compound had fallen victim to.

And Nate! Was he going to die with Becca? The two people I loved most in the world—the *only people I had left*—and Ms. Strepp had sent them off to *die?*

Ms. Strepp had done so many horrible things to me, Becca, Nate, Tim—everyone we knew. She'd made us fight, pretended to kill our friends, had starved and scared us—but we'd learned that she was training us for the apocalypse. That the dark and awful things we'd learned would help keep us alive.

But how would Becca's death help anyone? How would Nate dying get us any closer to answers?

I brushed an angry tear from my eye and downshifted to handle this curvy mountain road in the dark. Becca couldn't be dead. I would feel it. But goddamnit!

CRASH!!!!

It was like getting struck by lightning and running into a brick wall at the same time. Though we didn't roll, my ears filled with the sounds of buckling, scraping metal, breaking glass, the sound of Tim slamming against the dashboard, our belongings flying everywhere. The front windshield shattered, and my vision darkened as something huge burst through the broken windshield right at me. A shocking, searing pain shot through my shoulder as a hot, furry mass snapped my head backward. I couldn't breathe, couldn't move.

And just as fast, everything was quiet again. No engine noise, no breaking sounds, nothing except my muffled attempts to breathe and Tim groaning in pain.

"What the fu—" Tim began. "Oh, no. No, no, no!"

73

"I CAN'T MOVE," I MUMBLED into the—it was fur. Warm fur. "Can't breathe." Every breath brought the sharp scent of wild animal into my nostrils. My shoulder hurt so much that it had gone numb, as if my nerves had been like, *Nope, too much, we're shutting down.*

I heard Tim moving, but couldn't see anything.

"There's a huge animal face in here. Looks dead. You okay? Anything broken?" he asked in a shaky voice. I heard him climbing out his window.

"I think maybe so," I managed. "You?"

"No. Maybe some ribs." Now his voice came from outside the vehicle.

"You hit a—an elk? It's huge. I've never seen one in real life."

"It hit *me*," I said, turning my head. Even that movement brought a keen pain back to my shoulder. "I didn't even see it. Can you—get it off me? I can't breathe." Hot blood ran down my arm and I hoped it was from the elk.

Tim managed to open my door with a jerk. He saw me smashed against my seat, something pinning my shoulder. His eyes met mine soberly. "Shit," he said.

I was trying not to cry. Tim's nose was bleeding a bit, and a pink blotch on his face would soon turn into an ugly purple bruise.

"His antler is in your shoulder," he said.

"No shit," I said, my voice wavering.

"Okay, let me think," Tim said. "This thing must weigh...like a thousand pounds. Goddamn." He went to the front of the ATT and I heard him groaning and muttering. He came back around and said, "That was me trying to shift this thing. I grabbed its leg and pulled as hard as I could. But I have an idea—hang in there."

Like I had a choice.

He opened the back of the vehicle and came back with the jack. He wedged it between the elk and the steel beam of the window and started cranking. For a minute nothing happened. Then the animal shifted a bit and I bit back a scream of pain.

"I'm sorry," Tim said. "We gotta get you out. But this is going to hurt like a sonofabitch."

Tim cranked the handle as fast as he could, but it was torturous agony an inch at a time. I'd figured the antler was three or four inches in, but as Tim cranked, the pain went on and on. Blood flowed down my shirt. As soon as I could move a little bit, I pressed my other arm against my mouth. Tears ran down my face and I felt faint and sick.

It seemed to last a week. My head hung limply by the time he was finished, and I still couldn't move. All I knew was pain, a pain that radiated out of my shoulder and reduced the rest of me to a weeping kindergartner.

"It went right through you, through the seat." Tim's voice seemed to come from a distance. I felt him lift me, walk with me, lean me against a rock? A tree?

He cut off my shirt with a knife. I didn't care. "Holy shit," he breathed, leaning me forward so he could use the car's headlights to see my back. When he poured alcohol into my wounds, front and back, I sobbed. Then he pressed one large, cool hand against the hole in front and his other hand against the hole in my back. He kept pressure on them for a long time, till I knew his arms, though ridiculously strong, must ache. Finally he gave me some pills to swallow, packed the wounds with gauze, and bandaged them the best he could. He buttoned one of his shirts around me, keeping my left arm pressed against my body. Slowly I leaned over and slept.

74

BECCA

ON BUNNY'S STOMACH WAS WRITTEN "They will." In blood, a dark red against her dark skin.

On the back of Mills's neck: "the Loner."

I ran back to the car where Nate was stowing everyone's gear.

"Ansel is gone," I said abruptly. "But he seems to have left a message."

Nate tried to pull away as I started lifting his sweatshirt, pulling his collar. When I pulled the neck of his sweatshirt down, in small letters below his collarbone were the words "take you," in blood, already drying and flaking off.

"They will," I said, pointing to Bunny, "take you," I pointed to Nate, "to the," that was Jolie, "the Loner." On Mills. "They will take you to the Loner."

"You don't have anything written on you?" Bunny asked.

Last night I'd been asleep in the car with Nate, apparently cling-ing to him like lichen. Somehow Ansel had opened the car door, lifted Nate's shirt and written on his chest, and closed the door without waking any of us. The thought made my face burn. Slowly Jolie started looking at the back of my neck, pushing up my sleeves, finally tugging my raggedy sweater up to show my belly, white as a trout's. Nothing.

Suddenly Mills crouched and pushed up my pants leg. "Chip? Sorry," he read.

On my leg. My *leg*. While I *slept*. "'Chip? Sorry'? What the hell does that mean?" I practically snarled. "What does any of it mean? God! Let's just get in the freaking car! I'll drive!"

Later that day, we found that Ansel had been right: This big city was the capital, and its name was Chi-cah-go. How did we know? There was a huge sign a couple miles outside the city that said WELCOME TO CHICAGO: CAPITAL OF THE UNITED.

That had been an important clue. But what did "They will take you to the Loner" mean? What did "Chip? Sorry" mean?

The road we'd been on had gotten slowly bigger, the way a creek becomes a stream, then a river. We saw many more cars, the fancy kinds from the factory. No one seemed to notice or care that five kids were driving around by themselves. Maybe that was normal here.

When I crested a bridge and we first saw the capital, I almost slammed on the brakes so we could just...absorb it. But the car behind us honked, so I sped up and tried not to completely lose my mind.

"It's..." said Nate in wonder, and Mills said, "Yeah."

"It's so unbelievably huge," Bunny said, which didn't begin to cover it.

There were so, so, *so* many *people.* Just the people walking along the streets were more than ever came to a cell festival. The buildings went up and up, almost to the clouds.

"There are people in those buildings," I said in awe. "There's enough people here to *fill* those buildings." I couldn't imagine it, and pictured one or two people per floor.

Most of the buildings had lit signs on them, some of them the company's name, some with enormous ads two or three stories high, saying drink this beverage, or eat these noodles.

There was so much traffic here that we were moving slowly, and I could see a checkpoint up ahead. "We should ditch the car," I said reluctantly. "I'm sure they know it's stolen by now and are looking for it."

"That sign says park here," Bunny said, pointing, and there was an empty space between two other cars. I parked and we loaded up with all the hand weapons we could. I hated leaving the rifles, but we just couldn't hide them well enough under our coats. I locked the car—something I had never done in my life—and thought about home. It had been peaceful there, quiet. I'd known just about everyone, at least by sight. These two realities existed *in the same world.* It was unbelievable.

Jolie took my hand and, trying not to look too obvious, spelled P-O-L-I-C-E, and then made a circle motion with her finger.

I nodded. It was true—there were police everywhere. I'd never seen so many cops. If you have a ton of people, you have a ton of cops, I guess. At home people pretty much followed the rules. Was it the same here?

One of the billboards flashed, BUY TRUMAN BRAND SHOES— THE BRAND YOU CAN TRUST. Then that picture winked out and we had the more typical sign: THE UNITED IS BUILT ON TRUST. YOUR LOYALTY IS TO THE UNITED FIRST. It gave us a few seconds to absorb this, then changed to, UNITED, THEN COMPANY, THEN FAMILY. THE UNITED ONLY WORKS WHEN EVERYONE COMPLIES. That was more like it. We had the same signs at home.

I started looking at small building signs—if we found a doctor, could we risk having her check out Nate? He hadn't complained lately, and he looked okay, but—

"Arms, please!" The cop was wearing riot gear, with visor, bulletproof vest, the works.

"What arms?" I blustered, my brain immediately whirring with possible escape routes.

"Your *arms*, smartass," said the cop, holding out his own arm, wrist up.

Real arms. Okay.

One by one, we did the same, holding out our left wrists.

The cops pushed our sleeves back, then scanned us with a UV light. Nothing showed up, and the cops frowned and looked at each other.

"Where's your chip?" one asked, just as another punched a button on his comm and alarms sounded, along with a canned voice: INTRUDER ALERT! INTRUDER ALERT!

Instantly we had our weapons out and were in attack stance. This was exactly what we'd been trained for.

75

THE *SITUATION* WAS EXACTLY WHAT we'd been trained for, but these big city cops were on a whole new level. The United soldiers we'd taken out before were nothing in comparison. These guys were a highly trained, professional team, armed with weapons so new I barely recognized them. Five teens, even armed to the teeth, didn't faze them. One of them even smiled. My heart started pumping, and without being aware of it my brain quickly calculated order of attack and key areas of vulnerability. I heard a high-pitched whine and recognized the sound of a taser charging.

"Let's get crazy," I said under my breath, and the team knew I meant *like at the Crazy House* and whirled into action—literally. I spun away as if to run, then sprang up to snap-kick the closest guy in his helmet. He staggered back and pulled out his gun, but his aim was off and the bullet whizzed by my ear. Another kick from me knocked the gun out of his hand, and his expression went from stunned to furious. I kept it up, mostly with kicking since his flak jacket would break my knuckles if I punched him. He whipped out a billy club and smacked my thigh with it, almost dropping me to the ground. I wouldn't have thought that a stick could hurt so much.

Finally I got in a lucky kick that snapped his head back, and as he came forward I managed a flat-palm smash against his nose. He fell.

There was a one-second opening and I jumped in. My squad had been doing their best—Mills and Bunny had even been shooting at them—not a good idea in such close quarters. But the cops' bulletproof vests made the shots painful annoyances rather than death blows. We were all fighting dirty—street fighting the way we'd been taught—but this high-tech armor was defeating us. All of us were wounded. I was limping, Mills was holding his right arm close to his body, and Nate could barely see because of the blood running into his eyes.

Dodging blows while aiming a kick perfectly at one cop's nuts, I heard a zapping sound, then a body hitting the ground. Someone grabbed the back of my neck, so I slumped to dead weight, then stomped his instep and followed it with a kneecap-shattering kick. There was another buzzing sound and the cop I was facing grabbed his arm, stiffened, then fell like a bushel of wheat seed. Right next to him another cop went down. The team stood back, as mystified as I was. The last two cops we'd been fighting were lying on the ground twitching, their eyes open. They'd been tased, clearly, but by whom?

Then I saw them. They weren't dressed all in black or anything, but there was a look in their eyes—the same look I saw whenever I got a glimpse in a mirror.

They were armed and wore blue kerchiefs rolled up and tied at the back of their heads. Scanning quickly, I counted five people, male and female, some looking as young as us. Glancing from them to the cops helpless on the ground, I got it right away: these were rebels. Big-city rebels. Potential allies? Ansel's message, "They will take you to the Loner," popped back into my head. Had that been a clue, or a *warning*?

I stepped forward, ready to make contact with the one who seemed in charge. She pointed her rifle at me, and a guy held up his Taser.

"Hold it," she barked, and I froze.

Within seconds, a black van with tinted windows screeched to a halt right next to us and its doors slid open. Before I could yell for the team to scatter, we'd been grabbed and thrown into the van. Inside, in the darkness, waiting hands immediately cuffed and hooded us.

Awesome, I thought grimly as I was tossed into a corner like a sack of turnips. Just like old times.

76

'COURSE, I WASN'T A SACK of turnips. I was a soldier-kid with anger-management issues and an extremely strong dislike of being cuffed and hooded. I sensed someone in front of me, someone who smelled different from my team, and automatically I pulled back a booted foot and slammed it forward as hard as I could. I heard someone hitting the other side of the van, and they swore. Then someone punched my leg and said, "Kick me again and I'll tie you up like a pig!"

Suddenly I slumped with an exhaustion so complete that it surprised me. I was just so... tired. Tired of fighting, being on guard, working a mission I wasn't even sure of. A bit more than a year ago my biggest concern had been my calculus final. I was too tired to think of the weird path I'd taken to end up here. My concerns now were to keep myself and my team alive and, oh, yeah, *try to overthrow the government*.

I lay quietly, breathing in dust on the floor of the van, and when Mills whispered a question at me, I pretended not to hear him.

After about half an hour I quit measuring time. We were in darkness, on unfamiliar roads and streets, in a huge city we hadn't known truly existed till two days ago. So all I could tell was that the drive took forever. Another skill the Crazy House taught me came in handy right now: the ability to fall asleep instantly, almost anywhere and under any conditions.

Who knew how long later, I got shaken awake. The business end of a rifle prodded me hard in my ribs and someone yelled, "Get up!"

Recognizing the slightest grunts and groans of my squad, I knew we were all still together, still alive. Cuffed and hooded, we were pushed along by a couple different people who said nothing, explained nothing, threatened nothing. Bunny was first in our line—I heard her hiss as she stumbled. The air I breathed smelled damp, a bit musty. My foot hit something, and I realized we were being herded up steps.

I concentrated on trying to hear anything around us as I climbed: voices, water flowing, people working, vehicles that might tell me where we might be. I tried to jump-start some brain cells, enough to memorize the route we were taking, the twists and turns. I was concentrating so hard that it took me several moments to realize I now heard only three sets of footsteps: mine and two others. Two unknown others. *Where was the rest of my team?* When did we get separated?

A door swung open and I smelled wood smoke. Someone yanked off my hood and I blinked in the sudden brightness. I was in a small, fancy room, its walls covered with shelves holding more books than I'd ever seen. There was a fireplace with a fire blazing beneath its carved marble mantel. I smelled pipe smoke, old books, some things I didn't recognize. I blinked and shook my head—where the hell was I?

Behind me a voice said, "Thanks, Bets." I whirled to see my two captors step backward through the carved wooden double doors, shutting them. I turned toward the voice and saw one person, only one, standing ten feet away. I could take him without even trying.

I'd been trained to be hyper aware of my surroundings. Keeping the person in one corner of my eye, I did a fast three-sixty, memorizing doors, windows, any means of escape. And…did not see much. The person—quite tall—he must be six foot six—was also very slender with shaggy blond hair and clear blue eyes. He gave me a half smile that I didn't return.

"There are two double doors," he said, pointing to the ones my guards had just left through. "The only windows you can reach are these little round ones, which won't do you any good." He met my eyes again, an odd, almost sad expression on his fine-boned face. "Actually, Becca, the only way out of here right now is *up*." He pointed toward the turreted ceiling and I saw, maybe fifty feet up, several large, open windows, letting in light and air. He'd seen me look, knew I was searching for an escape. So he was a former soldier—or maybe a former prisoner?

"How do you know my name?" I demanded.

He didn't answer my question. "People here call me the Loner."

77

CASSIE

I LET MY BREATH OUT in little pants, following Tim as we walked along the road. My whole right side was soaked with blood and I couldn't feel or use my right arm. My rifle was slung over my left shoulder, but we both knew I probably wouldn't be able to use it one-handed. Not fast enough to make a difference, anyway.

We'd left the car roughly two hours before at daybreak, though it felt like at least twelve hours. Tim had filled a backpack with the paper files about Becca's mission, the map of the city, the directions that should lead us to the Loner, and all the supplies he could carry, but it wasn't much.

We were headed downhill. At first he had tried to walk beside me but as time passed he'd started walking ahead, then farther ahead. I'd tried to keep up but I was getting light-headed from blood loss. Now he was so far ahead I could barely see him. He turned back as if to look for me, then leaned against the rock wall that bordered this mountain road.

When I finally reached him, his face was tight, and for some reason that made me mad.

"It wasn't my fault an elk committed suicide while I was driving," I said.

"I know," he answered, but I could tell that part of him believed that if *he* had been driving, the elk would have waited another ten minutes before charging across the road.

"Go on," I said coldly. "Leave me here. I know you want to."

"Becca would kick my ass!" he snapped.

So he really did want to leave me behind. It would be hard for me to survive without him, even for a little while. Knowing that made my blood boil. Usually I only got this mad at Becca.

"Leave, then!" I spit at him. "But you need me more than I need you! Unless you think you can read all the signs yourself!"

"I can!" he shouted. "I'm not *stupid*!"

In a way that used to infuriate Becca, I raised one eyebrow. It had the same effect on him and he stomped over to me, eight inches taller and outweighing me by at least fifty pounds.

Gritting his teeth, he snarled, "At least I didn't run into the world's biggest deer!"

"You couldn't have read the 'Warning: Elk Ahead' sign!" I yelled.

"There was a freaking *sign* and you ignored it?" He stormed away, tearing at his hair.

"No, you *idiot*!" I shrieked. "There *was* no sign! I would have *read* the goddamn sign!"

"Don't you call me an idiot!" he roared so loudly that his voice echoed back at us.

That was what it took to instantly shut us both up. Knowing that we were giving away our presence and position shocked us into silence.

At that point, I realized I was about to faint. There was a convenient boulder and I sank onto it, then put my head between my knees.

"Shit," he said quietly.

78

I DIDN'T RESPOND.

I heard him walk away, but he'd left our packs by my feet, so I knew he planned to come back. My head started to clear but I felt awful—and even worse, was trying not to cry. I would have happily bled out right there before I let him see me cry.

His footsteps returned. "Hey," he said softly.

"Mm," I said, not looking up.

"This is the bottom of the mountain," he said. "And you won't believe what's on the other side."

I did glance up then, and on his face was a mixture of confusion, wonder, and fear. Not a good look.

Very slowly I stood up, relieved to find that my faintness had passed. Wordlessly he pointed past the rock wall. I walked past him, and it was as he said: the mountain ended abruptly, and on the other side was . . . desert.

I looked back at where we'd come from: mountain. Now we were suddenly at the edge of a desert. I stared at Tim. "Oh, my God, have we been heading *west* all this time?" I cried. "The deserty parts of the United are in the west, right?"

Double-checking, Tim looked up at the sun. "No, we're definitely heading east. But there shouldn't be a desert here, for damn sure."

A desert. Surprise #428 of our list of surprises so far on this journey. Without another word, he retrieved our packs. I let him continue to carry mine, out of spite. With effort I hitched my rifle up onto my left shoulder, and we headed down the slight slope toward the desert. I looked around, shielding my eyes from the setting sun, and saw nothing but sand, a very few small plants, and some tumbleweeds that spun in the wind like someone was playing invisible soccer with them.

We had plenty of water—he was carrying it, and I smirked at the thought—but I wasn't sure how smart it was to set off across a desert without knowing how wide it was or where it led. All I knew was that we were still headed east, the sun setting behind us. Then I saw some shadows on the sand. I traced the shadows and saw...two yellow arches? Poking up out of the sand, maybe eight feet high?

"What in the world are those?" I asked, pointing.

He'd already seen them. "No idea," he said. "But—I've seen them before. I know I have."

Now that I thought about it, they seemed familiar to me, too. Yellow arches. Two yellow arches...

He snapped his fingers. "They were on that little cardboard box, in one of the piles! Those arches were printed on the box!"

"Right, right," I said, remembering. "It said…McDonald's French Fries." I looked at the buried arches again. "So this was his house, I guess. But—what made all this sand? Where did it come from?" I whirled to look at him. "Is this a beach? Have we gone so far east that we're near the ocean?"

He frowned. "I don't think so. Those old maps made the ocean look much, much farther away."

"So basically we still have no freaking idea where we are," I said.

"Basically," he agreed, and I wanted to punch him.

79

BECCA

THE GUY HAD A—GET THIS—RED cloak draped around his shoulders. He was huge, well over six feet, but skinny and his back looked slightly bulky, as if he had a thin backpack on underneath. Without looking at me, he sat down in front of a big roll-top desk.

"Your mother named you the Loner?" I asked sarcastically.

The Loner gave me that half-smile again. "I never had a mother. But enough about me—your mother named you Rebecca."

Again I demanded, "How do you know that?"

Meeting my eyes, he went on calmly. "You're from a dinky farming cell hundreds of miles southwest of here. Your parents are dead. Helen Strepp sent you here, to the capital. And luckily, Ansel sent you to me. Do you know why?"

For the first time, I felt a tingle of fear. He knew too much. Ansel had known these rebels would find us. Had his whole "rescue" been an act? In that case, there were six dead United soldiers who hadn't been in on it. But what had seemed so random and unplanned now looked like the inevitable conclusion to a much bigger plot I wasn't aware of. *What had Strepp done to me?*

"Who are you?" I asked, trying to keep my voice strong, my face blank.

"I told you. I'm the Loner. I've been waiting for you." The look he gave me wasn't exactly kind, but it didn't seem too hostile, either. "Strepp sent you to me—by various methods. You're the one who's going to carry out the mission."

My head was whirling. "So you and Strepp—and Ansel—are working together?"

He started stacking pens in a little square, hardly paying attention to me. "It's not that formal of an arrangement." His little square was four pens high. "We know about each other. We have skills that can help each other."

I crossed my arms across my chest, feeling like he was speaking in riddles. "Okay, her skills are forcing people to do things they don't want to do and basically scaring the shit out of kids. What are *your* skills?"

The guy smiled, a private smile at an inner joke. "Well . . . I like to blow things up."

I hadn't expected that—didn't know what I'd expected, but it wasn't that. His little pen square was maybe ten pens tall now, looking like a log cabin with no windows or doors.

"I always have," he explained mildly, "even as a kid. Mostly I stay hidden here in the capital and every once in a while I blow up a key bridge or an important United building. It throws a wrench into their system and gives me...a thrill. Win-win."

This guy was creeping me out—but at the same time he didn't actually seem evil.

"Why am I here?" I asked clearly.

The Loner smiled. "You've been trained to be an assassin. Strepp sent you here to fulfill *your destiny*. We're *depending* on you. You're the Chosen One. Now that I've seen you, I agree with her assessment. You're here to complete the mission."

"What. Freaking. Mission?" I asked, letting irritation sharpen my voice.

He looked up at me again. "Your mission to kill the President of the United."

80

WE WERE BOTH SILENT FOR several minutes. The Loner—what a dumb name—was playing with his pen log house on the desk as if I wasn't there.

Several thoughts raced through my head: 1) Strepp had known about this mission but chose not to tell me. 2) This was probably the most important thing anyone in the Resistance could do. 3) No one could kill the President of the United and live to tell about it. 4) Strepp had knowingly sent me and my squad on a suicide mission. She had expected to never see us again. 5) She had knowingly separated me from my sister, and from Tim. Forever.

Maybe Strepp was doing anything she could for the greater good of cellfolk, but she was an asshole, all the same.

I looked over at the Loner, who was still occupied. The desk lamp shone on his shaggy, pale blond hair, his fair skin, his slender arms, long, graceful fingers. This guy was a weirdo.

"Huh," I said, and he looked up. "My mission is to kill the President. Of the United."

"Yep."

"Where's my squad?"

"They're no longer your responsibility," he said mildly, dismantling his pen structure.

My entire being stiffened, getting ready to beat the info out of him. His blue eyes suddenly became alert and his long fingers tensed. So he knew enough to pick up on danger signals. And man, I was sending danger signals out of every cell in my body.

"I'm afraid I disagree," I said politely, my fingers itching for a gun. "I will need to see my squad immediately."

He started to say something but I interrupted him. "The only answer here is, 'Sure, Becca.'" My voice was heavy with steely ice and he tensed as if he was about to spring out of his chair.

"They're needed for other missions," the Loner said.

"I will see them now." My voice had never been so hard.

He hesitated for a moment as I calculated angles of attack, then punched a button on his desk. "Bets? Becca wants to see her squad. Can you come get her?"

When he looked back at me, his blue eyes were just as icy as mine, and his lean face had hardened into bone. "I'll see you back here in twenty minutes."

Bets came to get me as ordered, and we walked down several flights of winding stairs. Finally she stopped in front of a heavy wooden door. I didn't know what to expect; didn't know if my squad had been imprisoned, tortured, disposed of. They were probably terrified, wondering what had happened to me.

Bets opened the door and there they were: Bunny, Jolie, Mills, and Nate. They were sitting at a big, old-fashioned table that had all kinds of food on it, and they were happily stuffing their faces.

"Becca!" Bunny said, waving a drumstick at me. "Look at all this stuff!"

Bets turned to leave. "You have twenty minutes."

81

CASSIE

I HOPED MR. MCDONALD WASN'T still down there, buried beneath all this sand. It was a creepy thought. Ahead of us we saw more shapes, more shadows in the deepening dusk, and we plodded toward them. Without my asking, Tim made sure I'd been drinking enough, to help make up for all the blood I was losing. Now I was starving, but I refused to ask to stop for food before he did.

"That's a chimney," he said, kicking sand at a tall stand of bricks.

"There's another one," I said. "This must have been a street."

A much bigger shadow loomed in front of us and we walked steadily to it. It was dusk, I was feeling faint, and we needed shelter for the night. It had already dropped at least fifteen degrees since the sun had gone down.

It was a big, two-story building, completely dark, its wide picture windows broken, some boarded up. The roof was flat and the store's name was still right below it in big yellow script: CABELA's.

He pulled out his handgun and motioned me to be quiet, since I obviously had just fallen off a turnip truck and had no idea how to act in times like this. I rolled my eyes at him. Silently he stepped through one of the broken windows and did a few minutes of recon before coming back for me. I'd maneuvered my rifle into position and was ready to back him up, but he shook his head *No* and reached for my hand.

"Everything look okay?" I asked, stepping over the broken window.

He nodded. "Nothing here. No rats, no birds, no bats. But..." He grinned. "It has everything else you could possibly want."

"A hot shower and then a banana split with everything on it?"

"No," he said, frowning. "Normal things."

"Like what?"

He waved his arms around. "Whatever a *normal* person would want!" He strode over to a staircase. "And look!" He shone his flashlight downward and I saw that there were two floors *below* the sand as well as another floor above us.

Even just standing here, I saw canoes, tents, bicycles, weird machines that looked designed for torture, where you put different weights on them.

I smiled at him for the first time in a long time. "It's paradise," I said, and he grinned back.

"Can you hold your flashlight?" he asked, and I nodded. It was understood that I would continue to carry my rifle. I tried to flex the fingers on my right hand and could move them a tiny bit. It was a good sign—maybe the elk's antlers hadn't done any permanent damage.

At first we stayed together, starting at the top and working our way down. We hadn't seen a living creature since the formerly-living elk, but as Strepp had drilled into us a thousand times: You never know. There could be squatters hiding here, there could be wild animals—anything could happen at any time.

"Oh, my God, clothes!" I said, forgetting to keep quiet. There was a huge section of women's clothes, annoyingly colorful but blood-free and clean, except for the dust. I carefully pulled off my blood-stiffened coat and Tim's shirt, and he muttered something about not being into fashion, and left.

He was back sooner than I expected, when I was in front of a mirror, staring with horror at the mangled hole in my chest, right below my collarbone.

"I found a shitload of great stuff," he said, and set up a little camping lantern that surrounded us with an almost cozy glow.

From a large Cabela's shopping bag, he pulled out medical supplies, field kits, boxes of pain medication. I realized with surprise that he'd been able to read the labels.

He ripped open a package of wet wipes with his teeth. They were dry, of course, but he'd found bottled water.

Ten minutes later, I was de-blooded, dressed in warm, dry, slightly sandy clothes, and was contemplating a wide array of unappealing camper food.

"Expiration date: 2040," he read, and opened an envelope of

freeze-dried beef stew. Mixed with water and heated with canned fuel, it was bearable.

"Oh, geez," I said, looking around with sudden understanding. "It was the plague. Everyone here died."

"But what happened with the weather?" Tim asked, opening a can of something. "It wasn't always a desert."

"I don't know."

After we ate, I felt 70 percent better. I could flex my whole hand and didn't feel as light-headed. We grabbed some sleeping bags and hunkered down in a corner of the store. Just as I was falling asleep, I put out a hand and touched Tim's arm. "Thanks for not leaving me behind," I murmured.

He didn't say anything, just stared up at the ceiling.

82

I WAS DREAMING—IT HAD TO be a dream. Ma was inside, making dinner. Pa was outside with our oxen, Ed and Ned. This was before he got his secondhand tractor. The huge animals were gentle and slow as they plowed Pa's fields, and I loved them. In my dream I was feeding Ned a carrot, but instead of carefully lipping it up, he was growling at me. *Growling?*

I blinked awake slowly without moving, as we'd been taught. It was still mostly dark, but a dim light came from the left. I blinked again, controlling my breathing, staying completely still. My shoulder was killing me, throbbing and burning with pain, worse than before. Very slowly I turned my head and saw nothing. Stifling my groans, I sat up and glanced over at Tim to see if he'd heard the weird sound. My heart stopped.

He *wasn't there.* He'd been lying next to me when I'd fallen asleep, but now *there was no sign of him*—his sleeping bag was *gone,* his pack was *gone,* his weapons were *gone.* Oh, my God—instantly I was wide awake, my pulse throbbing in my neck. *He'd left me.* He'd waited till I'd fallen asleep and then he'd *left me.* Hot tears filled my eyes—I was furious, but also couldn't blame him. He'd made the right choice, the choice Ms. Strepp would have approved of. I was holding him up. We'd both known it. Oh, my God. Quickly my brain turned to survival: I could find useful stuff, could even maybe just stay here till my shoulder healed up. Then I could head east alone. Maybe meet up with him somehow. Brain him with a rock or something.

Grrrrrrrrooooooowwwwwwwwll. The noise was so low my chest vibrated. I'd never heard such an utterly menacing sound—it turned my blood to ice. Moving as little as possible, I turned my head and saw a large, gangly, smooth-coated dog hunched down, staring at me, its lip curled. Not—a wolf. Maybe a mastiff? A Rottweiler? It was about ten feet away.

My shoulder thudding painfully, I scanned the area and used every muscle I had to suppress a scream. Oh, God—there were more of them. Many more. Ten? Twelve? Their eyes reflected red in the darkness. They had snuck up on me as silently as Tim had snuck away.

I didn't swallow—didn't make a sound. Just tried to keep my shit together and assess the situation, as I'd been taught. The animals' ribs were showing. Well, we were in a desert and we hadn't seen any small prey. I wished I could tell them there was an enormous dead elk only a couple hours away....

The largest dog inched forward, head lowered, growling. Clearly the pack was thinking I would provide at least one meal, between them.

Shit, shit, shit. Could I run, jump up on a display? Where was my gun? My fingers drifted to where it had been and then my terror turned to stunned disbelief. *My gun is gone.* Tim had left me with *no weapon.* That goddamn asshole! You need to leave, fine, leave! But give me a fighting chance!

Think, Cass, think. There'd been bows and arrows somewhere. My mouth was dry, my eyes hot. I had no idea where the bows and arrows were. I'd been so exhausted last night I hadn't memorized the store layout. Ms. Strepp would think I'd deserve to die just for that.

My sleeping bag provided zero protection. Wait—I had a knife tucked into my boot. I'd have to be super close to the wild dogs to use it. Deathly close. But it was all I had. I gripped it in my left hand and faced the animals, pulling my knees in so I could jump up. I couldn't swallow. After everything I'd been through, it was weird that this was how I was going to finally die.

I'm going to die today, a dim part of my brain registered. *I'm going to die today. Tim deserted me, and now I'm going to die. And I'll never see Becca again.*

83

BECCA

"YOU ARE SHITTING ME," I said flatly. The plain gray dress, its white apron tied neatly around the waist, lay over the back of a chair. The Loner patted it with one long, thin hand.

"It's the best chance for success," he said smoothly. "And it's taken us almost two years to set this up, so don't blow it."

"A *maid*," I said. "A *housemaid*."

Nate turned from warming his hands at the fireplace. I hadn't seen him or the others since dinner last night. I wonder where they slept. "Wouldn't she have to have, you know, like *domestic skills* for that?" he asked, not even bothering to hide his smirk.

"I have domestic skills," I insisted. I didn't admit that in fact Cassie had inherited that gene. *My* domestic skills included *almost* being able to boil water for tea.

"*You* will be working in the kitchen," the Loner told Nate, and handed him a pair of black-and-white checked pants and a white jacket. "The President entertains a lot and the kitchen is huge and well staffed. You're going to start as a dishwasher."

I thought of how, as a Provost's son, everything had been done for Nate since he was born.

"Huh," I said thoughtfully, putting one finger to my chin. "Wouldn't he have to, you know, have *any kind* of skill for that?"

Nate's face flushed, but he had no comeback.

"Two years," the Loner warned us. "This plan has been in play for *two years*. Don't tell me that Strepp sent me a couple of clowns."

I glared. Two years? That meant the Loner had no intention of keeping Nate away from me—was yesterday some kind of test? He wanted to see how I'd react at being separated from my squad? I've had enough stupid mind games. "Okay," I said. "Give us the brief."

The Loner did, turning on the bank of large monitors that surrounded his desk. We saw several bird's-eye maps of the President's palace, and then a schematic map of each floor: four floors in all, and then a basement below.

"Memorize these," the Loner said. "I've heard there's been some remodeling of some areas, some redecoration. I haven't been able to have that confirmed. But until you get inside to assess, this is the best we have to go on."

We nodded.

"Once you're there, Nate, you'll report to Mal in the kitchen," the Loner said. "He'll show you what to do."

"Washing dishes," Nate said dully.

"Yes," the Loner said, then turned to me.

"You're starting as an undermaid, which is basically maid backup. You'll do whatever they ask you to do."

Nate snorted and I tried to change the mulish expression on my face.

"This will be great," Nate said. "I'm sure that'll come naturally to her."

The Loner looked at us seriously. "You will do as you're told," he said. "You will not give away your identities or the fact that you're on a mission. If you should be captured or found out, no one will admit to knowing you. No one will be able to come to your aid. Do you understand?"

I understand that I'm being screwed, I thought sourly, but said, "Yeah, I understand."

"Nate?" the Loner prompted.

Nate didn't look any more thrilled than I did, but he nodded. "Yeah. I got it."

"Good. Okay. You guys get changed," said the Loner. "And we'll go to the palace." With a flourish of the cape that mostly disguised his back deformity, he swept out, tall and thin like a stork.

"You know, I can't call him 'Loner' anymore," I told Nate. "He needs a new name." I thought for a minute, then smiled evilly. "Blondie McMystery Man. It has a certain ring to it."

"Fine," Nate said. "But can you see me taking on the kitchen staff, armed only with a rolling pin and a sink of hot water?"

"I'll be armed with a feather duster," I pointed out, then mused,

233

"Actually, I can think of seven different ways to kill someone with a feather duster."

Nate looked at me. "You're kind of scary and bloodthirsty," he said. "I like that about you."

I rolled my eyes and picked up the maid's uniform. "Only 'kind of'? I must be slipping." But I thought of his words over and over—was Nate flirting with me?

84

"YOU ARE SHITTING ME," I repeated, staring at the...*palace* that the President lived in. Sure, I'd seen pictures and floor layouts, but this was far, far beyond anything I'd imagined. It was *enormous*, taller than the United Bank and United Insurance buildings at home combined, and it went on and on, taking up a whole city block. The land around it wasn't divvied up into neat rows of vegetables for the family's use. There was no thought here of making every square foot count. For at least an acre in every direction it was lush, fragrant flower gardens. The precise symmetrical beds were lined with narrow paths of pale crushed stone. The tall iron front gates were wide enough to drive a farm combine through, and the drive itself was laid brick. Even the Provost back home had to make do with rutted concrete.

"I've tried to blow it up any number of times," Blondie McMystery Man said wistfully, breaking into our stunned silence. "But it's impregnable, even from above."

I couldn't respond. The President of the United and his family lived here—thanks to us, all the rest of the people. Cellfolk like me, Cassie, Tim and even Nate, *provided everything* these people ate, wore, drove, sat on... They were like fairy tale royalty. I thought back to the worn clothes Cassie and I had shared, the ancient radio in the kitchen where Ma had listened to Cell News. I thought about our dinky moped, our beat-up truck.

Looking at the pruned cherry trees, the carefully trained apple trees growing between windows, I thought of my mom, who had loved beautiful things. Her need for beauty had clashed so strongly with the reality of our lives in the cell that eventually she had been taken away for a mood-adjust. And had never come back.

Five years later Pa had killed himself, though it had been months between the poorly aimed rifle shot and his last breath.

People like *this* had caused our misery, all across the United.

And it was only *just now* that I *finally* got it, that the truth *finally* struck me with the clarity of a lightning bolt against a dark sky: It wasn't just *how things were*. It was *how things were designed to be*. By a handful of people. People like the President.

"Oh, yeah," I said softly. "This guy has to die. And I'm just the housemaid to do it."

"Excellent," Blondie said.

85

CASSIE

I COULD KILL ONE OR two, *maybe* three dogs before one of them ripped my throat out. Those were bummer odds, but if this was my death day, then it was my death day. The Crazy House had done that for me—removed any expectation of a Happily Ever After. I really hoped Nate and Becca were okay, wherever they were. I even hoped Tim was okay, wherever he was, however far he had gotten.

For myself, I was going to die here and now, and I was cool with that.

I saw the almost imperceptible tightening of the alpha dog's hindquarters. It was about to spring. I knew getting bitten would hurt. I just hoped I'd be dead before they started in on their feast. The dog leaped and I yanked the knife out of my boot.

Blam! The gunshot was deafeningly close. The large dog dropped out of midair and landed heavily not three feet away from me. Should I hunker down and be rescued, or throw myself into battle, armed only with a knife?

I jump-rolled out of my sleeping back and landed in a crouched ready position, ignoring the agony in my shoulder. Within seconds more shots were fired and several more big animals hit the ground. A straggly husky type lunged at me, and though it weighed less than half of what I did, it easily pinned me to the ground, standing on my chest, growling meanly.

I almost felt sorry for it as I adjusted the knife in my hand. But it was me or the animal, and I chose me. My hand went up in a hard, practiced move, and I stuck it right between the ribs. Still it lunged for my face, its hot breath mingling with mine, but in a second I saw the light leave its eyes. It collapsed slowly on me, a smelly, furry body, and I pushed it off, feeling like I might be sick.

Two more quick shots and the remaining pack members turned tail and raced off howling into the desert.

Looking up, I saw Tim lowering his rifle. It was a different rifle, one I hadn't seen.

"I thought you left," I said.

"Left? No. Exploring," he said shortly. "Guess what? They have guns here!"

"I had a gun *here*," I retorted. "What the hell did you do with it?"

"I was gonna clean 'em, but then I found better ones," he said. Then he took a good look at me, pale from pain, splashed with blood from the dog at my side. He frowned. "How's your shoulder?"

It took me a second to register the waves of numbing pain radiating out from yesterday's injury. "Not great," I admitted.

"Like, 'I'm in pain but I'll live,' not great? Or 'I'm probably gonna die,' not great?" he asked.

I shrugged, which hurt, so I winced.

"Okay, well, look what I have here." He knelt and upended his backpack. A hundred things fell out.

"We have more bandages," he said, "and we have needle and thread."

Needle and thread? I narrowed my eyes.

"The bleeding isn't stopping," he said, pointing at my shoulder. "You already look like you're ready for the funeral pyre. You can't lose any more blood. Not if you want to keep going."

With me went unsaid.

"Take off your shirt," he said, threading the needle.

Feeling somewhat sick, somewhat embarrassed, I did, revealing the lacy camisole underneath. I'd gotten it here, for once choosing something pretty instead of practical.

But Tim might as well be working on a sheep for all the acknowledgment he gave of me as a woman.

He poured alcohol on his hands, then swabbed the front and back holes that the antler had left in my body. I tried not to yelp at the cool, burning sensation.

"This is going to hurt," he warned. "Find something to bite on." He cleaned out the wounds, using alcohol liberally. He was going by rote, following the procedures we'd learned in our field-medic classes. For myself, I was gripping two legs of an overturned chair and biting as hard as I could on a retriever's toy duck.

When he was done, I threw up into a portable compost pail, fixing its lid on tightly. I felt wrung out and exhausted and wished my arm would just fall off so I could leave it behind.

Tim was busily opening ancient camping food packets. "We're going to stay here the rest of the night," he said. "But we have to go first thing in the morning."

Or else went unsaid.

86

BECCA

I WAS A SOLDIER. AN assassin, even—call me what you will. I was one of the best that Strepp ever trained. I could kill people silently with whatever I had at hand. Now I was getting a list of my duties as a *housemaid* at President Unser's house. And the head housekeeper, Mrs. Argyle, made Strepp look like a pansy-ass amateur.

Some of the house rules: speak only when spoken to. The President was called sir, Mrs. President was called ma'am, young master Kirt was called Master Kirt, and young mistress Mia was called Miss Mia. Never say "yes," only "yes, sir," "yes, ma'am," "yes, Master Kirt," etc. When a member of the household passed by, you stopped what you were doing and cast your eyes down.

No curtsy? I almost said snidely, then remembered Blondie McMystery Man and the two years it'd taken them to place us in the employment agency where Mrs. Argyle got new recruits. I clenched my teeth and said nothing. I wondered how Nate was faring in the kitchen. The fact that he was no doubt elbow-deep in suds cheered me up a little.

I was shown to my quarters—a tiny room in the attic, but it had a small window—and then was given a quick tour of the house, which was mind-blowing. The riches, the beautiful *everything*, the things I had no idea existed. I was shocked and awed and then filled with rage again at the gross, *gross* injustice. I wished Blondie had given me a bomb so I could blow this place sky-high right now.

Unfortunately I had gone through a metal detector at the door—every door on the first floor had them, as did every balcony door upstairs. Not only that, but I'd been thoroughly patted down by her. Finally, the uniform Blondie had given me had been taken away and replaced. So if it had had a tracking or listening device sewn into the hem, it was gone now. Burned in the incinerator.

"Rebecca, your job is to attend to Miss Mia," she said, and I almost choked.

I held up two fingers. "One, everyone calls me Becca," I said. "Two, I don't have, uh, much experience with attending...young ladies. Maybe I could just dust instead?"

Her look would have burned holes in a lesser maid. *She* held up two fingers. "Number one, here you will be called Rebecca. Two, here are the directions to Miss Mia's room. Don't get lost."

Yes, I needed *written directions* to Mia's room because the place was so effing big that I could be lost for days before anyone found me. I'd planned to do recon on the way, but soon noticed I was never alone. There was always some other servant within sight, dusting, mopping, arranging flowers, straightening pictures. No wonder the house was so hospital-clean already. Or was this on purpose? So they weren't only keeping an eye on the new staff, but on each other?

As I passed a girl close to my age, I stopped. "Hey," I said, and the girl actually startled, like a deer, then gave a quick look around.

Her responding "Hey," was almost soundless. She stood frozen, the soft paintbrush she was using to dust an ornate picture frame dangling from one hand.

"I'm Becca," I said. "One of the mistress's attendants. I'm from Cell B-97-4275. How about you? Where are you from?"

The girl frowned slightly and cocked her head to one side. I resolved to use that expression later 'cause it looked awesome.

"I'm...Nell."

"What cell are you from?" I was taking a risk, lingering like this. Nell would get in trouble, too. But I had to start somewhere, and time was a luxury I didn't have.

"What do you mean?" she asked. "What's a cell?"

87

EVENTUALLY I FOUND MISS MIA'S room and knocked on the heavy wooden door. *What's a cell?* There's someone in the United who doesn't know what a *cell* is? *How?*

No one answered my knock, so I knocked louder. Finally I just opened the door, thinking I could tidy or straighten or whatever I remembered seeing Cassie do back at home. For a moment I stood in the doorway as my eyes tried to comprehend what I was seeing. This girl's bedroom was as big as the entire first floor of my parents' house. Pale pink curtains framed giant windows. The white bed was enormous, with four posts and a curved top. Thick, pale-green carpet made my first tentative steps feel like I was walking on a sheep. It was the most beautiful room I had ever seen, and my throat closed in a weird, overwhelmed reaction. A person could be happy in a room like this. Anyone could.

"What do you want?" It was a girl's voice, full of snide rudeness. Back at school, anyone who talked to me like that usually ended up crying.

Despite my sniper-vision training, it took me several seconds to locate Miss Mia. She was sitting on an overstuffed sofa in an alcove that had its own round window. She was around my age, I guessed, or a bit younger. She was holding a fiddle and bow.

"Well? What do you want?" She looked at me as if I still smelled like farmyard.

"I'm your new maid," I said bluntly. "My name is Becca." Well, it's not like I went to maid school. I went to soldier school.

She looked surprised for a second, then shrugged. "My laundry's in the closet," she said dismissively, looking at sheet music on an ornate stand. "You can make my bed, dust, or whatever. Just be quiet and don't disturb me."

My fingers instinctively felt for my gun and of course found a dust cloth instead. I pressed my lips together hard and managed to nod. My blood was boiling. This kid was obviously brought up to be a princess. Back in my cell, there were no princesses. The fanciest person there was Provost Allen. This house made him look like a beggar.

She ignored me as she bent her head to her fiddle and began playing. After twenty seconds I realized this was a whole other level than the fiddle playing I knew back home. It was unlike anything I'd ever heard. It was like—like if a river or a tree or a rock or something could cry. If it could wail in despair, it would make sounds like this. I guess that sounds pretty stupid.

I did actually dust, but I also noted there was only one door in and out, that the three windows opened onto tiny balconies and were three stories up, that there were a million hiding places and another million things that could be used as weapons. The windows looked out onto what seemed like a main street, four lanes wide and full of cars from the fancy car factory.

I tried not to listen to the sad, wailing music as I moved around the room, dusting, neatening, tidying. It was like I'd died and been forced to come back as Careful Cassie, atoning for my messy ways.

In the closet, which was as big as my bedroom back home, I collected the clothes strewn on the floor, and subtly tapped all the walls, listening for a fake front or hidden exit. Nothing.

The bathroom was all mirrors, white and gold. My head was spinning by now and I moved like an automaton back into the bedroom. Almost one entire wall was bookcases, with cupboards beneath. Her own bookcases in her own room, filled with hundreds of books, like she was a library.

I'd never been a great student, except for Unexpected Kill class, but suddenly I felt hungry for books. I mean, I'd loved story time in my younger grades. As I dusted, titles caught my eyes—some were fantasies, some sounded like romances—there was a whole encyclopedia with twenty-seven volumes! If she left, I could go crazy and look at all this!

"What are you doing?" Her voice was accusing.

"Nothing," I answered, remembering just in time, "Miss Mia. Just dusting."

Her eyes narrowed. "Just keep your eyes on your job, you hear me?"

I nodded, attempting to look bland and maidlike. *Oh*, I thought, *I'm going to enjoy wrecking your life. And I'm gonna steal your books, too.*

88

CASSIE

TURNS OUT, IF YOU STOP blood from leaking out of your body, you feel better. My shoulder still hurt like crazy, but I felt less like the walking dead.

"How're you feeling?" Tim asked, coming up behind me so silently that I almost screamed.

I whacked the side of his leg. "Quit sneaking up on me!" I snapped. "You're lucky I wasn't holding a loaded gun!"

"Speaking of loaded guns," he said, "it seems that looters did get most of them. I found this one in the back storage room." He patted the rifle he'd used on the wild dogs the night before.

"Okay," I said. "We can do one last thorough sweep before we go, see if we can find one or two more."

"Yeah," he agreed, pulling yet more stuff out of his backpack.

"I also found more old paper maps—thought we might figure out where we are, where we need to go."

"Good thinking," I said, and he looked gratified.

At one of the dust-covered counters I found store receipts with the store's address printed on them: 2700 CABELA DRIVE, MOLINE, ILLINOIS.

"Look for Moline, Illinois," I told him.

He found it. "But who cares where we are if we don't know where we're going? The files said the capital, but we don't know if it has any other name."

"We should head for the biggest cell we can find," I suggested.

"Cells aren't marked on this map," he said with exaggerated patience. "Cells didn't exist back then."

"You know what I mean," I said, embarrassed to be caught in such a dumb mistake.

"Our best bet is to keep heading east," he went on. "There's a big *city* called Chicago there. Maybe it still exists and maybe someone there can tell us where to find the capital."

I nodded. "Let's load up. Meet you in thirty."

Half an hour later he came to the broken third-floor window where we'd first come in.

"You ready?" he asked.

I heard the impatience in his voice; he wanted to get out of here at sunrise. What other dangers were there besides wild dogs?

"Yeah," I said. "I'm just looking at this…boat." It was a little Sunfish, maybe nine feet long, covered with dust. Mr. Grogan had had one for fishing in Cattail Pond, back home. Sometimes he'd let me take it out by myself, sail it across the pond.

"Yeah, so?" he said.

I dumped my backpack into the rear of the Sunfish.

"Cassie. You remember the desert part, right? The great out-doors where tumbleweeds go to die?"

"Yeah," I said, walking around the small boat. "But look—it's attached to this trailer."

"We can't pull the boat across the desert," he said flatly.

"I *know*. But the boat's on a trailer, the trailer has wheels, and the boat has a sail, too. Could we maybe *sail* it across the desert? Save us some walking?"

His mouth dropped open. He stood back and looked at the boat.

Half an hour later, when we were about to ditch the boat, trailer, and everything else, our small sail suddenly caught the wind. It filled out, plump and beautiful, and Tim and I stared at each other for a second.

"Get in!" he yelled, and we threw ourselves into the boat.

I shrieked as the small boom almost knocked us overboard. Tim reached for the rudder, but I shook my head. It wouldn't help us steer since we weren't in the water; we'd have to go where the wind took us. Our only choice was to swing the boom back and forth, zigzagging across the desert.

I didn't even have the words to describe how I felt skimming along. Happy? Maybe. For once I didn't have a worried scowl on my face. I looked over at Tim and he seemed almost lighthearted with the wind ruffling his hair.

We nodded at each other, grinning. Then I gasped as a gust of wind sent us careening for just a second. I stumbled into him, and he grabbed my good shoulder, pulling me toward him. Looking into my startled eyes, he tilted his head and kissed me. A real kiss.

He pulled back moments later, looking shocked. I probably looked just as shocked, my face white, my fingers moving slowly to my lips.

Time stood still, for a while.

89

HELEN

MS. STREPP COULDN'T BELIEVE HER life's work came down to this. She'd thought she could drive this mission further. All those soldiers—no, those *kids*. They'd believed in her. They'd been *forced* to believe in her. But now instead of a training camp director, she was a prisoner. A prisoner! Her! It was unbelievable, except for... the reality—the horrible, infuriating reality of *now*.

The door of the dank metal shipping container opened with a rusty, goose-bump-inducing shriek. It was a guard, of course. A guard from the lowest echelon of guard school. He clomped up to where she sat on the cold, wet floor. He kicked her ankle in its shackle, knocking it several feet sideways. Ms. Strepp prided herself on not looking up, not moving her foot back.

"The Vice President will be here soon," the guard said. "She wants to meet you herself. Before you...disappear." He giggled at the last part.

Think, Helen, think, Strepp told herself. *Buy Becca more time.*

The guard left, clomping through the puddles, trying to splash her. She was stoic till he left, then let her face sag. Becca. She was the best Strepp had ever trained, ever seen. But it was a difficult journey, and there were so many ways it could've gone wrong. What if she never made it to Chicago as Strepp had planned? It was risky keeping Becca in the dark, but Strepp couldn't risk her getting captured and divulging their plans to the enemy. Even if she did make it, Strepp knew that Becca's was a suicide mission. They would probably both be dead long before they accomplished their goals.

90

BECCA

"NO, THOSE GET WASHED IN the sink and then hung to dry!" Mia snapped, yanking the flimsy lace bra out of my hands. "Didn't they teach you anything?"

Uh, they didn't tell me how to wash your undies, but I know a couple different ways to kill you with this hanger.

Right at this minute, I was ready to use all of my deadly skills on every single person in this joint. Whenever my eyes were open, they were assaulted by beauty, culture, art, luxury. No cellfolk anywhere had anything like this stuff—real paintings, actual statues, extravagant flower arrangements in enormous vases on round marble tables.

I'd come to the conclusion that the best solution would be to level this city, tear down every cell wall everywhere, and let everyone go free to choose their own lives. Total anarchy, in other words. It would be so awesome.

"Just go." Her snide voice broke into my fantasy. "I'm tired. You can do this tomorrow, after you bring up my breakfast tray."

It took a lot of willpower to keep my face expressionless, and to ruthlessly force down the shriek boiling up inside me over the words "breakfast tray."

But this wasn't about me, my feelings. I was on a mission. I was supposed to be an emotionless weapon, as I'd been trained. Somehow the last month had broken down some of my walls. I was tired, too.

I nodded to her, my eyes down, and backed out of her highness's room.

This job had no set hours—it was ten o'clock at night now, and I'd just been let go. If she'd wanted to keep me working till three in the morning, she could. That was one way living in a cell was better than here—we had regular work hours, by law.

The servants' rooms were up in the attic, but I took a chance and headed to the basement, where the kitchen was. I saw the occasional roving guard—sometimes we nodded at each other. The rest of the house was quiet—all the privileged people were of course asleep in their feather beds.

In the servants' dining hall, I found Nate asleep, his arms pillowing his head on the table. For just a minute I looked at him, remembering that Cassie loved him. He was no longer the smooth-talking, finely groomed Provost's son. Once upon a time, he may have fit in here at the palace. He was rougher now, his hair longer and unkempt, a shadow of red beard across his jaw. I saw his hands—they were red and chapped, almost raw. How the Provost's son had fallen.

I shook his shoulder—we had a lot of information to exchange. He woke, drowsy and grumpy. "Come on, Cinderella," I said briskly, and he frowned.

Just then the head housekeeper, Mrs. Argyle, came in. "What are you two still doing down here?" she snapped. "Get upstairs, and mind you be quiet about it!"

Nate looked at me, and I barely managed a shrug. The male servants slept in one attic wing, and the females on the other side of the house. We couldn't exchange info tonight.

Ten minutes later I lay on my narrow, hard cot (which was still heaven after the Crazy House) and wondered where in the world the President was. How could I kill him if I couldn't even find him?

91

THE NEXT MORNING, WHEN I delivered Miss Mia's breakfast tray, she wordlessly pointed to a small pile of lacy bits of cloth that barely deserved to be included in the clothing category. I took them into the bathroom and filled the sink with soapy water.

This was all bullshit, I fumed. This couldn't have been what Strepp had in mind. True, Blondie McMystery Man had seemed pretty solid in his creds and planning. But really? How was washing goddamn underwear part of the larger plan? I wondered how Bunny and the rest of the squad were managing in their new roles. Each of them had been assigned a role to play—not in the palace, like me and Nate, but still decent assignments.

I was rinsing the clothes maybe a bit too roughly when Miss Mia came in and I had to put on my ridiculously inappropriate submissive face.

"I'm going to a riding lesson," she said without looking at me. "Change the sheets on my bed and be sure to dust the bookshelves."

Okay. This was more like it. As soon as I was sure she was gone, I searched her room again, tapping the walls, listening for hidden doors to a safe room or an escape route. I found nothing. Simultaneously I looked for bugs and cameras, any kind of alarm system, any kind of surveillance, and to my surprise I found nothing. The only visible alarm nodes were on the windows. Strepp had explained that rich people usually had personal surveillance or panic buttons.

Next, the bookcases. Dust cloth in hand, my eyes raked the titles of hundreds of books, looking for anything that could help me. *The Proud History of the United* caught my eye and I pulled it out, then pushed it back in fast as the door was opened.

That was a quick lesson, I thought, but turned blank-faced to see—not Mia.

"Well, hello there," a guy said. I guessed he was from the family—he had Mia's dark hair and blue eyes but hadn't been so lucky in the bone structure or the acne-free skin. I just looked at him.

"I'm Master Kirt," he said. "Miss Mia's big brother."

92

RIGHT AWAY MY FINGERS ITCHED for a weapon. His oily voice made the hairs on my arms stand up.

"Sir," I said quietly, and continued to carefully dust the books.

"They said the new maid was a looker," Kirt said. "They weren't wrong."

I said nothing—all I needed was Mrs. Argyle hearing me telling Kirt to go stuff himself. She'd probably cut my tongue out.

He came closer. He reminded me of a snake, the kind of snake that farmers cut the head off of with a shovel.

"Are you assigned only to my sister?" he asked. "Or are you part of my father's entourage as well? He's due back today."

I almost stopped dusting. Finally! Something useful from this most useless of families! The President was due back today!

"I serve only Miss Mia," I said, trying to keep excitement out of my voice.

"Good," he said, and he actually reached out and touched my

hair, the few locks that weren't covered by my maid's kerchief. If I aimed the handle of the duster right, I could get it right through his ear and into his brain. I considered it, now almost shaking with fury.

"I'm glad you're not assigned to Father." His voice dropped. He was so close to me now that I could easily have chopped him in the kidney. He'd be pissing blood for weeks. "I hear that serving Father can be . . . taxing for the maids."

The blood drained from my face as I got his meaning.

Practically whispering in my ear, curling an escaped strand of my hair around his finger, Master Kirt went on: "But you don't have to fear the third-floor study. I'm much more reasonable, and I'm practically right next door."

So the President's study was on the third floor, not the first, as I'd assumed! For just a second I considered flirting with this gross schmuck to get more info, and in the second I let down my guard, he sprang at me, pushing me onto Mia's bed.

Becca, you idiot! I thought, as he became an octopus, all hands and mouth. If I used my instinctive fighting skills, he would instantly know I was a trained soldier, which would get me kicked into prison at best, and killed at worst. So I squirmed, ineffectually trying to push him away. The same way I had tried to push my teacher, Mr. Harrison, off me back in grade twelve. Before I was adept at killing people. While Master Kirt writhed on top of me, I dully remembered my horrible miscarriage and how incredibly heartless Strepp had been about it. Cruel to be kind.

I gritted my teeth and tried to fend Kirt off in a normal, outraged girl way, pushing at him, clenching my mouth shut, turning my head.

"Kirt!"

It took me a moment to identify the furious voice as Miss Mia's.

"Goddamnit, not again!" she shouted, and I heard the whiz of a riding crop slicing through the air and landing on Kirt's back. "Get off!" She whipped him with the riding crop again.

He scrambled off me, red-faced. "Watch it, you bitch!" he shouted. "She's just the maid! Goddamnit! What's wrong with you?"

"Get out of this room," she spat at him, and I was amazed at the different Mia I was seeing.

"Screw you!" he said, but he left the room and slammed the door so hard that a small framed picture fell to the floor and broke.

I sat up and pulled my uniform down, retied the kerchief around my head.

"Thank you, Miss Mia," I said, surprised to hear a convincing tremble in my voice. "I don't know—"

"Just don't let him get you alone," she said briskly. "Now help me get cleaned up—we're going out."

93

CASSIE

I FELT A SMALL BUG crawling beneath my untucked shirt but didn't move, keeping the binoculars riveted on the action below. I'd been sad to leave our boat at the edge of the hard, cracked desert but once the tall-grass prairie started, it'd been useless. For the last day and a half, we'd waded through sharp-edged grass taller than my head, with Tim breaking a path and me traveling miserably in his wake. The air here was heavy, cool but humid, and we kept being assaulted by horrible clouds of stinging gnats. After the dry, bugless air of the desert, this felt unbearable.

"Here." I handed him the binoculars, lying in the grass next to me. We were hidden well—the prairie ended here, but three feet into the grass, no one could see us.

He gave a low whistle while I smashed the bug and shook it out of my shirt.

"Right?" I said. "Like the biggest cell in the whole United."

He lowered the binoculars and looked at me. "It's not a cell," he said solemnly. "It's a city, like what we read about in the attic. Maybe even the capital."

Becca could be down there! Absently I rubbed my shoulder—it still ached. At least I could use my hand again.

"How far away do you figure?" he asked, and I guessed he was trying to be polite since he could estimate distance as well as I could.

"Three hours, walking?" I said. "Very visible for a lot of it."

"I'm seeing cars and people lining up to get through the gates," he said, peering through the binoculars again. "People are talking to the guards? Shaking hands or something? No clue."

With a hollow feeling in my chest I now realized that all the info we'd learned up in the camp attic had been too old to be useful. We knew how they had done things a hundred years ago—big whoop.

"Lemme see the map again," I asked, and he took it out of his shirt pocket, creased and falling apart. I lined up the pieces and peered at them. "Weird. Look, here's those two rivers we crossed, right? So we should be about here." I pointed. "But the map shows other cells—cities—and roads. So where are they? There's nothing here. No cities. No roads."

"Yeah," he said. "But still, *that* huge city must be Chicago, right? And since it's the biggest city, it's probably the capital of the United. There's no other city it could be."

"That isn't sound logic. But we should go there anyway. Just in case. We have to get through that checkpoint," I said, pointing out the extremely obvious. "Any bright ideas?"

He pinched his lips—the lips that he'd kissed me with days ago and never mentioned again. "I do," he said slowly. "But you're not going to like it."

94

HE WAS RIGHT—I DIDN'T LIKE it. It was dangerous, would probably not work, and would most likely end up with one or both of us dead or in prison. Unfortunately, I couldn't think of anything better that we could actually pull off.

So here we were at the city's checkpoint, waiting in line like a lot of other people on foot. During our twenty-minute wait, he and I automatically catalogued our surroundings, noting places to run, where we could breach the razor-topped walls, how many guards there were and how we could take them out. My heart was thudding heavily in my chest and I was still worried about the lameness in my shoulder. I didn't want it to let me down at a crucial moment. Because I knew that Tim would keep going without looking back.

"Metal detectors?" I asked, trying to see ahead of us in the long line of people.

He shook his head. "Weirdly, I don't think so. At least, not that I can see."

Across the road, a line of fancy cars moved more quickly. For just a moment my mind wandered away from the danger. I had relived his surprising kiss several times, but he'd been pretty distant since then. It felt like years since I'd seen Nate and with a flash of pain I realized I couldn't remember the feel of his arms around me, his body, slender and strong, against mine. I didn't even know if he was alive. Or if Becca was.

One thing I *did* know: if Becca *was* alive and in this city, I would find her.

We took another couple of steps closer, my gaze nervously darting here and there as I examined our options.

"So, razor wire," I said quietly, and he nodded.

"Doable," he said.

The thing about razor wire is that it's super scary looking, and if you don't know what you're doing, you could get stuck in it, all cut up. But if you *expect* it to hurt, *expect* it to cut you up a bit but not kill you, and you're really determined to just let it rip your clothes, well, you can usually make it over alive.

"I'm thinking razor wire, rooftop, sewer cap on the other side," I said.

He gave me a look of agreement, but murmured, "Or guns blazing, take the guards out, hop the turnstile, run down the street, sewer cap."

"Also a plan," I said. Inside, I was trembling. It had been weeks since I'd fought, either practice or real, and I was still weak from the accident. Could I still function? Would it really come back so easily?

The people in front of us moved ahead, and it was in fact a tall metal turnstile they moved through, one at a time. I looked up at the guard with an open smile and waited for him to demand whatever thing I didn't have to get into the city.

The guard snapped, "Your arm!" and I thought, no way am I giving up my gun.

"Your arm!" the guard said and held out his own arm. Mystified, I held out my actual arm.

He grabbed it, pushed my sleeve up, and held a small wand over the top, scanning it. He frowned, then moved the wand around.

"You're not chipped!" he said, and stepped backward to press a red button on his comm. "INTRUDER ALERT! INTRUDER!"

95

BECCA

I'D SEEN SOME OF THE city with Nate and Blondie McMystery Man, but with Mia I was in an enormous, chauffeur-driven car. It had two backseats facing each other, and Mia rode in the backward one. I tried not to crane my neck at this part of the city, which looked like paradise. I was supposed to be *from* here. This was all supposed to be *normal*, business as usual. I kept my gaze low but peered out from under my lashes to drink everything in. There were buildings here so high that I could barely see the top of them. I'd never seen so many cars, so many electric lights, so many people. The street plan seemed to be a grid, and I started memorizing street names, landmarks, certain buildings, etc.

"Here, Mattias," Mia commanded, and the driver smoothly pulled the car over to the curb. This building had huge glass windows full of fake people wearing clothes. Way creepy. I could barely take it all in as I climbed out of the car after Mia. About twenty feet away I saw a very tall, lean figure leaning against the building and stuffed down a gasp: It was the Loner, Blondie McMystery Man!

Why was he here? It was almost like he'd been waiting for the car, had *known* we were coming.

I kept my face still but inside I was glad to see him, this reminder of another life, a real plan, a purpose. It was only my second day working at the palace, but it felt like much longer than that.

Without acknowledging us in any way, he casually pushed off the building and walked in our direction.

"Come," Miss Mia commanded me, and I quickly caught up with her as she went through automatic glass doors.

I don't care about clothes on a good day so the next hour was torture, but an amazing torture. I didn't know that clothes like this existed. Mrs. Allen, the Provost's wife, had been the fanciest-dressed woman in our cell, and I'd assumed her matching skirt suits and impractical shoes were about as good as clothes got. But the things that Mia was picking out made Mrs. Allen look just regular.

Finally, *finally* Mia, with me trailing her like a hunting dog, went to the counter to pay. Behind the counter was a hall leading who knew where, and I tried to keep my eyes properly looking at my feet while the clerk boxed up all the new clothes and tied the boxes with wide satin ribbon.

With a flick of her hand Mia gestured to me to pick them up, and as I did so I glanced down the hallway. There was movement and I looked more sharply. Was that a flash of fair hair? It was gone in a second.

Back at the palace, Mia told me to unpack the boxes and put everything away.

"Remember that things are arranged by color and type," she said, sounding nothing like the angry girl who had used her riding crop on her brother. I nodded silently. Here I was, sorting clothes by color and type when the President might already be here, in this building, where I could kill him!

Burning with impatience, I flicked the lids off the boxes and unpacked ridiculous shoes that I had to line up on shelves next to hundreds of other shoes, more freaking underwear that could not be described as sturdy or practical, skirts made of wool and leather that got hung up next to similar ones (kill me now), soft, beautiful sweaters that were folded just so and arranged in paper-lined drawers, a long, gorgeous dress of amber satin that was kept in its white paper bag and hung up like that, and . . . *a gun.*

96

HELEN

HELEN STREPP HAD BEEN SITTING on this metal chair for what felt like twelve hours. She knew it had probably been about four. Four hours was the prime length of time to keep a prisoner waiting—not so long that they got angry and defiant, not so short that they retained hope.

Her hands were chained to a metal link welded to the metal table. They'd gone numb about forty-five minutes into this. She was still considering escape possibilities but the best scenario she came up with only had a seven percent chance of working.

Ms. Strepp considered herself unsurprisable, yet when the interrogator walked in, she was surprised. More than surprised. Stunned. It took everything she had to keep the shock off her face.

"Hello, Helen," said Ajana Nielson.

Helen realized she was staring at her and quickly looked away, striving for casualness. "Ajana," she said evenly.

Ajana laughed. "That's Vice President Nielson to you," she said, further shocking Ms. Strepp.

"Vice President!" Helen said. "What happened to becoming a minister, having your own church?"

The Vice President laughed again. The harsh white light in this room no doubt made Helen look older than she was, and unhealthy to boot. But it bleached Ajana's face to a sickly greenish mud, made her smooth brown arms look rubbery.

"I had a higher calling," she said with a smile, the smile that Helen remembered heartbreakingly well. There was a thick file in front of her and now she opened it, skimming the first pages. "You've been busy," she murmured. "Whew—an actual training camp! Looks like *you* had a higher calling, too."

An unusual feeling began churning in Helen's stomach. They'd known about the training camp? Did they know about the Knowledge Stash there? Her mind spun rapidly. She couldn't remember how she was captured—head trauma, or maybe she was drugged. Did they breach the camp?

"I'm afraid everyone in the training camp is dead," the Vice President said, making a *tsk*ing sound. Looking up at Helen, she shook her head. "It wasn't us that killed all those kids. It was the plague. The plague that's been emptying cell after cell." She turned a few pages while Helen struggled not to cough, not to choke. Then sanity washed over her and she calmed down. Her camp wasn't dead. They were fine. Ajana was making this up to break her.

She would have done the same herself. She relaxed and breathed again.

Finally Ajana closed the file, gave Helen such a familiar look that Helen wanted to cry for the first time in—

"Helen, Helen, Helen. I thought we'd seen the last of you. This is all just so silly, your little 'uprising.' Why don't you come back home and forget all this?"

"The palace isn't my home," Ms. Strepp said thinly. "Maybe it was once. But never again."

"How many years has it been? Ten, twelve?"

Ms. Strepp's lips were thin. "Seventeen."

"And what have you accomplished?" Ajana asked, looking as if she really cared. "What is all this about? Are you saying you don't want to live well, eat good food, have all comforts and conveniences available to you?" Her eyes were round, such a dark brown that Helen couldn't see the pupil, and so caring. So deceptively caring.

Helen made her voice strong. "Not at the price of my soul."

Ajana laughed again. "This is *me*, Helen. *Your best friend.* The girl you grew up with, played with, made plans with. Then you… betrayed us. Betrayed everything. And you never told me why."

"You *know* why."

"I know what you said. I didn't believe you. Not then, not now. Christopher Harrison wouldn't have risked his vice presidency for a mere girl."

Helen turned and looked at the wall. She'd never been so close to crying. Not in seventeen years. She had sacrificed everything when she accused Vice President Harrison of rape. She thought she was doing the right thing getting him demoted and sent to a remote cell, but in the end he just hurt more girls like Becca.

Ajana rapped on the two-way mirror and the guards came in.

"Put her back in her cell," the Vice President said.

Helen waited while one guard unlocked her and one guard stood five feet away, Taser aimed. Here, the word *cell* meant something very different.

97

BECCA

MIND: BLOWN. MIA WAS OUT riding *again* today, so I had a couple of hours to snoop after clearing up the breakfast dishes. I sat on the cozy armchair, reading one of her schoolbooks. I figured she must be in grade eleven—but the history was completely different. There were comparison maps of the earliest America, showing the Louisiana Purchase, the Ohio Territories, the Republic of Texas, etc. Stuff I'd never heard of.

Turning pages quickly, I found a chapter on the "States Period." It said that the country was mistakenly divided into unequal, inefficient "states" that served only to create disharmony and tension. Finally, after Civil War II, those boundaries were erased.

Then there was a Reclamation period that lasted fifty years, where the United was sensibly divided into its six even land sections, A through F, and further divided into evenly apportioned numbered areas. Like B-97-4275, for example, I thought bitterly.

"Put that down at once!" Mrs. Argyle had opened the door soundlessly and was now looking at me with rage coloring her red face even redder.

Shit! I leaped from the chair and quickly shoved the book back into the bookcase, picking up my dust cloth at the same time.

"How dare you!" she went on while I tried to figure out what a submissive servant should look like. "This is not your room! That is not your book! How dare you treat Miss Mia's things as if they're your own!"

I stood with my head down and my hands behind my back. In two seconds I could grab one of the books behind me and whip it at her pulsing temple. End of rant.

"Do you understand the difference between the family we serve and yourself?"

No doubt it was a rhetorical question, but I nodded.

"There is a hierarchy in this house, and *you* are at the *bottom* of it! Do you understand?"

She went on like this for several more minutes, and I nodded occasionally.

"Now, get yourself together—you'll be serving in an hour!"

Since I was always serving, I looked at her blankly.

"We're short-staffed, and the President is having a state luncheon," she said. "You will be serving."

Eh? What was that?

"You'll watch the other servers and do what they do," she said impatiently. "It involves putting plates down and picking them up. Surely you can do that?"

I bit the inside of my cheek to squash a snarky answer and nodded.

"You're done in here," she sniffed. "Present yourself to the cook downstairs."

"Yes, ma'am," I said, trying to channel Cassie's meekness.

She looked at her watch, gave me another glare, and huffed out of the room.

My chest was about to explode. *This could be it.* This could be when I *kill the President.* The end of my mission. My permission to go home, if I still had one. If I lived through it. I rushed to Mia's closet and delicately lifted cashmere sweaters until I found the gun at the bottom of a drawer. I popped out the magazine—and then stared in dismay. There. Were. No. Bullets. "Goddamnit!" I whisper-shouted. "Goddamnit!"

Then I thought, *Maybe the bullets are somewhere else.* I had to get downstairs but I took as long as I dared to search the rest of the closet—shaking out shoes, riffling through underwear, shirts, pockets. Nothing.

Shit. Well, thanks to the Crazy House, I had a million other weapons at my disposal. If I had to kill him with a soup spoon, so be it.

98

THE LONER

IF THE LONER KNEW THAT Becca called him "Blondie McMystery Man," he would have bent double laughing. Out of the many names he was known by, that was the funniest by far.

Right now he might be mistaken for just another hobo hanging out under a bridge. Except all the usual bridge-dwellers had mysteriously taken a hike. Very carefully, the Loner attached a plastic box to the underside of the main bridge strut. He wiggled it a little, making sure it was stuck on well.

Looking at Bets, he saw the young woman was leaning way back, covering her face, and he grinned. Seating himself more comfortably on a hunk of concrete, the Loner opened an app on his phone and clicked. The plastic box had a couple of small lights attached to it, and one lit up green.

"The last one," he said. "Lucky thirteen."

As they climbed the embankment, a street cleaner was unenthusiastically pushing a wide broom. He gave them one glance and barked, "Pick that trash up!" pointing to a crumpled piece of paper at the Loner's feet. As the Loner bent down to pick it up, the street cleaner sped up, pushing the broom fast away from them.

The Loner opened the paper and read it. He frowned.

"What is it?" Bets asked.

"Helen Strepp," he said thoughtfully. "She needs a...hand."

99

CASSIE

THE GUARD YELLED OVER THE alarms, "You're not from here! You're from *Outside*!"

Tim grabbed my arm. "Let's go!"

We ran past the guard, but guards were already spilling out of everywhere, racing to the gates, and my blood turned to ice water.

"Quick!" Tim yelled and made a step for me out of his hands. Without hesitation I launched myself at him and he propelled me strongly upward, over the seven-foot turnstile and *almost* over the razor wire. It caught my long coat as I twisted through the air, coiled for a landing. I heard shredding sounds but landed neatly on top of the guard shack, popping to my feet instantly.

Whipping out my rifle, I shouted, "Who came to work to die today?" and shot at the roof so they'd know I wasn't joking. The guards stood back, seeming confused about a citizen who fought back.

Tim scrambled up over the turnstile as I kept my gun pointed at the guards, waving it from one to another as they tried to intervene. Stepping on the lower wire, Tim held up the higher one so he could scramble through as the guards decided to take a chance and jumped up at him uselessly. Once he was on the roof, we both dodged bullets and ran, then windmilled to a stop at the far edge.

Below us, ladders hit the wall and guards started climbing up.

An alley separated this building from the next. I thought I could *probably* make it, with a running start. I looked up at Tim and we read each other's minds. We both knew *he* could make it for sure.

Damnit.

100

BECCA

"GRAB YOURSELF AN APRON OVER there," one of the sous-chefs snapped. I'd just stepped through the kitchen door and was already overwhelmed. It was enormous, several huge rooms connected by wide doorways. Servants rushed back and forth, all wearing crisp white aprons.

I didn't see Nate anywhere—the air was steamy and there seemed to be hundreds of people, all shouting. I tied an apron on, then sidled along one wall, looking for Nate and trying to figure out what to do. Who did I need to talk to in order to make sure I was in the dining room with the President?

One sideboard I walked past held ten, eleven...*fourteen cakes and pies*. All I wanted to do was throw myself on top of them, snorfling them up like a pig.

And I thought: These people do this *all the time*. This amazing food is *normal, regular*. I thought about our school bazaar, where everyone brought their best cooking. This kitchen made the bazaar, once big and exciting, look ridiculous and pathetic. Ma's pineapple upside-down cake used to win awards, and after she left for her mood-adjust, Cassie had made it and still won prizes. Now I looked at a three-tiered, finely iced chocolate thing dotted with sour cherries and I was filled with rage.

"Move!" I jumped when someone bellowed at me and darted to one side.

I was here on a mission, I reminded myself. I was here to right at least some of the wrongs these people had done to us cellfolk. And I needed to get cracking.

My goals:

—Find whoever was in charge of assigning waiters to the President.

—Get myself assigned.

—Kill the President, perhaps with a sterling silver fork, or maybe just pistol-whip him, since my still-bulletless gun was tucked into the waistband of my underwear.

Whatever happened after that didn't matter.

101

HELEN

THE TALL, DARK SHADOW SEEMED to come from the ceiling, and Helen Strepp blinked at it in alarm. Sitting up on her hard bunk, she tensed her muscles, made her cuffed hands into hard blades of flesh. But when the strip of faint, dusky daylight showed off his blond hair, she relaxed a tiny bit.

"Gaz?" she breathed.

"None other," whispered the Loner, and started to pick the locks on her cuffs.

"How did you get here?" she asked him.

His bright-blue eyes met hers for a second, then he made small flapping motions with his hands. She nodded. Of course.

"Is your part of the plan in place?" she asked as her cuffs popped off.

He nodded. "How about yours?"

"I hope so," Strepp said, rubbing her wrists. "Did you get Becca into the palace?"

The Loner sighed, sat back on his heels. "Yeah. A girl less cut out to be a servant, I've never seen. Well, okay—I've seen one other. But still."

"I know," Strepp agreed ruefully.

"Duck," the Loner said gently, touching her shoulder.

Strepp flung herself to the floor seconds before the wall of her prison cell exploded inward, showering her with chunks of concrete and dust. Alarms went off, people started yelling. Blinking dust out of her eyes, Helen saw that the large hole led outdoors, with sunlight and clouds.

"Come on," the Loner said, grabbing her hand. They leaped through, her feet feeling pillowed on the manicured grass.

Ajana—Vice President Nielson—had told her to come home. Well, Helen was. Just not in the way anyone expected. This time she was coming back to see the President die.

102

CASSIE

"GIVE ME YOUR BACKPACK," TIM yelled, and I tossed it at him. He threw it off the roof, along with his own, then jumped down after them. I peered over the edge—because of another fence, no guards were waiting below. *Yet.* When I looked behind me, I saw the top of a ladder and very quickly, the head and shoulders of a guard. I slung my rifle over my good shoulder and jumped down into Tim's strong arms, jarred only a bit by my landing.

"Okay, now we run!" he said, and grabbed my hand. Most of the guards were on the *other* side of the fence—excellent planning, guys—so we had a tiny bit of a head start. We stuck out like corn-stalks the reaper missed: the only citizens running, me trying to shove my rifle back under my somewhat shredded coat, Tim looking everywhere for a good place to hunker down.

And it had to be soon—you don't run as long as you can. You run a little bit and then hide and disguise yourself. Blend in.

"Here!" Tim threw back at me, his words almost lost as we raced by. He turned into a market street—I'd seen pictures of them in old newspapers. It was like a Co-op, but everyone got to keep their own stuff, their own money. Weird.

"Okay, okay," he muttered as we slowed down. My rifle was safely stowed and we continued to hold hands. It was time to hide—past time.

"Forty-seven, forty-seven," he said under his breath. I looked around us—the stalls were numbered. At stall forty-seven, he pulled me inside. I was blind after the sunlight of the street, and I tensed, stopping dead, until my eyes adjusted.

"Come *on*," Tim said, pulling me forward again.

"Where are we?" I hissed, seeing colorful fabrics draped from the ceiling, shelves full of pottery and glassware.

"I told you to memorize that little map!" he whispered back to me. "The one from the file!" He said nothing to the women who were working there, but the woman behind the chip reader met his eyes and made the slightest motion with her head. We took a sharp turn through lovely, draping silks, and before us was a long, dark, bad-smelling staircase.

Suddenly it occurred to me that I had put my complete trust in Tim sometime after we'd left the camp. Maybe when we were in the abandoned store with the wolves? When he hadn't deserted me? It had just happened; I hadn't noticed it.

So basically I had broken the very first, most important rule of Crazy House: *Never, ever trust anyone.*

103

BECCA

I WAS STUCK. I'D THOUGHT I'd be a lunch server, immediately leap through the air, knock the President out of his chair, and kill him somehow. I didn't care what happened after that.

But the "dining room" was in fact an enormous *dining barn* practically as big as the Provost's *house* back home. One wall was all windows opening to a beautiful garden. I had them pegged as one possible route of escape. The other walls were covered with gold-flecked wallpaper and lined with gorgeous sideboards laden with food and extra plates. I'd seen several easy-to-grab carving knives, if I could avoid the eyes of the armed guards stationed around the room.

So I had weapons and at least one possible escape route. What I didn't have was *proximity*. I was at the *opposite end* of the world's longest table, serving a woman with elaborate blond hair fading to pale green. There was one server per person, and she was mine. All I'd been able to do for the last endless hour was mimic the servers on either side of me: stepping forward to push chairs in, refill water glasses and wine goblets, remove empty plates, etc.

My bulletless gun hung uncomfortably beneath my skirt and apron, tucked into the granny panties they made me wear here. I shouldn't have even brought it.

I was trained to assess risk and outcome. The risk here was high; I judged my chance of success to be about 25 percent, and the chances of me dying at 100 percent.

I told myself I was biding my time, waiting to make my move, but in reality I had no firm plan on what my move might be. Also, I was learning a lot standing here like an herb-picker, listening to the table talk. Servants are invisible; we might as well be robots. As we kept refilling wineglasses, the talk got louder—and looser.

"Any more news on the drought in the western cells?" a man asked my personal assignment.

She tilted her head and made a face. "Little or no relief, and death tolls rising."

I glanced left and right to see if the other servers had "Oh, my God" faces on, but they looked expressionless and I quickly wiped my face to neutrality. They were talking about cellfolk. Cellfolk *dying* because of drought. While their big stag ice statue dripped silently into a silver tray of fruit.

The next time my neighboring server leaped forward to refill water glasses, I edged over to the sideboard and slid a long carving knife into the folds of my skirt. Over the next ten minutes I calculated how far I'd have to run to get close enough, how much time I'd have to do that, and how much force I'd use to sink the carving knife deep into the President's chest.

The woman next to mine leaned over and lowered her voice. I immediately drifted up with a chilled bottle of rosé. They ignored me.

"If you're planning to go south for a vacation, dear," the other woman said very quietly, "don't. Virtually everything south of here has been hit by plague."

I almost let the wine spill but caught myself and stepped back. Everything south of here? Like, *everyone* south of here? Every *cell*?

"I heard there was . . . trouble in the east," my woman murmured, and the other one made the very slightest appalled face, then took another bite of sorbet.

Okay, that was it. All I had to do was quickly slice a jugular, nick a carotid, swiftly run a knife beneath a rib cage—it would take two seconds.

I gripped the knife more tightly and took a step forward. Then one of the dining room doors opened and two guards admitted a tall man in a suit. I stared in disbelief and bit my lip hard so I wouldn't gasp out loud.

"Ah, *Provost Allen*, is it?" The President's voice drifted to me from far away. "From Cell . . ."—an aide whispered into the President's ear—"*B-97-4275*, right?"

104

CASSIE

"I'M SURPRISED YOU'RE ALIVE," MS. Strepp said to me.

I just gaped at her. Eyes wide in the dim light, mouth open like a goldfish. Slowly my head turned to Tim: he wasn't surprised at all. Finally I looked at the stranger with us; he was very tall, very slender, and wearing an oversize, bulky trench coat.

"They call me the Loner," he said, brushing fair blond hair away from his face.

Finally my brain could seize something. "Oh. *You're* the Loner?" My eyebrows raised. "Okaaaay." I turned away just as his blue eyes flared.

Time for some answers. I crossed my arms, feeling the comforting length of my rifle beneath my coat. "What happened?" I asked, narrow-eyed. "Why did you leave the camp?" Usually Ms. Strepp scared the crap out of me, but after all we'd been through, she was going to have to up her game.

"I was kidnapped," she said, sounding unlike herself, as if she still couldn't believe it. "I don't remember much. But I woke up hooded and handcuffed in a van. They put me in a prison cell—a room in a prison," she went on. "The Loner blasted me out of there today."

"Who kidnapped you?" I asked.

"The President. Or rather, his henchpeople." She sounded bitter. I saw raw red marks on her wrists. Was this another test? After wondering if I could trust Tim, could I trust *her*?

"Why would the President kidnap you?"

She looked me in the eye. "To stop me," she said. "From leading a revolt. From training an army."

I let out an exhausted breath. "So much for the army," I said, rubbing my hand over my eyes, as if I could ever unsee all those bodies.

"What do you mean?" she asked harshly. "I've sent word for them to join us, to make their way to the capital!"

"Did you get a reply?" Tim asked, sounding as beat as I was.

There was silence for a minute, and all I could focus on was the strong, mildewy scent.

"No...not yet," she said, looking back and forth between me and Tim.

"You won't be getting one," Tim said, sounding colder than I'd ever heard him. "Everyone at camp is dead. From a virus. They couldn't even fight back."

When she looked at me, I nodded.

Ms. Strepp almost fell back against a filthy wall, seeming horrified, stunned. I was pretty sure she wasn't acting.

105

MS. STREPP BREATHED HARD FOR a minute, her eyes darting around this small, dirty room. Then she looked at me, Tim, and the Loner.

"I can't believe—" she said, then swallowed and tried again. "That's an awful thing, for all those soldiers—all those *kids*—" her voice grew quieter. "How did you two escape it?"

"We were up in the attic," I pointed out.

She nodded. "Listen. I do have an army outside of the city—the second division. They're going to infiltrate through the subway tunnels." Strepp must've seen our looks of confusion. "The subway is like an underground train system. The Loner has been planting explosives all around the city, and he'll wire the tunnels after we've gone through."

"So we'll be trapped with no way out?" Tim asked.

"The way out will be *through*," she said, sounding more like her cool self. "Through the fine citizens of the capital. You, Cassie, and I will lead troops to the presidential palace. If the President isn't already dead, then we'll kill him."

"How would he already be dead?" I asked.

She met my questioning eyes. "Because Becca's there, and her only mission is to kill the President."

"Becca's there? Inside the palace, *surrounded* by United soldiers?" I almost shouted, then lowered my voice. "What about Nate?"

She looked annoyed by my questions, but too freaking bad.

"Yes, as far as I know," she said, then turned to Tim. "Now I want each of you to fully comprehend our mission. The President will die, *at any cost*. Do you understand?"

"Yes," I said, my mind still exploding with joy that Becca was so close. I just hoped we could reach her before she made her move. Ms. Strepp might have been willing to sacrifice Becca, but I wasn't. This wasn't some stupid training exercise—I was sick of Strepp's bullshit. I was not afraid to die, thanks to the Crazy House, but that didn't mean I didn't want to *live*.

"Kill anyone else who gets in your way," she ordered, staring at us intently. "Do you understand?"

"Yes," I repeated, and Tim echoed me. I understood I was getting Becca back.

"Then let's go," she said, and opening one of the doors, led us into darkness.

106

BECCA

MY THROAT FELT LIKE IT was squeezing shut. Provost Allen! I kept my eyes down but felt almost light-headed with shock. What in the almighty hell was *he* doing here? *Shit, shit, shit.* He'd recognize me, almost certainly. His presence here lowered my probability of success to practically zero. I needed a new plan, fast. *I had to get out of here.*

"*Psst,*" I said to the server next to me, a guy in a black suit. "I'm feeling sick."

"Too bad," he said out of the side of his mouth. "Shut up and serve."

You butthole. "You don't understand," I whispered. "It's...it's, you know, a *woman* thing."

He shrugged.

Provost Allen was shaking the President's hand.

"Look," I said more firmly. "*Aunt Flo has arrived*. I am *surfing* the crimson wave. *My visitor came*. This is a *code red*. So I can shut up and serve with *blood* running down my legs, or you can cover me for two seconds while I go take care of business!"

"Go, go, go!" he said out of the side of his mouth, looking grossed out. "I'll cover for you. But hurry up and get back here."

I slipped out into the hallway, trying to think. Provost Allen! It felt like two or three lifetimes ago since I'd last seen him. *God, what an ass!* Then I had an awful thought: *Nate! Did the Provost know that Nate was here?* Had Nate contacted him? *Had this all been a huge set-up?*

One way to find out. I raced to the cavernous, steamy kitchen and grabbed the first person I saw.

"Where's Nate?" I asked urgently.

The girl, her face red with heat, frowned at me. "Who?"

"Nate! The dishwasher!" I almost shook her, and she got angry.

"We have four dishwashers!"

"Uh...the tall, good-looking one?"

The girl glanced around. "He's not here."

I let her go and rushed back out into the hallway. *Shit, Nate, where are you?* Had he left or been taken by force? Had he joined his father?

"Well, hello, there," a low voice said, so close to my ear that I jumped. As my brain registered that it was the repulsive Kirt, he grabbed my arms hard and yanked me backward into a room.

Oh, like I need this now, I thought grimly, my fury igniting. I

295

spun easily out of his arms but he moved in again, pinning me against a long table.

"Bad touch!" I snarled, smacking his hands away. Kirt just grinned, gripped my hands behind my back and tried to kiss my neck. I gave a quick glance around—this was a walk-in pantry, so there were about five hundred things I could use as weapons.

"I'm going to scream!" I said, trying to free myself. Jeez, this loser was strong, and my hands felt crushed between me and the table.

"No one will hear you," he assured me with a smile. "Not with all the commotion in the kitchen. Now, quit pretending you don't want me. I'm Kirt Unser—I could do a lot for you."

"I'm going to do a lot *to* you," I promised. "Like break your nose and a couple of ribs."

He grossly stuck his tongue in my ear and thrust his hips at me—which was when he felt the long carving knife in my skirt, hidden by my apron. His eyes widened and he let go of me.

"What are you up to, bitch?" he asked. He didn't even sound scared, just curious.

I made a snap decision. "Kiss *this*," I said, and grabbed a cast-iron frying pan. He shot his arm up but I loosened my arc so it missed his face but cracked against the side of his head. It felled him like a tree, and he collapsed to the slate floor.

I looked around quickly. His blood was already spreading across the floor. Huffing and puffing a bit, I dragged him beneath a large worktable and rolled him against the wall. He was still breathing and bleeding like a stuck pig. I grabbed some ten-pound cans of lard and weighed him down. Then I rolled several bushels of potatoes and onions against him, followed by burlap sacks of coffee beans, rice, green peas, and tea leaves. They'd be good for absorbing blood.

I backed out of the pantry, listening for his breathing, straightening my clothes, and bumped into yet another hard body. Whirling, I saw...Nate.

Was Nate a *friend*...or was he a *foe*?

107

"WE HAVE TO TALK," I said quickly, scanning Nate as if a mere look was enough to tell me whether he could still be trusted. Somehow... I sensed that he *was* the Nate I knew—and not the double-agent I feared.

"This way," Nate said, leading me away from the hall of pantries and through a small door. Suddenly we were out in the garden—not the beautiful, landscaped garden for visitors, but the kitchen garden, enclosed by tall brick walls. Nate led me to the darkest corner, where we were surrounded by herby scents of basil, parsley, and sage.

"I guess you didn't do it," Nate said, letting go of my hand. "All hell would have broken out."

"You mean, kill the President?"

"Yeah! Our mission here!"

"I was just about to," I said, watching his face, "except suddenly *your dad* strolled in."

Nate looked shocked. Convincingly shocked. He stepped back and pushed his hand through his hair the way he did when he was thinking. "Whoa," he finally said.

"Yes," I said. "Whoa. Right when I was about to do a ten-yard dash with a big honking knife."

"He must've done something really good or really bad," Nate said slowly.

"Not that these people can tell which is which," I said. "So what now?"

"We still need to kill the President," Nate said in a lower voice. "Whatever else happens, we have to do that."

"No sh—" I began, but without warning, Nate took me in his arms and lowered his mouth to mine.

Shocked, I stood there, too startled to close my eyes. I felt the firmness of his mouth, the strength in his arms. This was the second time in ten minutes that someone had grabbed me, but Nate was the opposite of Kirt. Till now, Tim was the only guy I'd been with *voluntarily*, and Nate felt so different. But... not bad, actually...

"Hold it right there!"

The harsh voices made adrenaline instantly thread through my veins and we broke apart.

"There she is!" Kirt shouted.

"I can't believe he's already up," I murmured. "I'm losing my touch."

"And he's in on it!" Kirt, blood-covered and holding a bag of ice to his head, pointed at Nate.

"No, he isn't!" I shouted. "I clocked you all by myself, you rapist!"

"Search her!" Kirt screamed. "She has a knife! She's planning something!"

The guards patted me down roughly but I'd lost the knife back in the pantry, and they found nothing. Goddamn Kirt. I should have killed him when I had the chance.

Nate and I were cuffed and dragged to a different door that led to the cellar. A couple more locked metal doors and there we were, in a whole hallway of empty cages. We were thrown into one, and its heavy door was locked. Because of course there was a dungeon in this house. All the best houses had one.

108

CASSIE

"I WISH MY OLD TERRIER, Ratbane, was here," Tim whispered.

I nodded, casually trying to look behind me. Ms. Strepp had led us underground to a subway tunnel. It was filthy, stank of urine and human waste and the occasional dead rat or possum. We moved in pairs, walking between the two rails and staying far away from the third rail, as we'd been warned.

I stared through the darkness at my feet, trying not to trip on the wooden crossties.

I'd never seen a train that ran underground, never imagined there could be so many people who would need one. And I'd never imagined that Ms. Strepp would have a *backup army*. I looked back at Strepp's army. They filled the tunnel, hundreds and hundreds and hundreds of soldier-kids, or kid-soldiers. Ms. Strepp must have been collecting them for a long time.

"Once Ratbane killed twenty-three rats in one night," Tim said. "It was the year of no fuel, and no food had come in months. We ate 'em."

"You ate. The *rats*," I said, not even trying to keep the shock off my face. I remembered the year of no fuel—it hadn't affected our cell much, except that our crops piled up and some rotted. It had never occurred to me to wonder what effect no fuel would have on other cells. Tim had *eaten rats*.

Still staring at my feet, I walked right into Ms. Strepp, almost bouncing off her thin, hard body. I froze, waiting to get punished, but Ms. Strepp was looking behind me, holding up one finger.

She nodded shortly. "Train," she said.

Tim immediately said "Train" to the next pair of soldiers. On and on down the line, our followers heard "Train" and did as instructed: dropped to their stomachs between the tracks, flattened themselves as much as possible, and turned their heads to one side.

We did the same and I tried not to gag at the smell, tried not to think about what might have happened *right where my face was*. Tim and I looked at each other tensely. I prayed Ms. Strepp was right about train clearances.

In moments I felt the vibration, heard a distant rumble become louder. Soon the train let out an ear-splitting whistle. I squeezed my eyes shut and reached out for Tim's strong, scarred hand. Even if I had admitted being afraid, he wouldn't have heard me. But what if the ground vibrated so much that it bounced me right up into the wheels? What if the train rode much lower than Ms. Strepp knew?

This sucks this sucks this sucks this sucks.

The train was right over us, its heat and noise and smells of oil and fuel weighing on me. I wanted to cry. Gripping Tim's hand, I thought about how back home, I'd be out in the sunlight and fresh air, smelling the clean scent of corn ripening, freshly mown hay, the wild honeysuckle from which Becca and I used to suck the nectar...

My teeth rattled in my head. My brain shook inside my skull. I started to feel sick but was too afraid to even raise a hand to my mouth. Instead I clung to Tim's hand and tried not to breathe.

Suddenly it was gone. Its rear light shot down the black tunnel and disappeared faster than it had appeared. We all got to our feet, brushed ourselves off. I heard one kid whisper, "Ick," and another said, "Yeah."

I felt trembly and embarrassed that I'd been so scared, and my face heated when I saw Tim shaking his fingers slightly, trying to get his circulation going after I'd practically cut it off.

Turning to me and Tim, Ms. Strepp murmured, "When we get beneath the palace, the Loner will set off a bomb big enough to blow a hole in the floor. We'll swarm up over the rubble, and I want guns blazing! We need to cut the head off this elite monster, we need to *spear its heart*!" Her drawn, angular face was grim, her eyes dark holes burning with something I hadn't seen before.

"Yes, ma'am," I said, as Tim relayed the message down the line. I knew something he didn't: My days of blindly following Ms.

Strepp were coming to an end. When I climbed up into the President's palace, I'd have only one thought in my mind: finding Becca. If Becca was still alive, then Becca was my only mission. If Becca *wasn't* alive...well, it'd be time for me to strike out on my own. With or without Tim or Nate or whoever was left.

109

BECCA

"HERE WE ARE AGAIN," I said tiredly, pacing our small cell. It was ironic that they'd decided to call all their little nodes of factories, farms, mines, mills—*cells*. The cell we grew up in *had* been a prison cell. We just hadn't known it.

I sat down on the metal cot next to Nate, unwilling to meet his eyes. Yes, *of course* I knew his kissing me had been a diversion, a ruse. All the same, it had been...well, *not unpleasant*.

Then at the same moment, he and I looked at each other.

"You hear that?" he whispered, and I nodded.

People were arguing, faintly. But where? We peered out into the hall, walked the perimeter of our cell, trying to pinpoint the direction. I shook my head.

"It's above us," I said, climbing up onto the metal cot. "Give me a lift."

This was when I longed for Tim, big, muscled Tim who could probably lift me with one hand. The Provost's son was almost as tall and well-built, but no Tim.

Still, he held me on his shoulders securely, walking where I told him, not complaining.

"This is where the voices are loudest," I told him softly.

"Can you see anything?" he asked.

"Uhh...nope. Dungeon wall," I said, tapping against the stones. Then one of my taps went right through and I moved my hand left and right. "Oh, so gross!"

"What? What?" Nate said.

"There's a...grate in the wall right below the ceiling," I told him. "Clogged with basically the grossest stuff ever." Grimacing, I pulled it away like it was horrible, dirty witch hair. I pressed closer to the grate and could hear the voices more clearly. I slid off Nate's shoulders and we both stood on the metal cot.

"That's Dad," he said quietly. "I'd know that bellow anywhere."

My eyes narrowed. "Did you tell your dad where we were?"

His face flushed and he jumped to the floor. His hands made fists and when he looked back at me I realized I'd never seen him so angry. "Screw you!" he snapped. "You think I'd go through *all this* to *help* my dad? The dad who basically lobotomized my mom? You *asshole*!"

He looked ready to punch me, and I decided I was convinced of his loyalty.

With dignity I said, "Okay, I stand corrected."

Above us, Provost Allen was reporting grim conditions in his cell: crop failures, food shortages, people revolting—especially the teenagers—and worst of all, an outbreak of the plague.

"Shit," Nate breathed. "That's *home* he's talking about!"

"The plague?" I said. "I heard people talking about it in the dining barn. But what plague? Did you hear anything about it in the kitchen?"

Shaking his head no, his face paled and I remembered that his mom was in our cell. Barely living, but still. Both my parents were gone, and who knew where Cassie was? Still being Strepp's pet librarian, safely back at camp while our friends and neighbors were dying back home?

A heavy door slammed somewhere down the hall, and without speaking we both jumped down and sat on the metal cot with bored expressions on our faces. I didn't know what was coming, but I knew enough to look broken down.

The face that appeared on the other side of our bars was only too familiar, except he'd gotten his head injury bandaged. He stared at us with loathing, then smiled a horrible, knowing smile that made my skin crawl.

"Here it is!" he shouted back to someone down the hall. "I found the fire! Turn on the water!"

That's when I saw he was holding an emergency fire hose in his hands.

110

I DID AN IMMEDIATE SURVEY of our cell—the cot was fastened to the wall and there was nothing else. Nowhere to hide.

"Shit," was all I had time to say before the fire hose came alive in Kirt's hands. He struggled to control it, then aimed it right at us. I braced myself, my arms crossed over my face, but the full force of the water was like a cannon, easily knocking Nate and me flat on our backs on the stone floor. Keeping my back to Kirt, I struggled to get to my hands and knees but every time the water blasted me, I was flattened. If I was on my stomach, my face scraped against the stone floor. If I was on my back, Kirt aimed at my face with gleeful rage until I wondered if I had skin left. It was harder and harder to breathe— water filled my nostrils, blew my mouth open, peeled my eyelids back.

The violent, freezing water was like a living beast that couldn't be slain. If only I could grab it by the neck, crack its spine, break its nose. Instead it pinned me to the floor, to a wall, and it felt like my skin was being flayed from my bones.

Above the rush of the hose I got glimpses of Nate not faring much better than me. He was bigger and heavier and seemed to be trying to reach me but was shoved back by the powerful force each time.

"I'm going to drown you, you bitch!" Kirt screamed over the noise. "And then you're going to *hang* for treason, you and loverboy both!" Once again he trained the hose at my face, its power knocking my hands away, making me gulp water and gag. My lungs were starting to scream for air. He *was* drowning me, minute by endless minute of incessant assault. I couldn't scream, couldn't swallow fast enough, couldn't move. Was this how I was going to die? Being drowned in a dungeon cell beneath the President's house? The President I was supposed to kill? Not only was I dying, but I was dying a *failure*. I just needed to breathe, goddamnit!

When the water stopped abruptly I still heard its roar in my clogged ears. My skin burned. I was gagging.

"You are the biggest asshole!" a high-pitched voice screamed.

"Get the hell out of here, Mia!" Kirt roared in rage. "This is none of your business!"

Slowly, on trembling arms, I sat up, coughing up water, feeling it run out of my nose and ears.

"I swear I'm going to tell everyone you were wasting precious water, you prick!"

Nate was sitting up now, his face scraped and red, eyes bleary, coughing up water like me.

Throwing down the hose nozzle, Kirt stomped toward Mia. There was a lot of hushed, angry arguing, then Kirt trod heavily down the hallway. We heard a door slam loudly, and then Mia approached our cell.

"Sorry," she said abruptly. "He's a complete dick. Always has been."

"Can you get us out of here?" I asked, my voice raspy.

"I can't," she said regretfully. "Not until I ask my father. I'll try to get you out when I can, but he's super busy. Anyway, I brought you this—don't tell anyone."

She pushed a paper bag through the bars, then left quickly.

Nate opened the bag. Inside was a loaf of bread and a small glass jar of honey.

"Is there a hacksaw in the bread?" I asked, and he tore it into pieces.

"Nope," he said, shaking the bag for the last thing to fall out. It dropped into his lap and we both stared at it. Then, freezing, sopping wet, our skin raw, we started laughing. Mia had thoughtfully provided a monogrammed sterling silver honey-dipping spoon.

111

CASSIE

FOUR MORE TRAINS WENT BY. Each time I was *literally* inches from death. Each time I waited for my spine to be ripped open as it passed over me. Each time I clung to Tim's hand like a total wuss, unwilling to give up his strength. I wasn't afraid that a train would kill me. I wasn't afraid to die. I was afraid that it would kill me *horribly, messily, and for a long time.*

After each train we sprang to our feet and kept marching while I tried not to think about Tim eating rats. We were even columns, two by two, but then someone carefully pushed past me.

"Ms. Strepp?" It was a short, slight girl dressed in black.

Strepp halted, so the hundreds of rows of us halted, too.

"The President has just left the building," the girl reported urgently. "Something about a meeting. He's supposed to get back for a late dinner."

"Goddamnit!" Ms. Strepp said and looked at her watch in the dim light.

From far off, I felt the faintest rumble: yet another goddamn motherlovin' freaking train.

"Okay," Ms. Strepp said. "We probably won't get to the palace for another two or three hours anyway. Getting through these tunnels is slower going than I had anticipated."

Two or three more hours? Slower going than she'd thought? Gee, I don't know! *Maybe it's because of all the goddamn trains!* I shouted inside my head.

Ms. Strepp nodded briskly, then turned and headed back into the darkness. Softly, as if speaking to herself, she said, "By the time we get to the palace, the President might well be back. If not, we'll wait until he is. There's no point attacking the palace unless he dies."

112

BECCA

"WAIT, STOP," I MURMURED. "NATE, stop, hold on."

He paused in mid-chew and looked at me.

"We don't have time for this," I said, standing up. "We don't *have time* to be stuck in a *prison cell*. The President is supposed to be *dead* already!"

He pointedly looked at the stone walls of our cell.

"Do you have a sledgehammer on you?" he asked politely.

"No. But look—" I took a small piece of bread and rolled it into a tiny ball, then smeared it with honey and stuck it to my face.

"That's...so incredibly gross," he said, looking at me as if I'd lost my mind.

I did it a couple more times, putting one on my arm, another on my face, smoothing the edges.

"You look like a leper," he said conversationally. "A really horrible one."

"I look like I have the plague," I said. "They were talking about a plague!"

An hour later, Kirt came back to torture us again, as I'd known he would. He found us lying limply on the floor, covered with oozing pustules.

He shot back down the hall, yelling for a guard.

A tiny smile creased the corners of my plaguey face.

113

CASSIE

"THIS IS IT," **MS. STREPP** said, looking down at a hand-drawn map. "We're under the palace now, according to this."

Oh, thank God, I thought. Back at Crazy House, we'd been trained to jog ten miles at a clip, wearing loaded backpacks. But moving in these tunnels was so much slower and more tedious as we stepped over debris that seemed to have been put there deliberately to trip us. I pulled up the neck of my shirt and wiped the sweat from my face.

A fluorescent light flickered erratically overhead, showing us that the track stopped here. Half a mile back, the track had split and we'd taken the righthand one.

Ms. Strepp spoke into her radio, then turned to us. "The Loner says that the President's motorcade is about to pull up to the palace.

We'll give the President twenty minutes, and then the Loner will blow this ceiling." She pointed above us, where the tunnel ceiling dripped wetly. "In the meantime, make sure your weapons are loaded and ready to go."

I double-checked my rifle, every movement second nature by now. Everything I'd gone through, from getting abducted, trained to be a killer at Crazy House, and then trained for survival at the camp had led me here, to this moment.

Turning to the dark column of young soldiers, Ms. Strepp raised her voice, though of course she couldn't be heard by her whole army.

"Is everyone ready?" she shouted.

The *yes*es rippled toward us for minutes, as the question was relayed backward and the answer relayed forward.

"You're about to strike a death blow!" Ms. Strepp yelled. "A death blow to the users, the corrupted leaders, the rich who are living off of our work! This won't be the end of our struggle, but it is finally a beginning! Today, you will make history! This day will be written into history books that your children and your children's children will read in school!"

The murmuring behind us grew louder and I saw some kids raise their weapons over their heads in excitement. Did they realize that not all of them would live this day out? Would never have children or grandchildren?

Bing! went Ms. Strepp's phone—another message from the Loner.

"It's time!" Ms. Strepp said, her face alight with fervor. "He says it's time! Ten!"

We all echoed, "Ten!"

"Nine! Eight!"

We scrambled to take cover from where the ceiling above us would explode. I knelt behind a metal beam next to a side service tunnel about five feet wide, and that's when I heard a faint but growing roar. Like, water?

"Seven! Six!"

I peered down the tunnel. There had been the faintest light toward its back, but suddenly the light winked out.

Oh, shit. "Wait!" I yelled, waving my arms. "Wait!"

"Five!"

I cupped my hands over my mouth and bellowed, "Ms. Strepp, wait! Stop!"

Ms. Strepp stared at me, and all I could do was point.

Then a wall of water sluiced down the service tunnel and hit us full on, knocking most of us down. There was a reason the trains didn't come this far.

114

BECCA

WITHIN TEN MINUTES NATE AND I were surrounded by a team in hazmat suits. I allowed myself a small moan as they gripped our feet and shoulders and lowered us onto plastic tarps. I had no idea where they were taking us, but surely even a strict quarantine wing would be easier to break out of than a dungeon.

"They're still alive," one guy said.

The other one shrugged. "Won't be for long. Let's go."

It wasn't till I heard the zipper, felt the plastic closing over me that I realized with horror that they were putting us into *body bags* to take to the *morgue*. My heart started beating fast and I wanted to claw my way out, but then I realized that a morgue was still better than a dungeon.

The hazmat guys grabbed the handles on our bags and dumped

us on a small flat cart. I was dying to know what Nate was thinking or planning. We had made a decent team, and not being able to talk to him was hard.

They wheeled us down a long hallway. Inside my plastic bag, I was trying not to breathe too fast or too loudly. As soon as they left us in the morgue, I was going to tear out of here and then Nate and I would try to rendezvous with the Loner again, find out what the hell was going on.

Our cart stopped. I heard a heavy metal grate being lifted, heard the grunts of effort from the hazmat guys. They grabbed the handles at the head and foot of my bag and picked me up off the cart. I braced myself, sure that I was about to be thrown into some vehicle, or maybe onto the ground.

Instead, the hands swung me, then *let go*. I was falling and falling and falling....Just as I started to scream, I hit ice-cold water. I clawed at the zipper over my face, but of course the tab was only on the outside. Still, I should be able to—

A heavy weight landed on me, knocking the breath from my lungs, pushing me deeper underwater. I heard Nate's muffled shouts but couldn't understand him. He was, no doubt, coming to the same horrible realization that I was:

The sewers were the morgue at the President's palace.

115

CASSIE

AS THE COLD WATER SWIRLED around us, I barely had time to grab one of the tunnel supports. It was an I-beam set in concrete, and I hoisted myself up, trying to keep my gun dry. Tim clung to a vertical beam a couple of yards away, and kids were clambering like rats up anything they could grab on to.

Some weren't so lucky, unable to grab anything, too small or light to withstand the onslaught of water. I watched helplessly as some of my unknown soldier comrades were simply washed away by the rising tide. As one kid rushed past like flotsam, I stuck my leg out. She grabbed it and worked her way over to the support to hold on next to me. She was tall but skinny and already shivering from the cold.

"It will stop soon!" Ms. Strepp yelled, but the water flooded on, giving no sign of letting up.

"This is sewer water!" Tim yelled.

Bags of garbage, some busted open, spun around us before pouring down the tunnel. An old chair crashed into my ankle and I swore, unheard, as the water roared in. The frigid water was up to my knees now, making my feet numb. I held on as tight as I could, praying I didn't slip off the thin rim of concrete.

A kid screamed close by—hundreds, thousands of rats lived in the tunnels, too, of course, and they were being washed around us like the rest of the trash. They were swimming desperately and grabbing on to anything they could find. Such as soldier kids clinging to I-beams.

"Oh, no, no, no!" I cried as they reached me. Their tiny claws plucked my pant legs and they immediately ran up my body. As a farm kid, I'd seen a lot of rats in my life, mostly dead after Pa or a barn cat had killed them. These were large, gray, and greasy, and when they reached my hair I shrieked. Most of them ran right on over me and up the tunnel beam, but some stayed to enjoy the warmth of my body. I looked at the two kids holding on to the same beam and saw that the tall one was crying silently as rats swarmed up and over her.

"It's okay!" I told them loudly over the rush of the water. "It's okay!" Total lie.

Numbness was creeping up my legs and I felt like the cold and the shaking would never end. I was doing this for Becca—and Nate. Were they still alive? It seemed like years since I'd seen them.

My teeth chattered painfully. My hands spasmed into claws. I didn't know how much longer I could hold on.

116

BECCA

STAY CALM, I ORDERED MYSELF, but I'd already started freaking out long ago. I still scrabbled at the zipper of my body bag even as icy water seeped in. Next to me, Nate was struggling; I knew because he kept bumping heavily into me.

Don't panic. Strepp's words knifed into my brain. *Panic means mistakes. Panic means death. Keep your cool and work the problem.*

Okay. I tried to breathe more slowly. I didn't have long before water filled up the body bag and dragged me under.

I wedged my fingertip into the top of the zipper seam. It budged! I worked another finger in beside it and started to push down. Water gushed in over my face and I had to force myself to keep pushing. Finally I got my entire hand outside! I grabbed the effing zipper tab and pulled that sucker down, immediately surrounding myself with cold water. I kicked the bag free. My lungs were about to burst from lack of air. The water was freezing and dark, but I could make out Nate's form swimming toward me! He looked as panicked as I was trying not to be and he seemed to be pointing at something.

I had nothing left to give. My lungs were about to explode and my consciousness was threadbare. I had to get air. With my very last shred of strength I kicked upward—and slammed my head into something hard, metal, and solid. My awareness slipped away, and I dreamily noticed all the bubbles escaping from my aching mouth and the cool water rushing in.

117

CASSIE

I COULDN'T HOLD ON MUCH longer. I accepted this calmly even though my whole body was shaking from the cold. At first I'd been numb; now I was so cold that it was a burning feeling working its way up my body. Four kids clung to this beam; we were all in one another's way but it couldn't be helped. There had been a fifth, but she'd let go and was whooshed away.

Looking down the tunnel, I saw hundreds of wet heads, hands grappling for anything. They had been thousands strong, but not anymore. Every few minutes, someone let go and was swept screaming down the tunnel.

"The water is lessening!"

Dully I looked over at Strepp, who was clutching the top of the maintenance doorframe. Her face was white and determined; her dark hair hung in rough, wet strands.

Had she said something? I couldn't tell. My mind was dead, I couldn't focus my eyes. Even the noise seemed to be fading out of my consciousness. I turned back to watch the water still flowing out of the smaller tunnel. I blinked in numb confusion as a large dark shape was swept out and swirled for a few moments in a horrible eddy in front of me.

I blinked again even as adrenaline woke my brain. Suddenly I felt the pain and the cold all over again, I heard the rush of the water and the screams of the kids.

It was a body, facedown and limp, slowly bumping and turning closer to me. I stared—the shape, the hair, that tan hand, hard-knuckled from training...

"Becca!" I screamed. Holding on to the beam with one hand, I reached out, leaning over as far as I dared. I swiped at her and missed. But on the next try I grabbed Becca's shirt and pulled her to me. I jumped down into the chest-high water, bracing myself against the I-beam so I wouldn't get torn away.

"Becca!" I yelled again, and with difficulty turned her over. My heart stopped, my eyes stared in disbelief, and I almost threw up. Her face was pale blue and ice cold. Her lips were white, and a thin trickle of water came out of her mouth.

"Becca!" I shook her as hard as I could, and it was like shaking a limp, heavy doll.

Becca, my *twin*, my sister, my only living relative—was *dead*.

118

"TIM!" I SCREAMED, LOOKING FOR him. He saw me, saw Becca, and instantly leaped into the water, fighting its strong current to get to me. We both held her and I saw the same horrible realization on his face. *Becca was dead.*

The water had slowed and the level was now barely past my waist.

Becca! I cried silently. *Why now? Why couldn't you have held on just a little longer?*

Something bumped into me—another body. My mind was in such chaos that it took me several seconds to recognize Nate. I grabbed his pant leg and pulled him toward me. He swirled against a wooden barrier, hitting his head, and the jolt seemed to wake him up. His hands limply reached out, then clawed at the wood to hang on.

"Nate!" I shouted, but he didn't hear me, just draped himself over the wooden barrier and lost consciousness. Leaving Becca with Tim, I waded through the water and put my hand on his head.

"Nate! It's me, Cassie!" He didn't open his eyes or move. Was he close to death?

The water was definitely receding. I went back to Tim, still holding Becca. His face was ashen. Of course. He loved Becca. He loved *Becca*.

One by one, kids were dropping off whatever they'd held on to. They stood, some hunched over, in the knee-high water.

"She can't be dead," I told Tim hoarsely. "She can't be dead because *I'm still here. I'm here.* There's no Cassie without Becca. And no Becca without Cassie."

"Becca?"

I whirled to see Nate standing weakly next to me. I threw my arms around him, and he hugged me back. It felt like I was holding him upright.

"She hit her head," Nate wheezed. "I couldn't reach her."

I looked into his eyes, and all of our memories rushed back. Nate. He was here, alive. But not Becca.

"Here!" Tim said urgently and put Becca upside down over his knee. He patted her back with increasing firmness while I held her hair out of her face, unable to breathe. This was Becca. Becca's body. Nate stood behind me, his hands on my shoulders. He looked sick and bruised and we were both trembling. He didn't have to say it—I could tell: He'd almost died himself.

Ms. Strepp splashed through the water, taking count of who was left, helping kids back on their feet, checking weapons. She glanced at us, saw us working on Becca, and gave me an uninterpretable look.

"Assemble!" she shouted down the tunnel. "Weapons ready! This is it! We have fifteen seconds!"

"She's going to blow the tunnel no matter what!" Nate said.

"She's got a schedule to keep," Tim said grimly, and whammed Becca's back again. More water trickled out of her mouth.

"This isn't working!" I said. I started CPR, quick pushes on her chest to the count of five, then listening for a heartbeat. Then the world exploded.

119

INSTINCTIVELY WE HUNCHED OVER BECCA'S body as the ceiling detonated above us. Chunks of concrete and wood rained down on and around us—Tim grunted every so often, his large body taking most of the blows.

When the fallout stopped, I wiped dust out of my eyes and looked up. What was left of Ms. Strepp's army was scrambling like termites up the mound of debris, up through another subway tunnel and then into a house. Two stories above us, a large, fancy room was now missing a floor. That was the President's palace, and it was like we were looking up into an elaborate dollhouse.

I coughed, dust filling my nose and mouth. I looked down at my twin and knelt to begin CPR again. Becca *can't be dead.*

Wet, pale kid-soldiers passed by us, not glancing down. Despite looking shaken and cold, they attacked the mound of debris as they'd been trained, helping one another, hoisting themselves up. They held guns, rifles, shotguns, knives—whatever they'd managed to hang on to during the flood. Dust covered everything and everyone who'd been within a hundred feet of the explosion. Their wet hair was caked with it, and so was mine.

I gritted my teeth. One more time. I pinched Becca's nose shut and breathed into her lungs, then pushed on her chest quickly, one, two, three, four, five. And again. And again. And again. Tim reached out and touched my shoulder, tears in his eyes.

I ignored him, filling her lungs with my own breath. One, two, three, four, five.

Her eyes fluttered open.

Ten yards away, Ms. Strepp urged soldiers up the mountain of rubble. From above us we heard gunshots, shouting, people running. None of it meant anything.

I held her face in my hands, hot tears streaming down my cheeks. "Becca! Oh, Becca, you came back to me!"

Tim leaned down and carefully kissed her dusty forehead. Her brow wrinkled as she looked at us blankly. *"Who are you people?"* she rasped.

I gasped in horror, staring at her. Did she have brain damage? Had she been deprived of oxygen too long?

Then Reckless Rebecca gave a faint grin. "Just kidding," she said weakly, and coughed up some more water. I grabbed her and held her so tight. "I was so afraid you were gone," I whispered into her ear. "I was so afraid. There's no Cassie without Becca."

"And no Becca without Cassie," she whispered back.

"My turn," said Tim, and he swept her up onto his lap. They looked so happy to see each other. It was kind of weird, after I'd spent so much time with Tim.

"That seems kind of weird," Nate whispered to me. "I mean, I've been traveling with her for ages."

Still crying, I hugged him, my Nate.

Ms. Strepp strode over. "The Loner is going to blow this tunnel in two minutes," she said tersely. "Either come with us now or stay here and be buried."

"Can you walk?" Tim asked Becca, and she nodded.

I found my rifle slung across some metal fencing and shook the water off it. I couldn't help holding Becca's hand—she was alive, and we were together. And I held Nate's hand, too, my heart feeling like it was about to burst.

At the mountain of rubble, we released hands and started to climb. Though Becca looked weak and faintly green, she started climbing. Tim grabbed a discarded gun for her and she slung it around her shoulder.

Nate and I started climbing, followed by Ms. Strepp. We were the last.

In the subway tunnel above, there was a somewhat twisted metal ladder leading upward. This was it: We were storming the President's palace. A horrible, deadly battle was ahead. We might not survive, any of us. But I was here with my three favorite people in the world, and we were okay. Well, okayish.

I hiked my gun farther up on my shoulder and grinned at Nate through my tears.

"I'm just so happy," I said.

120

BECCA

I FELT LIKE SHIT ON a stick and couldn't actually believe that I was alive. I had a memory of floating above myself as I was washed down the tunnel. It hadn't hurt or anything. I'd felt peaceful, not worried, watching myself get carried away.

The next thing I knew, someone was pushing on my chest hard enough to break my ribs. I'd been able to ignore it at first, but then it was like I'd been sucked back into myself, and Cassie was there and Tim and Nate.

I was alive. And storming the President's palace. Because I hadn't fulfilled my mission of killing him. Panting, nauseated, and weak, I looked up to see Tim—strong, solid Tim—holding out a hand to me. I gave him half a smile and shook my head.

"This is the presidential dining room," I said when we had scrambled onto the rim of its floor.

"Follow the sounds of gunfire!" Strepp ordered and rushed ahead of us down the hall. In the foyer the massive double doors were open. I saw a lot of our army—they'd been assigned to take out or immobilize all military and law enforcement. The streets were a chaos of shots and shouting.

But we ran after Strepp as she raced down the wide, flagstone hallway.

"His study is on the third floor!" I shouted, glad I could contribute this info.

Strepp ran up the wide staircase. She looked back at me and I pointed to the doors at the end of the hall. She sped there, tried the doorknob, then shot the lock off.

Inside his study, a group of angry, flustered men were trying to get into the President's gun safe. Cassie, Nate, Tim, and I spread out in a circle, our guns trained on the men.

"Where is he?" Strepp yelled.

I saw the surprise on Cassie's face as she saw Provost Allen braced for battle, holding a fireplace poker.

"Provost Allen!" she blurted, but he'd just seen Nate.

"Son!" he said and waved his hand at us. "What are you doing?"

Nate shook his head and kept his gun trained on the group. "What you should have done long ago."

The Provost's face turned to ice and he raised the poker.

"Where is he?" Strepp screamed, sounding like a banshee.

None of the men answered her.

"You'll be punished, you and your unpatriotic pals!" one man shouted.

"Who are you to question the natural order?" another man yelled.

"You'll be exiled to a desert, and I'll laugh!" cried one of the female ministers.

"Boring!" I yelled and shot a volley of bullets at their feet, making them shut up and leap around. "Now. Where. The. Hell. *Is that asshole?*"

Tim had to shoot very close to their feet before someone said, "He has a safe room! Off his bedroom!"

The wide marble staircase was teeming with people, bodies, and blood.

"This way!" I said and led them to the narrow servants' staircase, where we went up one more flight.

I was wheezing, feeling sicker, and I lagged a bit behind the others. Tim looked back and held out his hand, but I ignored it and ran on, determined to make it on my own, not willing to hold them back, even as I fell farther behind.

On the next floor Strepp raced down the hall, as if she already knew where the President's bedroom was located. Suddenly a hard arm shot out of nowhere and yanked me into a dark room. A second later I felt the sharp, stinging blade of a cold knife pressed to my throat.

"You just won't stay dead, will you?" Kirt hissed in my ear.

121

"KIRT, YOU ARE A SACK of shit," I got out between clenched teeth, and he pressed the knife into my skin. A moment later I felt the warm trickle of blood on my neck.

"And you are a goddamn bitch who's going to get what's coming to you!" he said, pulling me backward.

Then the room flooded with light, and my sister stood at the door.

"Becca, you're missing the uprising," Cassie complained, raising her gun.

"She's gonna miss the rest of her life!" Kirt said, and swung me in front of him.

If I had been 100 percent, I'd have flung him over my shoulder by now and kicked him where it hurts the most. Since I had just died and come back, my reflexes were nowhere and my brain was going, uh...

"Yeah, I don't think so," Cassie said, taking aim.

"You can shoot," Kirt sneered, "but you can't guarantee that you won't hit *her*." He swung me from side to side, moving his head, making Cassie hit a moving target.

Which of course was second nature to her. The tip of her gun followed his movements and I could almost feel her waiting for the moment between breaths when you pull a trigger.

Cassie caught my eye. It was as though I heard her voice inside my head, and I did what she wanted. On the silent count of three I slumped, a dead weight in Kirt's arms.

Cassie shot, and Kirt's knife didn't even have time to cut me as he dropped like a pile of cow manure. I staggered, Cassie ran over and grabbed my hand, and we tore out of there. But not before I'd seen that Cassie had nailed Kirt cleanly through one eye. That bastard.

When we raced into the President's bedroom, we found him sitting calmly in a chair, while Strepp pressed her gun against his temple.

122

"GO AHEAD, SHOOT," THE PRESIDENT said. "And you'll live in ignorance and prison for the rest of your pathetic lives."

"Look outside," Nate said. "You'll see a distinct lack of people capable of putting us in prison."

The four of us had surrounded the President and Strepp, covering them from all angles. Now the President's eyes slanted toward the windows, where the sounds of gunfire, alarms, and shouting rose from the streets below.

"Your time is over," Strepp hissed. "You're the past! We're the future."

"You," the President said, looking at me. "I should have let Kirt kill you when he wanted to."

"Gee, thanks for *reining him in*," I said drily, sighting him down my barrel. "But don't worry—he won't be hurting any more housemaids for...ever." Just the memory of Kirt brought bile into my throat. I thought of him lying dead a few rooms away, a neat hole through one eye, and all I felt was relief.

"Get up," Strepp told him coldly. "We're taking a walk."

Just then the door flung open and several kid-soldiers bustled in, pushing Mia ahead of them. Her hands were cuffed behind her.

"Dad, what's going on?" Mia cried. "Kirt is dead!"

For the very first time, I saw the President show emotion. *"My son is dead?"*

"Yeah. And your daughter is in handcuffs. Not that that matters," Mia said.

"You killed my son!" the President screamed at Strepp, and lunged toward her. Tim whacked the back of his knees with a billy club and the President fell to the ground.

"No. *I* killed your asshole son," Cassie said, keeping her aim on him. "So don't push me."

"Becca," Mia said to me. "I knew you were different. Is this a revolution?" She looked excited rather than afraid.

"Yes," said Strepp.

"Oh," Mia said. "What now?"

"I've been thinking about that a long time," Strepp said. "I've got some ideas."

"I bet," the President sneered. "You worthless, stupid piece of— ow!" He was interrupted by Nate swinging his gun, butt-first, and smacking the President in the head.

"The tables have turned, Ron," Strepp said calmly. "You're not in charge anymore. Now, take me to the Thousand-Eye Room."

123

"I HAVE NO IDEA WHAT you're talking about," the President said.

"Becca, there's a Taser in the nightstand," Strepp said.

How could she know that? I went and got it, also grabbing a pair of pliers. Who keeps pliers in their nightstand? What a creep! I gave the pliers to Cassie.

"Mia, you don't want to see this," Strepp said, not sounding sorry.

Mia hesitated for a moment, then nodded. "I'll go direct the palace staff to surrender peacefully," she said, and a soldier opened her handcuffs. *What the hell? Does Strepp know Mia? Just who is Helen Strepp?*

"Good idea," Strepp said. "Thanks." Once Mia and the other soldiers were gone, Strepp asked again: "Take me to the Thousand-Eye Room."

"Screw you, you scarecrow!" the President snarled, and Strepp nodded at me.

I tased him, he jerked and twitched, then fell to the ground. Once he recovered, he got that unattractive sneer on his face.

Before he could speak, Cassie clicked her pliers a couple of times. "I've always wanted to do this. Let's see how many fingernails he really needs," she mused.

He stared at her in horror, then tried to bluff. "You wouldn't—"

Cassie leaned over him, giving him that creepy smile that used to piss me off so much. She waved her pliers in the president's face. "Guys, hold him."

Tim and Nate each grabbed an arm and got the President to his feet. Strepp snatched one of his struggling hands and held it out for Cassie.

"Fine!" he cried. "Fine!"

With the boys keeping a good hold of him, the President led us to the backstairs, the servants' stairs I used to use.

He pressed a spot on the wall that I couldn't make out and a section of the stairs slid sideways, revealing a short hallway. At the end of the hallway was a door, and Strepp held out her hand for the key. The President almost stabbed her with it but gave it up.

When Strepp unlocked the door, we were in a room as big as a bowling alley, and every foot of every wall was covered with monitors—hundreds of them. Thousands. My jaw hung open as I saw they were labeled: everything from Cell A-1-1 to Cell F-69-430. Covering the whole country.

Even Strepp looked appalled, watching cellfolk going about their business. Some screens were divided in halves or fours, some had only one picture.

"You are such a goddamn freak show," Strepp murmured, looking at the screens.

"It's the only way!" the President said angrily. "You don't know the world our grandparents inherited! The people were rebelling! Oceans were rising! World War III almost destroyed the planet. Then the plague rose up! Chemical weapons! This is the *only way* humanity can survive. This is the only way that makes sense!"

"It might make sense to *you*," Strepp said, still looking at the monitors in horror.

I was trying to find the monitor for Cell B-92-4275. My home cell. But there were so many and I *did* have to be ready to put a bullet through this guy's head.

"But the world you live in isn't the world I want the next generation to inherit," Strepp went on, surprisingly calm. "We can do better. We *have* to do better. Take them out," she told me and Cassie, waving her hand at the walls of surveillance equipment.

"Nate and Tim? Please take this person to the dungeon."

The former President roared and tried to pull free, so I tased him again.

"I know where the dungeons are," I heard Nate tell Tim.

Cassie began firing, shattering screen after screen, and I raised my rifle and did the same. It sounded like a thousand rocks busting a thousand wine glasses, and I would be lying if I didn't say it was damn fun.

Five minutes later the room was nothing but a dark cavern full of broken glass, wires, and smoke. And a former President, sobbing on the ground.

124

CASSIE

"WE HAVE DONE THE UNTHINKABLE!" Ms. Strepp yelled into a microphone. The front terrace of the presidential palace stood twenty marble steps above the shouting crowd. Some people were protesting, and we had hundreds of armed kid-soldiers keeping their eyes—and their guns—on them. But not everyone looked outraged; at least a thousand people looked curious, and more than a thousand people—people whose clothes showed that they were servants, cooks, maids—were apparently thrilled and eager to hear more.

"We have begun the revolution!" Ms. Strepp shouted, and punched her fist in the air. Behind her, twenty feet high, Nate had rigged up a display of pictures from books and files we'd found in the President's study. The projected pictures shone brightly in the night. They showed cellfolk plowing with horses or oxen, other cellfolk winding thread through weaving looms. These were jux-taposed with city people lounging by swimming pools or having fancy drinks with sunsets in the background.

Many in the crowd also punched their fists in the air. Could we pull this off? Ms. Strepp had been planning this for more than ten years. None of us, her followers, had had a choice about doing our parts in it. As Ms. Strepp continued her victory speech, I felt shocked about how completely I had followed her. We all had.

Becca and I were on the wide porch behind Ms. Strepp, with Nate and Tim and about twenty others. We watched the crowd for any sign of a weapon or threat to our leader.

Still, the show played on. It was fascinating. First there would be a fantastic masquerade ball in some city. Then it would show one of our harvest dances with straw on the floor. Watching the crowd, I saw how most of them looked shocked and confused. Could they really have not known?

I edged closer to Becca. "I can't believe this is actually happen-ing," I murmured.

Becca nodded, not looking at me. "I...I think I'm done with this," she said, watching the crowd, her gun ready.

"Me, too, sister," I whispered back. "So what now?"

"We finish this," Becca said. "Then we take off."

"There has been a toxic imbalance in our country!" Ms. Strepp shouted. "And I say country, because this country is made up of ten actual cities, but thousands of cells! We will sweep this country, we will free the cellfolk—not by tearing down fences, though we will, but by educating them!"

Many of the crowd shouted in approval. I saw others look at each other in concern.

"Together we will remake this country into what it should be, what it always was—communities of people, all kinds of people!" Ms. Strepp went on. "Every kind of person living in every kind of community! No more cells! No more fences! No more predestined lives handed down by a faceless government!"

Becca let out a deep sigh and gave me a glance. "Let's say three weeks?"

I gave the barest nod. "Three weeks. Then we make our own destinies."

125

"**IF YOU CAN'T KEEP UP**, you need a different vehicle." Becca sounded irritated, and I rolled my eyes at the walkie-talkie.

"We can keep up!" Nate said. "I'm still getting used to it! This tank has two clutches!"

I watched him as he peered through the eye slit and with difficulty switched gears. "I love our tank," I said.

As the capital had come apart and new loyalties were established, a lot of resources became "available." After Ms. Strepp had given us her blessing to leave, we'd had our pick of vehicles. Nate had chosen an army tank, for practicality, he said.

"We have no idea how some people will react to this revolution," he'd said. "I want to feel safe!"

I felt safe. Totally safe. But also super-heavy and slow.

Nate ground the gears, switching his hands and feet rapidly. He nodded at the big black SUV in front of us. "When those two get surprised by, like, angry cellfolk or rabid elk, they're going to be begging us to let them in this tank!"

I grimaced at the word "elk." My shoulder still ached sometimes and I had a big, ugly scar. It was weird to think that I'd been with Tim then, not Nate.

"Sorry," Nate said, remembering all the stories I'd told him. Over the last three weeks, we'd done a lot of catching up. But I'd never mentioned Tim's kiss. And I never would.

"Well, it's true," I said loyally. "There could be rabid elk or something. Their SUV wouldn't last five minutes!"

A surprisingly loud "Woo-oo-oo-oo" broke into our conversation, and I looked down at Anka.

"Even Anka agrees," I said. Among the various provisions we'd liberated from our evil oppressors had been Anka, a ten-week-old puppy. Brown and tan, with enormous batlike ears and paws like saucers, she had captured my heart as soon as I'd laid eyes on her. If I could just get her tank-trained, she'd be perfect.

I spread an old paper map out on the instrument board and hit Talk on the walkie-talkie. "Okay, so the capital was almost in the middle of the country," I told Becca. "We probably have about a week's journey to get to the coast."

"Yeah," said Becca. "Hope your ass can take those metal seats for that long." Her voice faded as if she'd forgotten to turn off the Talk button. "Honey, could you flip my cup holder so it'll keep my water cold? Thanks, babe." She had not "forgotten" to turn off the Talk button.

Nate gave up on the eye slits and flipped on the front camera so he could see where the hell we were going.

"And what happens when we get to the coast?" he asked.

I picked Anka up and held her in my lap. "Well, we go either up or down the coast," I said. "Find the real capital, the old one. I said we would help Ms. Strepp find some of the holdouts and Cell Deniers. She's convinced there are some."

"Okay, but I'm not up for a whole palace takeover," Nate said. "With the pretend plague and the body bags and the sewers and the almost dying. Maybe just a few small gunfights, stuff like that."

"Got it," I said.

Nate held out his hand. I took it. Anka licked it sleepily.

"It's been a long road," Nate said solemnly, and I remembered how we'd found Provost Allen dead—a suicide. "I'm so glad we're alive, and together."

"Oh, me, too," I said feelingly, and held Anka in place as I leaned over to kiss him.

126

BECCA

"I CAN'T EVEN SEE THEM!" I said, looking at the rearview screen.

"That would be because of the relative slowness of a *stupid tank* as opposed to a four-wheel Galaxy Max," Tim said drily. He flipped the screen to be forward-facing with the map, then pulled over to one side of the road and stopped the car. "Might as well give them half an hour to catch up."

"Which also gives us half an hour to catch up," I said, and climbed across the center console to sit in Tim's lap. "I missed you so much." I loved being back with Tim—I'd gotten along okay with Nate, but Tim and I just fit each other so much better. Every once in a while I remembered making out with Nate, the night we got caught in the kitchen garden. I'd left that part out of all my stories. No need for Tim to know it—it hadn't meant anything.

I did miss my team, though. Bunny, Jolie, and Mills all survived the attack on the palace. I thought about asking if they wanted to come with us, but they were all good soldiers, eager for their assignments in the new Resistance-led government.

"I'm just glad I'm back with the right twin," Tim said, and kissed me. I wrapped my arms around him and kissed him back, wondering just how much time we had.

127

HELEN

"I COULD REALLY USE YOUR talents," Helen said, looking up at the Loner. "We've won the capital—that's certain. But there will be other battles."

The Loner lounged against her desk, remembering fondly how he'd blown up the capital's DMV. "Fam needs me, too," he said. "I miss the kiddos, nieces, and nephews. But I'll be back." He gave Helen a brief smile and loped out of the room.

Helen wanted to look out her window to search the sky, but just then her assistant came in with that day's reports.

"Things are looking good," she said, placing a folder on Helen's—once the President's—desk. "Supply structures in place, rioting down."

"Thank you, Mia," Helen said, giving her a smile. "You're a huge help."

128

BECCA

"THIS … MAKES NO SENSE," I said, not believing what I was seeing.

I heard the heavy clang of the tank lid opening.

"I don't understand," Cassie said, climbing out the top of the behemoth with the freaking puppy she picked up from somewhere.

"We've only gone about three hundred miles," Tim said.

Nate spread a paper map on the hood of the tank. "We should need to go at least another four hundred miles," he confirmed.

"Oh!" said Cassie, putting her finger on the map. "Is this a big river? Is it the … Miss-iss-ippi?"

"No," Nate said. "This is much bigger."

Anka squirmed out of Cassie's arms and bounded to the unending expanse of water, where she yipped at the waves.

"This is an ocean," Tim said. "Once we found it on old maps, up in the library, I knew I wanted to see one someday."

"You're seeing it," Nate said drily.

"All our maps are wrong," Cassie said in disbelief. "Our maps showed we had to get through West Virginia and Virginia. How can two states be missing?"

"There's something wrong," said Tim. "There's not supposed to be an ocean here."

Instinctively I put my arm around Cassie. Had we lost one home and now lost the possibility of ever finding another one? It felt like—we weren't tethered to anything, or anyone except each other and Tim and Nate. Suddenly it felt like we were the only four people alive in the United. Or...whatever Strepp was going to call it.

Cassie put her arm around me. "Wherever we go, whatever we do, I want us to do it together," she said softly. Something hard inside my chest melted a bit and I felt less freaked. Home would be wherever Cassie was.

Nate stood next to Cassie and held her hand, and like a mirror Tim did the same to me. These people were my family. And the dog that had just piddled on Nate's boot without him noticing was partly my dog. I guessed.

The four of us stayed there, linked, and stared at the endless sea.

ABOUT THE AUTHORS

James Patterson received the Literarian Award for Outstanding Service to the American Literary Community from the National Book Foundation. He holds the Guinness World Record for the most #1 *New York Times* bestsellers, including *Confessions of a Murder Suspect* and the Maximum Ride series, and his books have sold more than 385 million copies worldwide. A tireless champion of the power of books and reading, Patterson created a children's book imprint, JIMMY Patterson Books, whose mission is simple: "We want every kid who finishes a JIMMY Book to say, 'PLEASE GIVE ME ANOTHER BOOK.'" He has donated more than one million books to students and soldiers and funds more than four hundred Teacher and Writer Education Scholarships at twenty-one colleges and universities. He has also donated millions of dollars to independent bookstores and school libraries. Patterson invests proceeds from the sales of JIMMY Patterson Books in pro-reading initiatives.

Gabrielle Charbonnet is the coauthor of *Sundays at Tiffany's*, *Crazy House*, and *Witch & Wizard* with James Patterson, and she has written many other books for young readers. She lives in South Carolina with her husband and a lot of pets.